CHAIN OF VENGEANCE

Also by William Beechcroft:

Position of Ultimate Trust
Image of Evil

CHAIN OF VENGEANCE

A Novel of Suspense by

William Beechcroft

DODD, MEAD & COMPANY
NEW YORK

Copyright © 1986 by William Beechcroft

No part of this book may be reproduced in any form
without permission in writing from the publisher.
Published by Dodd, Mead & Company, Inc.
79 Madison Avenue, New York, N.Y. 10016
Distributed in Canada by
McClelland and Stewart Limited, Toronto
Manufactured in the United States of America
First Edition

Library of Congress Cataloging-in-Publication Data

Beechcroft, William.
Chain of vengeance.

I. Title.
PS3552.E32C5 1986   813'.54   85-20761
ISBN 0-396-08664-0

CHAIN OF VENGEANCE

ONE

Tʜᴇ ʜɪss ᴏF ᴀᴜᴛᴜᴍɴ ʀᴀɪɴ was not shut out by the ill-
fitting window. He reached for the light toggle, but
the shrunken figure in the bed fluttered a hand.

"No, Vincenzo. No light. The window is enough."

He knew she wanted the refuge of late-afternoon shadows, didn't want him to see her clearly, not like this.

He moved close to the rumpled bed. It smelled of mil-
dew, but he didn't hesitate.

"Take my hand, Vincenzo *caro*." A claw already cold
with the inevitable. He held it in both of his.

"There is something you must know." Her voice was
parched with age and the feel of death that hovered low in
the room.

"Some *vino*, Mama?" He moved to reach for the bottle
on the corner table. Her fingers splayed to hold him.

"No, no wine, Vincenzo. Time is left only for words. You
must listen. Then you must swear. You must swear to me
that you will do as I ask. My last wish, *figlio mio*."

Then she told him, her words as dry as the rustle of old

leaves but ultimately more infuriating than any insult he had ever received from the lowest *buffone* in his lowest of professions. When the quavering voice stopped, he rose from his knees beside the bed. He was bathed in sweat and he shook with rage. At last he understood the nightmares, the awakenings in sodden bedclothes. And, yes, the humiliating failures with women.

Blood pounded in his ears, drowned the rain. She saw his fury, and she smiled, a mirthless grin that showed yellow teeth. She looked eighty. He realized with a jolt that she was not yet sixty-five. This accursed Sicilian climate had done that. He had been smart to leave for Rome when he became of age, to turn his back on the summer dust and soul-freezing winter rain.

It was more than climate. Now he knew she had aged so rapidly also because of what he had just learned, the ugly secret so obsessively bottled within her until this day. His hands clenched hers.

Then he heard the rain again. The ability to speak returned.

"You want me to—"

"Si, Vincenzo!" The dull eyes became bright. Now they were centers of flame. "Vendetta! Swear it on my grave."

"Mama, I swear it here. While you live."

"On my grave. This bed is my grave. A deathbed wish is sacred, *figlio mio*. So swear it now, on your mother's grave."

"I do, Mama!" He bent to kiss the crabbed fingers. "I so swear."

As she squeezed his trembling hand, the light in the sunken eyes failed. Then it was lost beneath the glaze of death. He lay the lifeless arm on the blanket, closed the eyelids with his thumb and forefinger, reached in his pocket, and placed a coin on each eye.

He straightened and brushed floor dust from the knees

of his Gucci suit. He looked down. So small she was now. All the years added up to only this? A forlorn death in a lonely village forty miles into the Madonie Mountains south of Palermo.

Everything could have been so different, he realized now. He'd been convinced that the nightmares were rooted here in the rocks and dust of Sicily. He'd thought that to escape those night sweats, he had only to escape this place. But the sleep terror had followed him to Rome, persisted wherever he traveled.

He'd blamed her because he knew no one else to blame. Sent her money, not out of love but out of guilt. Now, too late, he knew she was blameless, surely more tortured than he.

She would be avenged. He had sworn it on her grave.

He nodded at the three women in the front room, neighbors he barely knew. "She is dead. I will make the arrangements now."

"You must see Signore Podesto," one of the black-shrouded women said quietly. "At the top of the hill. She has already paid him, and he knows her wishes."

He pulled on his American raincoat and stepped into the downpour. It was warm, like blood. His thin-lipped mouth compressed. Blood. Only that would avenge her shame. Only that would expunge the nightmares and leave him in peace at last.

The engine balked in the dampness, then it turned over. The rented Fiat's right wheels bounced across the brimming gutter. He gunned the auto up the mud-slick incline.

He was planning already. Rollo could handle the business for as long as it would take. Cost was no problem. The cover? Simple enough. And he was no stranger to what had to be done.

Signore Podesto, *Impresario di Funebri*, had on file Mama's explicit instructions, as the neighbor had said. The funeral was prompt, austere, and plagued by the endless rain that drummed on the tiny cluster of black umbrellas.

Then there was nothing more for him to do here. He had done what was necessary, except for the final necessity. The Fiat rolled quietly out of Nocciola. Then the putter of its exhaust rose to a howl as he tramped the accelerator to the floor.

Let it begin. Let it begin *now*!

TWO

Roy Forrest shrugged grizzly-bear shoulders, bunching his blue shirt. "No bust in. No nothing. Just this security guard flat on his ass in the lobby. Two bullets in his brain by way of his right ear. Two shell cases—twenty-two rimfire shorts—on the floor."

Cousin Roy, Dan Forrest thought, certainly had a cop's relish for on-the-job detail. "I thought homicide dicks were suppose to have locked mouths."

" 'Dicks'? Jeez, 'dicks'?" Roy shrugged again. "This is in the family, Danny boy."

Dan nodded toward the slender redheaded woman in jeans hugging her knees on the floor beside him. "Casey's not family."

"Don't kid me." Roy leered.

"Don't I wish," Casey said.

"Behave," Dan growled at her.

"You want to hear this or not?" Roy opened plate-sized palms toward them. He was built square, like a van. Dan had heard that the guys in the squad room called him

Kong. "I never met a reporter who didn't get his rocks off on a homicide."

"Casey?"

"Are you kidding?"

Detective Leroy Forrest hunched forward, eager to impress. "We thought it was a botched B and E, you know? Some dirt bag, maybe a couple of them, go into the Candler Building for whatever. There's wholesale jewelers in there. A coin dealer. Silversmith. So they begin to jimmy the door."

"You saw the marks," Dan said.

"No marks, but maybe they haven't got really started when Helmsgaard—"

"The watchman."

"That's right. Helmsgaard the guard."

Casey rolled her eyes upward.

"We think he shows up and they get in and zap, that's it."

"What did they take?"

"Nothing. Nobody in the building reports anything missing or even a door forced. Nothing at all."

"They panicked and ran," Casey offered.

"That's as good as anything else we've come up with."

"What else have you come up with?" Dan was mildly intrigued, but this wasn't anything Charlie Lovett would go for. Charlie liked sin-and-skin a hell of a lot more than he'd like an obscure watchman getting plugged at three o'clock on a dank New York morning.

"We haven't come up with anything. In fact, if it was a heist, seems they would have dragged Helmsgaard into the rear hallway out of sight from the sidewalk. There's full-length glass doors on that building. But he was just off to one side. A graveyard-shift Con Ed man heading for the subway home spotted him. We figure they iced him, then ran."

"What makes you think there were more than one of them?"

Roy looked down at Casey. "Dunno. Maybe it was only one. One guy, two quick shots. Close range with that small a caliber don't make much noise."

"Sounds like a hit," Dan said.

"Don't it? But what kind of hit man rubs a sixty-one-year-old night watchman?"

"Depends on what kind of a night watchman he was."

Roy's caterpillar eyebrows climbed a notch up his forehead. "Standard burned-out security guard, retired from a draftsman job with some outfit called Consolidated Sheet Metal Crafters. Worked with GE, couple other companies before that. Problem was the bottle. Not a rummy, but enough to make him hard to get along with, you know?"

"Where'd you get all this?"

"His widow. Over in Queens. He'd never held one job long enough to build up a pension."

"Tell me about it." Dan's eyes were on the rug.

Roy ignored that. "So after he got too shaky to draw anymore, he ended up like a lot of them that have to keep working after they're too old or too beat to do it. Watchman job."

Dan absently ran his fingers through thinning, straw-colored hair. "Not much there."

"Not much else, either. One kid, a daughter, forty. Living in California. Divorced with two kids of her own. Boys. Widow tells me the daughter hasn't had an easy time of it either. Just your average, down-at-the-heels American working family. Nothing that tells you anything. But there he lay, flat on his butt, two bullets in the ear." Roy looked at his plate-sized wrist chronometer. "And it's late, and I gotta get home."

"Give my regards to Barb," Dan said automatically.

7

After Roy left, Casey said, "For a detective, he's sure got a compulsion to talk."

"Maybe because nobody at work talks much to him."

"Well, I shouldn't say this since he's your cousin, but he does come across as a bit of a jerk. How could the sons of brothers be so different?"

"We're not so different."

"Come on!"

"Come on, yourself. You think he's a jerky detective. I'm a jerky feature writer for a jerk of a publication."

She sprawled her unkempt lankiness in the chair by the TV, jeans-clad legs splayed, man's-shirted arms draped over the chair's low back, her new-penny hair a careless swirl. The rumpled picture of a New York working girl in repose.

"*NewScope* is read by millions. Five millions, to be specific."

"So we say, Casey. What we don't say is that it's a rip-off of the *National Enquirer* crossbred with the hairiest of the old Hollywood gossip rags. Godzilla of the print world."

"Totally titillating."

"You got it."

"Which brings me to another subject."

"I was afraid it would."

"Oh, Daniel, damn you! I'm fated to die the only virgin in New York."

"You've got time. You're just a kid."

"I'm thirty-five."

"You're thirty-four."

"I'm almost thirty-five. I will be in January. Look at me, Daniel. Don't you see the smoldering embers of repressed desire? Don't you want to fan those glowing coals into the consuming flame of . . . Oh, hell! I'm skinny, and I'm about as sexy-looking as Grant Wood's American Gothic

8

lady, and who'd want it? Look at this hair, for God's sake! Feathers in a windstorm."

"You've got to learn to subdue that high regard you have for yourself." He set the coffee cups in the kitchenette's steel sink and turned on the water.

"Yeah? How did I get such a used-looking bod when it's never been used?"

"It's used-looking? How can anyone tell? You dress like a bag-lady."

"I'm no good with clothes. Never have been. I try. God knows, I try."

"What's that from?" he asked over his shoulder.

"What?"

"That 'I try' quote. Sounds like Bette Davis."

"Oh, damn it, Daniel! Enough of this romance. When are we going to make mad, passionate whatever you want?"

"I'm an old man, you chippie." He walked back into the living room drying his hands on a red-checked dish towel.

"At forty-eight? The prime of life."

"Stop feeling sorry for yourself and feel sorry for me."

"You're six feet tall. Nobody feels sorry for men six feet tall."

"And I'm fifteen pounds overweight. With hair that lets the sun shine through."

"The jawline. The slightly mashed nose. You're sincere, Daniel, so sincere."

"It's the brown eyes. People trust people with dark-colored eyes."

"*That's* my problem!"

"Yup, those damned sea-green eyes. Like getting X-rayed. A cold look, Katherine Claudia Pickett."

"A mask for the fires within."

"I don't do virgins."

"I never should have told you."

"I would have known."

"The hell you would."

"Threat or promise?" He grinned.

"Try me!"

"Go back across the hall, K.C. Pickett. Play with your new computer terminal. Or get some sleep. Fiscal Processing Systems needs you fresh each morning."

"I can do that stuff with my eyes shut. I teach it to our customers, for Pete's sake."

"Never be overconfident."

"I never am. But one day, Daniel Forrest, I'm going to get you."

"This isn't the day, Casey. Now go to bed like a good girl."

"Story of my life," she growled.

Rollo's research and logistical support had been *eccellente*, right down to where Vincenzo Arbalesta would acquire the weapons. Automatic rimfire .22s, little cartridges with a detonation not much louder than a handclap. They had no long-range punch, but they would penetrate bone.

Because he would travel by air except in one instance, he would need to acquire a new pistol at five locations. It was possible to smuggle a weapon aboard an aircraft, but that required such elaborate planning and execution that it was impractical for his purposes. He knew that checked luggage was only spot X-rayed, but even that held too much risk. This mission had to be accomplished smoothly and so swiftly that the law-enforcement organizations involved would still be mired in confusion when he was safely back in Rome.

Were it not for Rollo Scorza's competence, Arbalesta would have been hard-pressed to carry out his mother's mandate. Shipments of refined product from Marseille would continue to arrive while he was absent, but Rollo would handle the deliveries to the U.S. distribution points as well as if Arbalesta had been in the Rome office himself.

If he hadn't been fortunate enough to have Rollo Scorza on staff? Arbalesta would have been forced to shut down the business to carry out the vendetta. He would have lost millions of lire, but Mama's wish, her deathbed wish, was sacred.

The green-striped Alitalia DC-10 put him into Kennedy at 4:47 A.M., Monday, October 15. Customs was uncrowded but suffused with that peculiar numbness that comes over night people at such an advanced time on their shifts. His cover—in New York to seek a supplier of copying machines for his burgeoning office equipment business—was perfunctorily accepted. Also taken at face value was the passport, a phony in the name of "Victorio Literri." He had other Literri documentation, including an Italian driver's license and an American Express gold card, all with a *Posta Roma* box number. The box had been rented, through several layers of dummy corporations, by Arbalesta's firm, Esportatore Varieta.

The bills he would incur were to be promptly paid by money order, then the accounts would be closed. The documentation would be turned to ash. It would be as if Victorio Literri had never existed. Where documentation was not required, he would use other aliases, thus further obscuring his transcontinental trail. The plan had risks, but they were reasonable risks directly commensurate with the speed of its execution. Arbalesta would waste no time.

The dawn limousine to Manhattan carried only eight passengers, but it offered several degrees more anonymity than would have an airport taxi. With his bag, he got off at the Statler-Hilton, then took a cab eleven blocks straight up Sixth Avenue to the Hotel Taft. From there he walked the additional two blocks to the Sheraton Centre, a mammoth, bustling convention hotel that he had correctly expected to be too engrossed in megalogistics to take any special notice of a single nondemanding guest.

He slept until 1:00 P.M. Then he showered, shaved, dressed in three-piece Italian-styled charcoal gray, slipped into his black raincoat, and walked two blocks east to Fifth Avenue, where he hired a rattletrap of a Checker. The afternoon sun had not quite dispelled the mid-October bite. A trio of short-skirted *ragazze* in front of a stone lion at the New York Public Library looked half-frozen as the cab bounded past.

Arbalesta paid off the driver near Union Square and walked several blocks westward. His destination was just another seedy wholesale outlet in a crumbling community of wholesalers. But this one was different. It was the address supplied by Rollo.

Arbalesta pressed the grimy mother-of-pearl button cradled in layers of paint, the current one a peeling green. Through the dusty display window, he thought he detected movement. The lock buzzed. He pushed the door open.

The showroom was crammed with rattan furniture, lacquered chests, and carved teak figures; it blazed here and there with the multicolored flash of intricate cloisonné. All of it was Oriental import. All wore a patina of dust.

From the shadows at the rear of the corridorlike showroom barked a high-pitched voice. "You like help?"

"Mr. Yung?"

"I am Mr. Yung." He moved into the wan light of the single fluorescent fixture in the high, stamped-metal ceiling. A small man, he wore a limp white shirt and vile green plaid sports slacks gathered at the waist with an overlong belt cinched to its final hole.

"I am Victorio Literri. You have a package for me?"

"You have ID?" The man appeared to be in the final

stages of something surely fatal. If the slitted eyes in the parchment face closed forever immediately after this transaction, so much the better.

Arbalesta offered the Literri driver's license. Yung disappeared into what was no doubt an office in the rear of the showroom. He walked with a peculiar hitch. Scuttled, Arbalesta thought, like a land crab. The aged Chinese reappeared with a package the size of a thick book and wrapped in soft brown paper secured with shiny Scotch tape, a lot of it.

"You mind if I inspect?"

Impassively, Yung reached into his incongruous plaid trousers and produced a red-handled Swiss Army knife.

Arbalesta slit the package up the side. The automatic was a Beretta model 950, chambered for .22 shorts. Four and a half inches overall with a two-and-a-half-inch barrel. It weighed only ten ounces.

He pressed the clip release. Full, but he'd need only two.

"Satisfactory," he said. "You have already been paid."

Yung offered a wan smile.

"*Grazie.*" Arbalesta slid the Beretta in the inside pocket of his suit coat to nestle beside the invaluable little notebook Rollo had detailed for him.

A thick overcast had diluted the sun. He decided to walk the entire distance back to the Sheraton Centre. He was fond of walking. He was proud of his greyhound slimness at forty-five, and he had time to kill.

He grimaced to himself. Worrying about his weight at this time of life was ridiculous for all the good his trimness had served him with women. He liked women, was fascinated with some of them, but had been successful with none. *Dio!* Not a physiological problem, but in his head. So he had been told by three *dottori*, three of Italy's most skilled specialists in such matters.

That did seem possible, coupled with the night sweats

he had suffered all his life. But the cause had eluded him—until Mama's whispered confession. No, confession was the wrong word. Her *umilezione.*

He felt obvious here in the sparsely peopled rundown wholesale district, a tall man, slim as a switchblade, with eyes set deep in a narrow, almost aristocratic face, a high forehead and a blade nose. He had shaved off his neat mustache and was displeased with the unexpected whiteness above his upper lip. A few blocks farther, foot traffic thickened. Now he blended in well. Anyone blends into a New York sidewalk crowd.

He returned to his room, field-stripped the pistol to check the components, dry-fired it, then slept until 8:00 P.M. He had a light supper in the Sheraton Centre's café, found a cinema not far from the hotel, and stayed through the idiotic feature twice.

Too much time, that was the problem now. He didn't want to be seen too often going in and out of the hotel. That was a holdover from the old days, a lingering paranoia, but one that was healthy. Interesting how it all was coming back to him so readily.

While the sidewalks were still busy, he walked past the Candler Building. The broad glass entrance was not good, but it was heavily tinted. The lobby beyond was probably not too starkly visible from passing vehicles, particularly since the bright interior lighting was no doubt subdued after the building closed. The doorway did not extend across the entire front of the lobby. The walls flanking it were not of glass but of decorative tan stone. That was good.

To use more time, he took a leisurely walk, ending in Pennsylvania Station. Then he burned off a long hour on a hard bench in the scruffy Penn Station concourse.

He arrived at the Candler Building the second time at 3:31 A.M., a lone, hawklike figure in black, the leather heels of his handcrafted Italian shoes ringing in the crisp air.

By now, the night guard had been on duty several hours. Through the heavy plate glass, Arbalesta saw a dumpy, dough-faced man with a shapeless reddish nose between puffy cheeks. His feet were propped on the little desk on the left side of the lobby. Blue uniform collar open, tie pulled down.

Arbalesta checked the street again. No traffic, sidewalks eerily empty. The night had turned cold. There was a trace of drizzle on the pavement.

He rapped on the glass with his gloved fist.

The guard looked up, startled from half-sleep. Arbalesta swung his head up and down the street, hoping to portray a man confused.

The guard swung his legs to the floor and stood uncertainly. Arbalesta knuckled the glass again. The guard shuffled to the double doors.

"What in hell do you want?" he called through the narrow crack between the panels.

"*Non molto bene, signore . . .*"

"What?"

"I . . . am not well. Sick. I need an ambulance."

The guard put his ear to the crack. "Can't hear you. Sick, you said?"

"*Ambulanza,*" Arbalesta muttered, reverting back to Italian. Americans were said to be possessed of an urge to help a foreign visitor.

"Oh, hell," said the guard. And he unlocked the door.

With a final glance along the sidewalk, Arbalesta slipped through before the guard could decide to stop him.

"Hold it a minute, damn it! I'm not supposed to . . ."

Arbalesta smelled cheap liquor, faint but unmistakable. "You are Helmsgaard, Phillip Helmsgaard?" The photograph Rollo's people had supplied of Helmsgaard was the worst of the group. Out of focus and not full-face.

The man's bloated face screwed up in surprise. "Well, yeah. What—"

"I have been asked to give you this." He reached in his breast pocket. Helmsgaard's fuzzed brain was obviously trying to make sense out of all this. He appeared more intrigued than suspicious.

"Wait," Arbalesta cautioned. "Not out here."

Helmsgaard, now thoroughly confused, allowed himself to be coaxed by Arbalesta's grip on his arm away from the exposure of the glass entrance into the relative concealment behind the adjacent stone wingwall. Only then did the man seem to have any inkling that something was decidedly wrong.

"Wait just a damn minute, buddy!" But Arbalesta had already produced the automatic. He rammed it into Helmsgaard's right ear before the man could spin around. Arbalesta jerked the trigger twice. All of this in one whiplash of motion.

The double crack of the little .22 sounded immense in the high-ceilinged lobby but probably made no sound at all in the empty street. Helmsgaard sagged backward, arms slack, legs buckling then straightening in reflex spasm as Arbalesta let him drop.

Almost no blood, Arbalesta noted. Just a trickle from the ear. He checked the front of his coat. Not a mark. This was the beauty of a .22. No blowing out the other side of the head as with a .45 or .357. Cannons, those things. The .22 was neat, surgical.

He stepped out of the building into the deserted street. *Eccellente.* He walked east. The time was now 3:37 A.M. He would find an all-night restaurant, use time there; find another, use more time. By then the city would be awake, and the hotel doorman would not think it odd that he was abroad after dawn.

In a corner booth of a grubby all-nighter near Broadway, he nursed one of the worst cups of coffee he'd ever tasted. He detested the place. The graffiti-scarred maroon paint of the booth was as far removed from his regular table at Rome's La Fontanella as a battered VW Bug was from his Ferrari.

This was a zoo. Three exhausted, pasty-white *prostitute* drooped over the counter; they could not have been yet twenty, any of them. A black man in a brown leather coat eyed them from a booth, himself stretching a cup of the putrid coffee. A pimp? Or *polizia* in street clothes? The rest of the clientele came and went, but these four stayed.

He didn't worry about the whores. The black man made him nervous. Or was it the hour, this dead of morning? This first operation had been amateurish. He realized now that he had allowed too much time. Thanks to Rollo, the acquisition of the weapon had been well-handled. And Arbalesta had easily disposed of it down a storm-sewer grate. But overall, the schedule had been dangerously loose.

He had made the errors of a beginner. It had been a long time since he had done street work. And there was more to do, much more in the days he had allotted himself. He had once been the best street man in the business. Now he owned the business, and he had grown rusty.

Assuming Helmsgaard would be alone, that was slipshod. But he *had* been alone. Assuming the street would be empty at the critical moment. As it had been. Luck had seen him through in both instances, but depending on luck was the amateur's mark. As was leaving himself so many predawn hours to eat up afterward and assuming he could do so in the open without being noticed. But fortune apparently still held up. Except for the man in the leather coat?

Then the black man slid from his booth and walked out of the place. Arbalesta felt tension at last begin to drain. Only in the impersonal chaos of New York could he have survived such a succession of stupid risks. *Si, stupido!* He had built those risks himself.

But the old sharpness would come back. The ensuing executions would be as swift, but cleaner. Helmsgaard was the only one who worked by night and slept by day. The others would be different.

Yet who paid much attention to the killing of a night watchman in this city? That would be only one more statistic in the already bloated dossier of apparently motiveless killings.

Which, of course, was why Homicide assigned the case to Leroy Forrest.

THREE

Each time the biweekly tabloid went to bed, Dan was bemused at how few editorial people *NewScope* had in its New York office. Just the Sweating Seven of Seventh Avenue. Quincy Harriss, a twenty-six-year-old journalism squirt with a mop of brass hair that he kept twitching off his forehead, turned out lead features. Most often they were "enhanced reverbs," as Quince himself called them— hyped rehashes of coverage by more respectable publications with their own people on the scene. Quince hardly ever went on the scene. He was a research-and-disgorge expert, as Dan put it, with a penchant for SF. Sleaze factor.

They all had that. They'd better have it, or it was out the door. The Three Muses had it. Corkie Brion, all one hundred sixty pounds of her, could detect a celeb scandal across two continents of wire service. CASTRO WAS HOLLY-WOOD EXTRA had been one of hers. Aliceanna Holmes, a raillike reciprocal of Corkie, could make the most mundane scientific "breakthrough" read like the second coming of Albert Schweitzer. EINSTEIN'S BRAIN IN WICHITA was an Aliceanna discovery that had stunned them all by being true. The third Muse, Melody Matso, her priggish little soul jeopardized by her aphroditic proportions, could turn a routine sports piece into an innuendo that would make a fight fixer blush.

Jonathan Blauvelt was another story; every issue, as a matter of fact. He covered the arts. Danced through them, Quince claimed, with both feet firmly planted six inches in the air. Dan was sure the pipestem pants with their constricted crotches and the deep-cut silk shirts were a disguise. "The guy's after a chorus or two of Melody," he assured Quince. "What better way than to con her into a crusade to show him there's a better way?" Blauvelt's copy was noted for its sardonic—some said bitchy—twists.

The other two editorial staffers were Dan himself and Managing Editor Charlie Lovett. Charlie saw to it that his little group of keyboard cutthroats turned out the kind of supermarket shitola that was impulse-propelled into grocery bags at checkout counters from Cape Cod to Apache Junction. "Next year, California, Alaska, and Hawaii," Charlie had confided to Dan. "Keep it under your hat."

It turned out that he had said the same thing to all six of them. Then he waited to see who would dump it first. They made sure he never knew.

NewScope was a Markelhenny Publication, owned by one grossly affluent resident of Cardiff, Wales. "A real Welsh rarebit," Dan had said to Quince. "We all know what we turn out is unadulterated crapola."

"Crapola is Markelhenny's international image. You don't like this work? Try a novel."

He'd already tried that. The investment in time had been prodigious, and the thing didn't sell. That was after his Scotch-powered years with *The New York Times*, then the *Daily News*, then a community paper on Long Island.

Even that little rag couldn't put up with his missed deadlines and, in the final stages, his impossibly sloppy reporting. Carole couldn't put up with him either. The same day he found the lock changed on his Garden City office door, she left him. He'd spun in and awakened to terror in a Long Island hospital ward. After that, he'd begun the novel and lived on part-time PR hackery.

A classified ad placed by *NewScope* saved him from boozing his brains out a second time. The magazine's incredibly lousy journalism had an interesting effect. Where it would have driven a conscientious sober talent to drink, it shocked him sober. But too late. The fire was out, and schlock journalism paid surprisingly well. He figured he could amble through whatever years he had left, jacking out the kind of crime copy that made Llewellan Markelhenny a Cardiff giant.

Dan had the first cell in Cubicle Row, the one adjacent to Charlie's glass-enclosed office. Dan's was an eight-by-eight like the other five. Each was lighted by a single fly-blasted fluorescent tube that painted its occupant a cadaverous pasty white. Only the abundantly endowed Melody could surmount the pallor of the crude lighting. No one looked at her face anyway.

The typewriters were IBM 71s, battered workhorses bought secondhand. They still carried the secretarial diddlings of office frustrations past. Dan's, a vile red, wore a bile-green sticker of a brontosaurus secured by a contact cement that defied any solvent available to man. He'd tried them all, choking on the fumes of several, then wondered what difference the damned brontosaurus made. It stayed, in a way symbolic of the ineradicable past.

Office SOP was to arrive precisely at 9:00 A.M. so that Charlie Lovett, arriving precisely at 9:10, could walk past each cubicle on the way to his glass cage and deliver his verbal goose. "Anything?" was his standard way of putting it. They all had learned not to reply in the negative more than three days in a row. Everyone had access to a battery of wire-service tickers in the machine room across the hall. The poor schlunk who couldn't pump a Markelhenny special out of half a teletyped hint was soon turning on a spit in Charlie Lovett's double-sized compartment, and in full view of those down the corridor through the not-so-sound-proof glass.

What kept everybody going in such a hideous working environment was the one thing Markelhenny had hit upon to make willing junk manufacturers out of otherwise intelligent people: the surprisingly high paychecks.

The morning after Roy Forrest's visit, Dan cut his arrival at *NewScope*'s tawdry offices a tad close. Charlie had his head in Quince Harriss's office when Dan edged past Charlie's imposing rear to clump into his own cell. He was impaling his now shapeless London Fog on the hook screwed into the plywood partition behind his chair when Lovett's voice exploded in the doorway.

"Anything?"

"Haven't checked the machines yet, Charlie. Locally, only the usual ethnic mayhem. And a geezer shooting night before last."

"A who?"

"Security guard in his sixties. Worked the Candler Building. Two slugs in the ear."

"That's only four, five blocks over." Lovett pulled his tie knot down and unbuttoned his collar, his reflex signal that the day was underway. By noon, the sleeves would be rolled up, too. "Didn't see a damned thing about that in the *Times*." He read only *The New York Times*.

"Too late for yesterday's editions. You'll find it in there this morning."

"So can you make anything out of it? Two shots in the ear ain't chipped beef."

22

"Nice way of putting it. What can I make out of a night watchman?"

"Yeah," Lovett agreed. He shambled away, a jowly, bulb-nosed, meringue-crested bear with a bear's beady eyes. Then he turned back. "Sure not a sex killing." His lumpy shoulders heaved in silent laughter.

"You ought to know, Charlie," Dan said. Lovett was fifty-seven.

"Uh-huh," Lovett said mournfully. "Check the wires, will you? We got to get our copy over to Newark by five tomorrow. I still got a hole in your linage. Get *something*."

The biweekly tabloid was written, or rewritten, here on Seventh Avenue, but the typesetting, composition, and printing was done in a huge commercial house on the edge of Newark. Every other Friday was a day of anguish.

He found Lovett's "something" on the Reuters wire. A Calcutta wife had joined her defunct husband on the funeral blaze of the outlawed practice of suttee. And there were suspicions that her conjugal death wish may not have been voluntary. Local authorities were investigating. WAS MATE GIVEN FLYER INTO PYRE FIRE? A mite redundant, but it made a nice two-line head. On *NewScope*, the writers had to come up with their own headlines, which relieved the printing house on the other side of the Hudson of the need for creative thought.

Dan's pyre fire copy embellished the sparse Reuters style. He threw in some provocative questions and began to conjure with a closing pun. *NewScope* readers were big on ironic wordplay.

The DC-9 to Baltimore was fifteen minutes late, but Arbalesta wasn't worried about his timetable at this point in the midafternoon. He walked out of the gray-carpeted Eastern Airlines Pier C, then rode the escalator down to baggage pickup. He retrieved his bag, used his Victorio Literri credentials to rent a car at the nearby counter, and took the courtesy van to pick it up, a metallic-gray Buick Skylark.

The day was overcast. As he merged from the airport road into the Baltimore-Washington Parkway, a film of light drizzle formed on the Skylark's windshield. He found the wiper switch, turned it to "Lo."

On the plane he had memorized the appropriate pages in his notebook. Bernard Latza, age sixty-five. The oldest of them, he noted. Lived in a retirement community called Beechglade on York Road north of Cockeysville, itself north of Baltimore. Arbalesta had already located York Road on the map of the area he had gotten from the automobile rental clerk. Latza, retired from a Baltimore manufacturer of aircraft components, lived alone. Wife deceased in 1980. This kind of thoroughness had taken Rollo several weeks. With such information, Arbalesta determined that he would complete his task in no more than fourteen days, fifteen at the most. The old instincts were sharpening, but he was now forty-five, not twenty-five.

The supplier this time was a gun store. That made Arbalesta oddly nervous. The fact that he found it so readily just off the Baltimore Beltway did not lessen his apprehension. He felt exposed here in this flat stretch of roadside businesses along the divided radial highway.

The building was ramshackle, painted gray with four red-bordered gold letters, G-U-N-S, in an arch on the big plate-glass window. He waited until two overweight, plaid-jacketed customers—or were they just loafers?—drifted out.

The proprietor was an extraordinarily wide man with a bushy beard that obscured the collar of his blue wool shirt. A youngish man with old, cold eyes. Arbalesta met them with his own hard gaze.

"You have an item for Literri? Victorio Literri?"

The big man blinked. "You him?"

"I am he."

"You prove it?"

Arbalesta displayed his bogus driver's license. "An Eye-talian license? You talk good English, mister. Almost like you was born here."

"Thank you. The item, please."

"The money, please."

Arbalesta's voice was hard as a nail on glass. "You were paid in advance, signore. If I were you, I would check my records most carefully."

The man's gaze wavered. Just a fraction. "You're right, buddy. Don't know what I was thinking of."

"We both know what you were thinking of. Get it, *per favore.*"

The gun-shop proprietor bent below counter level and came up with an object wrapped in oily cloth. He laid it on the glass-topped display counter, glanced nervously at his empty customer parking lot, and spread open the wrapping.

An American Arms TP-70, a pistol a little over twelve ounces, heavier than the Beretta had been but still less than five inches overall. It used .22 long-rifle cartridges, an inch long, a third more propellant than the Beretta's .22 shorts. More noise, of course, but not much more. Arbalesta thumbed the release and checked the clip. Full.

He slipped the little automatic into his breast pocket. "You will keep in mind, naturally, that the sum you were paid was also intended to guarantee silence."

"You kidding! This little transaction here never happened. Count on it."

"We do," Arbalesta said. "*Grazie.*"

He held the proprietor's eyes until he noted the glitter of

sweat behind the hair on the upper lip. Only then did he turn away.

He guided the Buick back to the Beltway. The drizzle had become a steady, cold rain. Traffic, four choked lanes of it, crawled past the Security Boulevard exit, where thousands of home-bound employees from Social Security's national headquarters, a mammoth complex to his right, added to the traffic crush.

He did not reach the York Road interchange until nearly 5:00 P.M. The traffic was abominable, but by Roman standards incredibly disciplined. Not an impatient horn had blared in the whole clogged fourteen miles from the onset of congestion. On his two previous trips to America, years ago when he was beginning to expand Esportatore Varieta into Miami and New York, he had decided that American drivers were among the most disciplined on earth, despite their professed low regard for each other's proficiency.

York Road, a highly commercialized main artery that arrowed almost straight north from deep in Baltimore City eventually to twist into open country ten miles north of the city line, took him past Beechglade at 5:18. And here he found a problem. Beechglade was a security-conscious compound, a cluster of individual multi-unit buildings flanking a larger central structure. All of it was built of brick and stained wood with slate roofs.

But it was not the construction that attracted his major attention. It was the seven-foot-high wrought-iron fencing, surmounted with decorative yet fully functional spear points at five-inch intervals. The fence enclosed the entire development, an obstacle broken only by the double-gated entrance, itself under the surveillance of a uniformed guard seated in a small brick gatehouse. These were items that Rollo's American contacts had not checked adequately or had deemed inconsequential.

Arbalesta had taken in all these details without slowing the Skylark. Two miles farther north, he turned around in the driveway of a private residence. Then he cruised south past Beechglade once again. Getting in there was not impossible, but it could be even more perilous that his incautious actions in New York. There would be far less risk were Latza persuaded to come from behind his wrought-iron security.

Bernie Latza liked summer a hell of a lot better than winter at Beechglade. In the hot months, of which this part of Maryland usually had five, he could laze around the pool and keep an eye on the women whose figures had not yet lapsed into advanced middle age. Latza considered himself a pro when it came to poolside observing. All you needed was a pair of sunglasses. Keep your face straight ahead and let your eyes do the walking.

Only Mrs. Fogelson had caught on. "You old roué," she had chided, perching on the chair beside his. "You had my bathing suit skinned right off, didn't you! I could feel it, even down at the deep end."

She took him aback with that, but not for long. "At my age, it's my only pleasure of the flesh."

"Oh, in a pig's eye! I know you flat-bellied old men. I was married to one who became that after our thirty-three years, God rest his soul. Don't tell *me* your fire's out."

"Not even banked," he said, taking off the sunglasses to give her a good look at his china blues. That's what Terri used to call them. His china blues.

"How long?" he said. A widows' and widowers' code phrase.

"Poor old Marvin faded away three years ago." She had a nifty little twinkle. She reminded him of a comfortably padded Toby Wing. Did anybody remember Toby Wing?

She rubbed her chubby legs with a terrycloth towel. "How 'bout you?"

"Five years for me. Three of them here. Tried to numb it with work, then mandatory retirement caught up with me."

"Sad thing, mandatory retirement."

"Well, maybe. Sad thing to drop dead on the cutting-room floor, too."

"You were in movies?"

"No, no. Design of electronics components. Like what goes into the nose cone of a missile. Where we worked on the prototypes, we called it the 'cutting room.' "

"So now you lurk behind your glasses and ogle the widows."

"It passes the day." He chuckled. "Not only the widows."

"You're evil," she said with a delighted grin. "I'll bet you're an old dog with tricks."

But within a week, she had taught him a couple, one of them so pulse-pounding that he'd almost lost the game before he was in it.

That had been in August. In September, Myra Fogelson had left to spend six weeks with her sister in Fort Lauderdale. Now it was October. Beechglade maintenance drained the pool the day after Labor Day. They did that come rain or come Indian summer. Bernie Latza's warm-season entertainment ended at that point. He tried hard to concentrate on reading his way through B. Dalton's suspense thriller rack at nearby Hunt Valley Mall.

He was halfway through something titled *Spiral of Doom* when his Japanese phone offered its cricket chirp.

"Mr. Latza?" The man's voice had a touch of some accent Latza couldn't place.

"This is Bernie Latza."

"I am Tony Podesta, a friend of Michael Josaitis."

"A friend of *Mickey's?*" God Almighty!

"Yes. He and I are in Baltimore on business. He has been delayed in the city, but he asked me to invite you to join us tonight. For dinner."

Had to be an Italian accent with a name like Podesta. "My Lord," Latza said, "I haven't seen Mickey in years. Where are you staying?"

"The Free State Motor Inn, north of Towson." He pronounced it "Toe-son." Foreigner, all right. "You know the place?"

"Sure, I know it. It's here in Cockeysville."

"Yes, Cockeysville."

"What time?"

"We are here only this one night. At eight?"

Eight was far later than Bernie Latza habitually heated up his frozen dinners, but the sudden prospect of seeing Mickey Josaitis made that of little concern. "Eight's fine."

"What kind of car do you drive?"

"A LeBaron. Light blue." It had been one of the few extravagances he'd allowed himself after Terri died.

"At eight, then. We will watch for you."

Latza replaced the receiver with a little quiver. His initial anticipation had been gut reaction. He hadn't seen Mickey Josaitis in God knew how long. They'd been through a lot together, Mickey and him. And the others.

But did he really want to relive it? Seeing Mickey again would sure as hell bring it back, all of it. Even if neither of them said a word about that particular subject, it would be there, hanging between them like that bird in the poem. What was it? An albatross? Bernie Latza didn't know precisely what an albatross was, but it didn't sound good.

That thought crossed his mind, then he forced it away. It should be great to see Mickey again, no matter what.

29

Something else had crossed his mind: the odd fact that Mickey's business associate had called him "Michael." That was Josaitis's real name, but he'd always made a point of his hatred of it. Nobody who'd ever met him for even as long as a handshake had ever been allowed to call Josaitis anything buy Mickey. Maybe the years had changed him. Enough years changed everybody.

Arbalesta hung up the phone in the outside booth at the Free State Motor Inn. He didn't trust phones in hotel rooms. Didn't they go through the hotel switchboard for billing purposes? That made them accessible, he assumed, for other kinds of monitoring.

Latza had seemed an easy enough target. Arbalesta had selected Josaitis from the list simply because Josaitis lived a great distance from here. Arbalesta suspected that such a distance, 2,000 miles of this huge country, would make it unlikely that Latza and Josaitis maintained frequent contact. Still, it had been a risk.

Also a risk was the blatant fabrication concerning "Tony Podesta" and Michael Josaitis traveling together on business, and the thin excuse for Josaitis's not calling Latza directly. Yet, as Arbalesta had correctly assumed, Latza had swallowed the whole lie in his excitement at seeing an old friend.

The eight o'clock time was essential. What the Americans called daylight saving was in effect, and Arbalesta had noted that darkness did not fall until eight. He needed darkness.

Bernie Latza set out at seven-fifty. He waved at the gate guard as the powder-blue LeBaron exited the womblike security of Beechglade and turned south on York Road. He flicked the headlights to low beam and joined the sparse traffic into Cockeysville. The rain had stopped, but the pavement was still wet. An overcast reflected the peculiar golden glow of Baltimore ten miles to the south. The evening was mild, and Latza had decided he didn't need a coat.

Full darkness had fallen when he spotted the shield-shaped red and yellow neon of the inn. He hit the right turn signal and pulled off York into the parking area. There was a space near the registration lobby. He locked the car and started for the entrance.

"Mr. Latza?"

The voice came from behind him, the same voice he'd heard on the phone. A tall man with a narrow face. High cheekbones. Deep-set eyes. And with thinning black hair combed straight back, like a photo a couple decades old.

He wore a black overcoat. The harsh neon almost directly overhead made holes of his eyes, black holes in a face that flashed alternate blood red and metallic yellow.

"I am Tony Podesta." He offered a hard, dry hand. "Michael is at our car. We have reservations at Hunt Valley. Come, we are parked in the back."

Michael. Podesta had called Josaitis Michael again. Bernie Latza was pondering this when he realized he was being escorted to the darkest corner of the big parking lot, a corner out of reach of the lighting at the street entrance.

Hunt Vally was much closer to Beechglade than the Free State Motor Inn. Why hadn't they simply met him there? And with spaces available up front, why had they parked back here?

Something was wrong with this setup. "Why are we—"

The hard pressure of metal against his right ear came as a shock. Then things fell into place.

"My God, did you have to go to all this trouble for a mugging?"

"Keep walking, Mr. Latza." The voice was impersonal and chilling.

"Why me, for God's sake? I'm an old retired fart. I got forty bucks on me. Right hip pocket. Take it. Go ahead, take it."

An icy worm of deeper fear squirmed down Latza's spine. This wasn't the kind of guy he'd visualized as a mugger. He should be a teenaged black with a knitted jungle cap, or a drugged-up pasty-white kid with crazy eyes. This guy had to be in his forties.

And there was the mystifying Josaitis connection—

"Between the cars," the man ordered in his foreign-tinged cadence.

They edged between a ghostly white Cadillac and a smaller, dark car that had been backed into its space. He tripped on the macadam curbing that edged the lot. Then he was stumbling downslope in tall weeds. His prized all-wool trousers would be covered with burdock and other seed stickers damned hard to pick off. Shit.

"Listen, take the damned money and just—"

Those were Bernie Latza's last words. His ear exploded. A lightning bolt spun around the inside of his skull. He didn't hear or feel the second crack of the .22. Only Arbalesta heard it. York Road's truck-traffic roar obscured the two small detonations for everyone else who may have been in earshot. The two small, white flashes were shielded by Latza's head—and because Arbalesta had forced him down a five-foot embankment.

Bernie Latza's body tumbled into a weed-choked drainage ditch between the Free State Motor Inn and a welding-supply outlet immediately to the north. It surely would not be discovered until morning.

Arbalesta hurried back up the slope and slid into his already unlocked Skylark beside the looming Cadillac. He eased out of the space, careful not to turn on his lights until he was headed toward York Road.

He had spent the night before in a motel two miles south. He had needed that sleep. Now he would drive north, deep into Pennsylvania. Because he would travel there in the Skylark, he had no need to dispose of the little TP-70 before he would use it to execute Walter Rose.

FOUR

Bernie Latza's body was not found at first light, as Arbalesta had expected. Latza wasn't found until midafternoon, and then only because of a Siberian husky. The overweight tourist from Kansas and his travel-worn, equally overweight wife clawed out of their Ford as if they both were ninety years old.

"That's the last time we drive five hundred miles at a stretch, Herb," the woman announced.

"Okay, Bess."

"And the last time we travel with that damned hairy horse of yours, Herb."

"Okay, Bess."

"And the last time we stay at a motel this far from where we really want to be. Harborplace must be a million miles from here. Next time, Herb, *get reservations!*"

"Sure will, Bess." Herb was preoccupied with snapping the leash on the husky and getting the big gray-and-white dog out of the back seat of the two-door car. Trouble with the husky was that you couldn't let him run free. He'd just keep going until he was in the mood to turn around. So Herb spent a lot of time on the end of the leash, wondering who was leading whom. Same thought struck him about Bess from time to time.

"Couldn't you have found a parking space closer to the unit?" she grumbled as she stretched into the back seat for her coat. But by now Herb was halfway down the lot's steeply sloped shoulder.

"Gol dammit, Snowball, you're hauling us through the biggest weed patch in Maryland." The dog had pulling power like a team of mules.

Then the husky froze. The guard hairs on its shoulders crested. Herb felt the vibration of a low growl travel up the taut leash.

First he thought somebody had thrown a pair of perfectly good shoes into the burdock and goldenrod and milkweed down here at the bottom of the swale. A pair of composition-soled woven-leather shoes.

Then he saw the ankles in brown socks. He forced himself forward. Snowball inched ahead, too, but hung in right beside Herb's left leg. Herb reached out, parted the weeds with his free arm.

"Great Lord Almighty!"

Bernie Latza lay on his back, his left arm thrown across his chest, his right arm twisted beneath him. There was a stain of dried urine at the crotch of the nobby buff-colored trousers. The middle button of the tan suit jacket was still neatly fastened.

Herb Collier from Kansas would remember all of this as if it were a photograph he'd had printed smack in his brain. He'd see it in his sleep, and when he was awake sometimes, too. And what he'd see most often would be the dead eyes, wide open, staring straight up into the cloudless October sky.

The story got on the UPI wire in an unusual way. Peter Farnhurst, a Baltimore-based syndicated news feature writer, had been looking for a grabber to lead off his long-researched piece on the increase of violent crime in major city suburbs. When the discovery of Bernie Latza's body burst on all three Baltimore network TV channels, he grabbed it. The story hit the national newswire a day later.

Two small slugs in his right ear ended the life of 65-year-old Bernard Lanza in quiet Cockeysville, MD, October 18. The gang-style killing with a pair of .22-caliber slugs typifies the terrifying invasion of violent crime into suburbs, where locking your door in the daytime used to be considered an antisocial action . . .

The teletype machine clacked and dinged on, turning out fifty more lines of Farnhurst's feature, none of it on the victim mentioned in the lead.

Dan straightened, tore the buff copy-paper free, and took it back to his dinky office. Coincidence, of course. But this was a slow day so far. He picked up his phone.

An exasperating ten minutes later, he had learned that Cockeysville, Maryland, had no police department. Or even a sheriff. It was not an incorporated town. In fact there were no incorporated towns or cities in all of Baltimore County. But there was a Baltimore County Police Department, which was entirely separate from Baltimore City's police department. All very confusing, and Dan feared the worst when he was finally shunted to the Baltimore County Police Department public information office.

"Dan Forrest, *NewScope*. In New York."

"Arnold Snyder. What can we do for you?"

"About the Lanza killing."

"That's Latza."

"Oh, it was Latza?"

"L-a-t-z-a," Snyder said patiently. "UPI had it wrong. Bernard Stanley Latza, with a *t*, not an *n*."

"Two shots in the ear."

"Two shots in the right ear. Fired with the muzzle against the head. Autopsy showed powder burns radiating out from the muzzle blast. How come you're interested? Isn't *NewScope* one of those scandal sheets my wife brings home from The Giant?"

"That's why we're interested, Mr.— is it 'Mr.'?"

"Yeah, I'm not a cop."

"Mr. Snyder. Sex angle, anything like that."

"You kidding? The guy was sixty-five. And he didn't get it in somebody else's bedroom. He was found in a drainage ditch next to the Free State Motor Inn in Cockeysville. Not exactly Sin City."

"Maybe there's a motel angle there somewhere," Dan suggested. Charlie Lovett had been particularly insistent this morning that *NewScope* carry some kind of crime headline this time around.

"We thought of that," Snyder admitted. He had the unflappable, ingratiating voice of the experienced PI officer, a rich baritone. This was no hack with his feet on the desk and a cigar stuck in his jaw. Forrest visualized Snyder in a white shirt, regimental tie, and fresh haircut.

"And?"

"I'll give you what they've given me. Latza's car was found parked in the motel lot, about fifty yards from where he was found. Nothing in the car. Only his prints. He wasn't registered there, but that figures. He lived only four or five miles north in one of those retirement communities. Place called Beechglade."

"Married?"

"Widower. Five years. Moved from a house in north Baltimore three years ago. Retired systems designer with an aircraft components manufacturer here. Stayed on two years after his wife died, then mandatory retirement caught up with him. He sold his house and went the retirement village route."

"You people have been busy," Dan said.

"We do what we can. What makes you so interested in this particular case? There's got to be bigger game in your own backyard."

"A Manhattan security guard was gunned down in what looks like the same way last week. Two in the ear. Two twenty-two slugs, with the muzzle right against the skull."

Snyder was silent for a moment. Then he said carefully, "You got a name for him?"

"Phillip Helmsgaard. That's 'gaard' with a double *a*." He knew by the silence that Snyder had begun to take notes. "You want more?"

"We'd sure appreciate the name of the investigating officer, Mr. Forrest."

"It's Forrest, Leroy Forrest."

Snyder was confused. "I meant the officer's name."

"That's it. Leroy Forrest. Two *r*s."

"A relation?"

"Cousin. Manhattan Homicide. You want the number?"

"I'll have our investigating officer handle it."

"Can I have his name?"

"We prefer that all press contacts be made through my office, Mr. Forrest." Snyder had a finely honed career instinct. "I'll be glad to give you whatever can be made public. Anything we can give out to reporters here, you can have as well."

No favor there. Professional, courteous, a hard man to dislike, but Arnold Snyder, PIO, wasn't going to be a source much better than the local newspapers.

"I'll be in touch," Dan said by way of a ring-off, and he dialed Roy. *NewScope*, in keeping with office austerity, was one of New York's last bastions of the rotary dial.

Roy's voice sounded as if he'd just been jangled awake from a bitch of a night.

"Roy? Dan."

"Yeah?"

"You're about to be called by the Baltimore County Police in Maryland. Some old guy down there was plugged a couple nights back."

"So?"

"In the ear, Roy."

"Uh?"

"With two shots, Roy."

"Oh."

"With a twenty-two."

"Jeez."

"Thought you'd like to know."

"Some coincidence."

"Think it is?"

"You don't, Dan?"

"Ask the county cop when he calls."

"Yeah, I will. I will."

Dan pictured Roy Forrest lurching back heavily in his battered chair, fiddling with the abalone-shell handle of the letter opener he'd picked up on a rare vacation he and Barbara had squeezed in down the Jersey Coast. Dan had been to Roy's squad room once, on a story that didn't pan out. Roy had a desk in the middle of a lot of desks. The letter opener had "Lavallette, NJ" on it in yellow script.

Dan punched the IBM's On switch. The typewriter began its rhythmic metallic whisper. He hadn't been able to make anything out of the Helmsgaard shooting, but now he could throw in the Latza murder. TWO .22 TWO-SHOT KILLINGS COINCIDENTAL? Loose, but as Casey would put it,

40

titillating. He flexed his fingers and bent over the keyboard.

Two small-caliber slugs in the ear were the grisly finds of coroners' offices in Manhattan and Baltimore County, Maryland, October 16 and 19. Both shootings, just two days apart, were by .22-caliber weapons. Or was it the same weapon?

Here we go again, Dan realized. Implication by question, a *NewScope* specialty. But it would hold up because Roy didn't expect ballistics reports until next week, and *NewScope*'s deadline was less than an hour from now. If the same gun was used, it would be an infinitely better story.

The small caliber used is the preferred weapon of crime syndicate hit men. Despite its size, it can be more destructive than a larger caliber. "The heavier gun has more punch," a ballistics expert has pointed out, "but its slug often enters and exits in a relatively straight line, making only a flesh wound. The small .22 slug with its lower penetration power can ricochet off bone and tissue and create internal havoc before its force is dissipated."

Dan had found the quote in the small criminology library he kept on two woodchip shelves behind the door.

Such was the case with Phillip Helmsgaard, a 61-year-old Manhattan security guard from Queens, and Bernard Stanley Latza, 65, a retired mechanical engineer in Baltimore County, Maryland . . .

Not bad for what he'd had to go with, Dan decided. He had done worse with more. Maybe he was getting a real feel for *NewScope*'s kind of saffron regurgitation. He

41

stopped his four-finger typing. The thought wasn't a soothing one. Then the phone rang.

"Thought you might like to know that Baltimore County called." Roy sounded like he hoped Dan would be impressed.

"That was quick. Anything new?"

"Routine, Dan."

"That went out with 'Dragnet,' for God's sake. What did they have to offer, Cousin?"

"Not much."

"Come on, make me proud."

Roy gave. He always did. It was that compulsive need to impress. But what he gave was what Dan already had. Spokesperson Arnold Snyder had leveled.

"So what does Homicide think, Roy?"

"What do I think?" That wasn't quite the same thing. "I think it's a coincidence, that's what I think. These two guys didn't have a damned thing in common except age, more or less. A watchman and a retiree two hundred miles apart. One's scratching for a buck, the other's living in what sounds like a pretty plush retirement setup. One had been a hand-to-mouth machine-shop draftsman, the other guy'd been an aerospace engineer."

"Similarity there?"

"Not much of one, Cousin. Two kinds of peas in different pods." Roy always did have a knack with clichés. "You can't make much out of that."

"I already have."

"The usual 'who struck Joan,' no doubt. Big questions, no answers."

"At least I had the decency to leave your name out of it."

"Good thinking, Dan. Appreciate it. Because we got nothing, you got nothing. El zilcho."

"And the guy from Baltimore County PD's got nothing."

"That's right. Except the guy's a girl. Detective Willy Constanz. All business, but she don't know anything either."

Dan had a sudden thought. "Anybody check for rap sheets on the victims?"

"Oh, boy," Roy groaned. "Yeah, we ran computer checks. Clean as a hound's hind leg, both of them. There's nothing there, Dan, I keep telling you. Get off my case."

Arbalesta had been surprised to discover that the forty-mile stretch of I-81 between Frackville and Wilkes-Barre dipped and rose across the rolling tops of Pennsylvania's flattish Pocono Mountains without a single roadside motel. He drove straight through to Scranton, a two-hundred-mile pull from Baltimore, most of it in the bleak darkness of the Poconos.

He checked into a motor lodge on the south edge of the Lackawanna Valley just past midnight. He undressed, took a long, very hot shower. Then, wearing only blue silk underwear shorts, he stretched out on the huge bed and studied Rollo's notes.

Walter Henry Rose, West Main Street, Dalton, twenty kilometers north of Scranton. Age sixty-two. Lives with wife, Adele, in her midfifties. Rose is half-owner, with Peter McClay, of Rose, McClay Jewelers. . . . One store, on Lackawanna Avenue, Scranton. General appearance: heavy, bald, medium height . . . This time, the photo was sharp.

Hit Rose at work? Hit him at his home out in the countryside? Either had its advantages and problems. No, in the American manner, call them challenges. The old stirrings were sharper now. This was becoming more than a sacred fulfillment. More like the old days when a lean, lightning-reflexed Arbalesta had stalked Milan, Bari, then Rome, his favored Belgian-made 9mm Browning changing the face of the *Sindicato d'Amici*, eliminating those too incompetent to realize their own employee was the one called *Il Sciacallo*—The Jackal.

Ah, what times, those days of the ruthless hunt. And the moments of realization in the final widenings of so many stupid men's eyes. That made the blood race, as it was beginning to race now.

Those had been the exciting days. Except for the women. He'd been cursed all those years with their disbelief, with their desperate attempts to help him, even with taunts of the unfeeling ones. Yet he had failed consistently, humiliatingly. He had searched endlessly for the reason. "Physically, Signore Avillano"—he was using the name "Salvatore Avillano" for that ineffective visit to the private clinic in Florence—"physically there is nothing we can discern that may cause your difficulty. Only the blood pressure somewhat high." Small, and ironic, wonder. There had been recent trouble in the Marseille processing location. An informer, who was now the diet of fishes at the bottom of the Mediterranean. And the entire operation had to be relocated.

"Therefore, Signore Avillano, the problem has to be one of a psychological nature. Might you consider seeing a psychiatrist? I can recommend an excellent man who specializes in problems of this nature."

No psychiatrists, Arbalesta determined. Not for a man in his line of business. He would have to work this out on his own. That had proved to be an impossibility until his mother's deathbed revelation. What else could be the reason for the years of humiliating sexual defeat? *Logico*. And just as logical was his conviction that carrying out the vow he had made to her would at long last free him of this lifelong curse.

"Different weapons, Dan." This time Roy had called

44

him. "Just got the Maryland ballistics photos. No doubt about it. No match. So much for your connection theory."

Dan tilted his chair back on its creaky spring. "It wasn't a theory, Roy. I was pointing out a similarity."

"Leave police work to the police, Cousin. I don't try to write your stories."

"You don't think it's an interesting coincidence?"

"Sure. But we see them all the time. Psycho copycat killers. Drugged-up kids who think it's funny to give us a hard time. Poor, pathetic bastards who glory in the press attention."

"By shooting a stranger in the ear? Come on, Roy. Keep me in mind if anything else turns up on this, will you? Remember, I'm the guy who sent the Baltimore County cops your way."

Roy was silent for a moment, then he said, "It was a nice, simple watchman killing up to then."

"Not so simple. There was no apparent motive."

"You realize how many homicides there are like that in this city? Who needs a motive with the world going nuts?"

"My wife makes me feel like somebody," Walt Rose said to Pete McClay as he opened his brown-bagged lunch. " 'Somebody forgot to cut the grass. Somebody forgot to take out the garbage.' You know what I mean?"

Rose was a stocky man, wide with meaty shoulders. His hair was a bushy halo that ringed a freckled bald spot the size of a saucer. His nose was a blob stuck in a cheery Santa Claus face. A clumsy-looking man, except for his hands. He could have been a big-city surgeon, so Adele often said. She had especially pointed it out when business went into the bucket in the late seventies. Instead, he was a jeweler in a city that once was big but that had lost nearly half its population since World War II. You build your whole economy on only one commodity—coal—then you shouldn't be so shocked when something easier to use and cheaper, like oil, comes along, Walt had told anyone who'd listen. But that explanation didn't slow the erosion of the business.

McClay watched Rose unwrap his cheese and bologna on rye. Then he wrinkled his thin nose in distaste.

"Twenty years of that! Come on, let's close the place for an hour, go over to Pregio's, and get you a decent lunch. Minestrone, maybe a nice lasagna. Real food, not that cardboard. That's for steelworkers forty floors up and old men on fishing trips."

"I'm not so young, Pete." Walt buried his teeth in the sandwich.

"Neither of us is so young," Pete McClay said. Rose looked at his partner leaning on the cheap-charms-and-nicklenacks counter. That's what Rose called the lines Pete had insisted on bringing in. They had downgraded the store, in Rose's opinion, but the schlock had also seen them through the worst days.

"This is Lackawanna Avenue, Walt," McClay had said in his spiel to sell the idea, "not Fifth Avenue. The money's leaving. There aren't enough big bank accounts left in Lackawanna County to keep us pure."

Pete McClay was a little shrimp of a guy with a mournful face. A basset. An itch, because he kept changing Rose's pure dream of a quality shop. "Nothing but quality," Walt had vowed to Adele when he'd signed the lease back in the fifties. "It's Lackawanna Avenue, all right, but right around the corner from Washington." Lackawanna hadn't been so bad then. Still had the Hotel Casey and the Riviera Theater. Not now.

McClay had signed on in the mid-1960s when Rose desperately needed the partnership money. They laid off a full-time clerk and a part-timer. That was when Rose began to bring the brown bags.

"So I eat alone," McClay said. "Be back at one-thirty." The floor-pad buzzer sounded as he left. Walt looked up in reflex, as he always did when he heard the buzzer. That was when he noticed the man in the black coat.

Was it the way the guy walked, small steps with no bounce to them? The precise cut of the coat and exact length of the trousers? Most men wore them either too short with some sock showing, or too long with crumpled breaks and the backs almost dragging on the ground.

Or was it the fact that the man seemed to be loitering? Watching. Was he watching the shop? After two burglaries in the dark hours of morning three years and one year ago, and a stupid midafternoon robbery six months back by a junked-up kid who'd been so nervous he'd dropped his cheap gun and run, Walt Rose was excusably paranoid about people hanging around outside.

Not that the guy over there was in the hanging-around category. It was just that he didn't seem to fit in. Too well-dressed, too confident-looking for Scranton. Was that it? Was he getting suspicious of people who didn't look beaten down by a city with problems?

Then the guy was gone. When McClay reappeared, Rose told him about the black coat across the street.

"You'd hang a guy because you thought he was out of place and watching you across Lackawanna Avenue? This is the widest street in Scranton, and the old eyes h'aint what they used to be, partner."

"He looked too successful to be standing around over there."

"That's a native for you. You're just not ready for a local comeback. Look up the street. That's a new Hilton there. They took that rotting pile of rock that was the DL & W Station and made a success of it. We pulled Steamtown right out of New England. Those are part of a comeback, Walt, and you're worried about a man looking successful

47

on Lackawanna Avenue. Should have gone for lasagna with me."

Rose rubbed his hand over his rubbery face. "You're right. Forget about it."

Which Pete McClay promptly did. But only for a short time.

Arbalesta had wakened at nine. The nonstop drive from Baltimore had been remarkably tiring. He had a leisurely breakfast in the motel coffee shop—scrambled eggs, bacon, toast, coffee. The marmalade came in a little plastic box no bigger than a postage stamp, and he had trouble opening it until he discovered the slitted access corner. America was fascinated with hard-to-open packaging.

At noon he drove into Scranton, became lost for several minutes, then found Lackawanna Avenue through the fortunate circumstance that it was perpendicular to the broad street, Wyoming Avenue, on which he was traversing downtown.

Traffic was heavy, and he was unable to see much on his first pass by Rose, McClay Jewelers. He decided that cruising the rented car's black-and-white Maryland license plates around and around the block was an unnecessary risk. He parked in a garage four blocks distant, walked back, crossed Lackawanna at Washington, and looked back across the wide street. There were two of them in there.

A bus roared across his view, adding its wake of diesel exhaust to the haze of the overcast afternoon. Arbalesta's eyes narrowed for finer focus. HOURS 9 A.M.–5 P.M., MON– SAT. Gold letters, three inches high, visible even at this distance. *Grazie*, gentlemen.

When the smaller man left, the man in the shop glanced up and seemed to look right at Arbalesta across four lanes.

Stared at him, then returned to his sandwich or whatever he was eating. No more than a bored shopkeeper checking the early-afternoon sidewalk traffic and hoping for walk-ins.

But Arbalesta automatically began to move, to blend in. Where Lackawanna Avenue curved to the left, he strode up the wide drive to the Hilton. A rebuilt railway station? Incredible. With their short history, Americans had absurd ideas of what was classic and should be saved. Near the entrance he dropped coins in a newspaper vending rack, opened the hinged panel, and took out a copy of *The Scranton Tribune.* He discovered that the lobby of the old station, a rococo cavern of a place, was now the dining room. He stretched his lunch of bean soup and a London broil into an hour and a half.

When he emerged into light rain, sidewalk traffic was becoming sparse. He cursed the weather and walked in the direction of the garage where he had parked, head bent against the increasing downfall. He passed a cinema, but it didn't open until seven. There was a coffee shop nearby. He ordered coffee and a sweet roll. The coffee was good, but the roll was far too sugary. He used up nearly an hour in the red plastic booth, making a pretense of reading the damp *Tribune.* Some of its ink came off on his fingers. He rubbed them clean on a paper napkin.

Now the hour was 3:24. Still time to kill. He walked the remaining block to the garage, guided the Skylark into Washington Avenue traffic, and drove northeast for thirty minutes. That took him out of the traffic-clogged central city into a middle-class residential section, then through a neighborhood of substantial homes with large, well-kept lawns. The rain grew heavier as Washington Avenue finally dwindled to a road through fallow fields, passed a gloomy, deserted construction he judged to have once been a coal-processing complex, then wound into a far less affluent suburb.

He turned around in a driveway and retraced his route. It was inconceivable that anyone plodding along the puddled sidewalks would even note the double passing of his Maryland plates, much less connect that with what he would accomplish here. If anyone did, the trail could lead only to Victorio Literri, a man who did not exist.

At 4:47, Arbalesta guided the Buick slowly along Lackawanna Avenue. Still too much time, the curse of this project. Then he found a parking space. He pulled in abruptly. Good fortune on a dismal day. Not only the luck of a parking space; there were twenty minutes left on the meter.

He was on the same side of the avenue as the jewelry shop, near the far end of the same block. Now if Walter Rose did not have an appointment somewhere, did not unwind at some bistro, did not take a bus—if there was a bus to the town of Dalton. Was not given a ride by someone. All of these possibilities would not alter Walter Rose's deserved fate, but any of them could delay it. Delay increased Arbalesta's risk.

At 5:03, he watched two men exit the store. The larger man turned back, rattled the doorlatch. Satisfied, he rejoined the smaller man. Together they strode along the sidewalk toward Arbalesta, passed him as he turned his face across Lackawanna. Not a chance that Rose, certainly the heavy man in the sharp, passport-size, full-face photo Rollo's people had provided, would realize that Arbalesta, the man in the shadowed car they so hurriedly passed, had been across the street earlier in the day.

In his rear-view mirror, Arbalesta watched the two jewelers walk into the parking area in front of the Hilton. A parking arrangement with the hotel, of course. They got into a metallic-green car, Rose on the driver's side. Unless they drove back down Lackawanna, Arbalesta realized, his own car was headed in the wrong direction.

They didn't. The green car glided down the drive to Lackawanna, then swung right. Luck didn't last forever. Arbalesta gunned the Buick, pulled out of the space abruptly, and executed a sudden U-turn across Lackawanna's four travel lanes.

Horns blasted behind him. In Rome, such a maneuver wasn't considered so unusual, but he had upset the more disciplined American drivers. He checked his mirrors. No police vehicles in sight. To hell with the horn honkers!

Four vehicles ahead, the green car—it was a Mercury— turned left on Mulberry. Arbalesta followed. Now there was only a small Japanese car between him and Rose's Mercury. He slowed to let another vehicle slide in ahead of him.

They crossed a long iron truss bridge, then entered a winding expressway. Arbalesta eased his speed. The Mercury pulled a quarter-mile ahead, and a half-dozen cars intervened.

A van drifted in front of him, blocking his view. Faster traffic rushed past on the left. When he was able to pull around the van, he discovered that he was racing into an interchange. Ahead on the highway to Carbondale, there was a growing traffic crush. He scanned the line of cars. A green— no, too light in color. Where in hell . . .

Then he spotted the Mercury swinging into an off-ramp to the cross highway. He floored the accelerator. The Buick leaped across the right-hand Carbondale-bound lane. Tires shrilled on wet pavement. He'd cut off one frantic driver, forced another to fishtail wildly. But he made it across to the off-ramp. He settled down a quarter-mile behind Rose, his heart slamming against the weight of the automatic in his breast pocket.

The expressway curved gracefully through a deep cut in the mountain ridge rimming the northwestern edge of Scranton's valley. Then they sped into hilly, open country. A small town spread itself along a lower parallel road to his left. The highway rode the shoulder of the mountain above it.

Two miles farther, the Mercury cut right, into the exit ramp of the Clarks Summit interchange. Arbalesta followed. Two cars were between them now. The brief parade crossed back over the highway on a long bridge, swung hard left, then reversed down into traffic on the lower blacktopped road.

The evening traffic here was thick. Arbalesta nearly lost the Mercury when a light changed between them, but the green car got caught at the end of a line beyond the light anyway. Then he lost sight of Rose's car altogether, had no choice but to drive straight ahead for more than a mile, then spotted it again in a tight line of vehicles at the crest of a long climb into what turned out to be the fair-sized town of Clarks Summit.

He got a surprise there. The Mercury pulled to the curb, and the small man got out, bent down in what Arbalesta presumed was a thank-you to Rose, and turned to begin a climb up a steep hill studded with small residences.

Arbalesta had no choice but to roll past the parked Mercury. In his mirror, he watched it pull out a half-dozen cars behind him. Ahead the road forked at the north end of town. Now what?

He kept his eyes on the mirror. Traffic ahead began to split into two lanes, one for a tight leftward swing, the other for the main highway, Route 6-11. Arbalesta bore ahead. Now far behind him, the Mercury obligingly followed. Luck had returned. A mile farther on, Arbalesta let

Rose overtake him. Then he accelerated to pace the green car a half-mile behind.

They passed a small blue-and-yellow sign: DALTON. The Mercury slowed, wound to the right down an incredibly tight ramp, and emerged in the little valley community. Arbalesta came down the ramp barely in time to see the other vehicle turn right again into Main Street.

At the stop sign, Arbalesta watched Rose pass beneath a bridge that supported the highway they had just left. Then the Mercury began a long climb, veering right at a fork partway up the hill.

The road was narrow two-lane blacktop now, potholed here and there. The houses flanking the road thinned at the top of the long grade. There were no other vehicles on this country stretch. Arbalesta felt exposed. He had no choice.

A quarter-mile farther, the Mercury climbed another, slighter grade, then rolled along a level stretch. The few homes here seemed to be former farmhouses rebuilt into country estates by professional people and business successes.

The Mercury followed a gentle curve to the right. Arbalesta stayed his quarter-mile back. When he rounded the curve, he saw the double flares of Rose's brake lights. The Mercury had stopped at a driveway. Rose's arm reached from the driver's window to extract something from a cylindrical silver container atop a waist-high metal stake.

Arbalesta rolled past. He held his head straight forward, but his eyes took in a lot. The box was marked SCRANTON TIMES. The Mercury was partially in the driveway, so this had to be Walter Rose's home. The house was set back from the road on an embankment, screened by a stand of dense spruce trees. Arbalesta judged that the end of the drive could not be seen from the house.

He drove another mile before he found a crossroad that

took him back down into the valley and to Route 6-11. He didn't want to retrace his route past the Rose house because he had already been forced to take too many risks today. He had been afforded only six seconds at most to observe the house and its grounds. That had been enough.

Now he knew where to kill Walter Rose.

FIVE

Yesterday Rose had had the creepy feeling that he was being observed, or even followed. It had begun with the hard stare of the man in the black coat across Lackawanna Avenue.

"That's nuts," McClay said, tidying up the cheap-charms-and-nicklenacks case from the depredations of the departing pair of barrel-shaped teenaged blondes who had bought nothing. "What brought all this on?"

"That guy yesterday. Haven't felt secure since."

"Jeweler's lament. Us and liquor store owners."

"More than that, my friend. It's a . . . This is going to sound stupid. It's a crawly feeling in my stomach. Like I swallowed a cold worm. Like something bad is going to happen."

"A holdup?" McClay's face sobered. "You did predict that, didn't you?"

"That kid with the gun? Yeah, I had the same feeling then that I have now. Adele says some people can sense that kind of thing. I think I'm one of them."

"I think you're letting yourself be a nervous poop of an old man, Walt."

"Wait 'til you're my age. What does a child barely fifty know!" He walked into the workroom-office at the rear of the showroom. Then he stuck his head back out the narrow door.

"You're right. It's an old man's fear of becoming older but no wiser."

Yet he couldn't shake it, this vague thing that squirmed in his mind. Not just in his mind. He couldn't get through Adele's carefully built liverwurst and swiss. On rye, yet.

It was a slow Saturday. He had too much time to fret, but only to himself. When he let Pete McClay out at the foot of his Clarks Summit hill, McClay said, "What a great conversationalist you've been today. But it all went on in your own head, didn't it? You all right, Walt?" The little man's long face showed real concern.

"It'll pass. All things pass. Have a nice Sunday." An inside joke. They had vowed to be the only merchants in the valley who would never say, "Have a nice . . . whatever."

Now alone, he found himself checking his rear-view and side mirrors. For what? Not much traffic on 6-11 this murky Saturday afternoon. Did the premonition, if that was what this was, concern a potential accident? Ridiculous, of course, but he edged the speedometer needle down to fifty. A truck howled past. Then came a battered van with a clatter of suffering pistons and a gray car with white Maryland plates, its tires sighing softly.

He swung down the fishhook turn into Dalton, stopped at the sign, drove beneath the culvert, then up the hill. How many years had he done this? How many Saturdays while most everyone he knew played or caught up with chores? How many years left? He wouldn't retire. To what? All he knew was diamonds and gold and rhinestones. A gardener he wasn't, nor much of a traveler. Retire to what? Adele?

He rounded the final curve, thoughtful and preoccupied. Then, a distance ahead, brake lights glared red. Did that car skid right at his own driveway?

When he pulled up behind it, the driver had gotten out and was looking at his left rear tire. Walt Rose rolled down his window.

"Trouble? Can I help?"

Then his voice was a solid thing obstructing his throat. The man wore a black coat. The same man. Rose knew without a shadow of Pete McClay's doubt that something terrible was happening here.

Yet when the man forgot about his tire and hurried toward him, he did nothing. What was there to do for a sixty-year-old fat jeweler? Blow the horn? Then Adele could be at risk, too.

"I don't carry any merchandise on me," he said. "You can have my wallet, sure." He was astounded at how calm he suddenly had become. Maybe from relief that his all-day worry had been justified. A little victory over Pete's sometimes aggravating pragmatism.

Then he thought how ludicrously he was acting, should the guy turn out just to be lost or something. He was gripped with sudden embarrassment until the man's right hand snaked out of his coat pocket.

Then it was too late to think anything at all.

"We got the gun," Roy Forrest said with immense satisfaction. "Found it in a storm drain, a block and a half from the Candler Building."

"And that's why you're here twice in the same week?"

"I like your coffee, Dan. I like to watch Casey work on you."

"Hey, back off there!" she protested.

"And, yeah, I wanted to tell you that."

"You could have called."

"That would be too easy. I wanted to see your face when I told you that you'd glued a story together out of match straws."

"You're a credit to your race, Roy. Did you find it in the storm drain personally?"

"I asked for the search. Garbage cans and storm-sewer openings. Prime stashes."

Dan had to give him credit for that. Roy beamed. "So we got what I thought we had from the beginning. A dumb-ass killing for no reason."

"Or a hit."

"You got to be kidding, Dan. The guy had no background for that. Only type who might be interested in icing Helmsgaard would have been a bar owner in a high miff over being stiffed for a big tab." Roy supported that with a bray of laughter.

"Look," he said, abruptly serious. "We checked him out with a fine tooth. There's nothing there." He set down his empty coffee cup. "It's a fluke killing. A drugged-up jerk with a pistol. A loose nut."

"That doesn't worry you?" Casey put in. She sat cross-legged beside Dan's chair, wearing baggy slacks of some shiny blue fabric, tight at the ankle. Dan had called them clown pants. Surmounting that was a rainbow-hued serape.

"Sure we're concerned. But we'd be a hell of a lot more concerned if we hadn't found the gun. A guy on a killing binge doesn't make a practice of throwing away a nearly new Beretta."

"You trace it?"

"No serial number. Chiseled off, then acid to boot."

"I thought there were ways to beat that."

"There are, and ways to beat the ways to beat that. No trace possible on that particular piece."

"You talk to Helmsgaard's wife?"

"Dan, let me up, will you? We interviewed her, sure. We interviewed everybody at the rent-a-cop service who had so much as ever said hello to Helmsgaard. We talked with anybody we could find in his apartment building who knew him. And we uncovered zilch."

"File closed?"

"Not on homicide, Cousin. Still wide open. But time is limited on this kind of thing if the file doesn't get any fatter. Any homicide department in the country will tell you that the day after a victim is buried, chances of breaking the case start to go right down the chute."

Casey got to her feet with a little squeak as she stretched cramped legs. "More coffee, gents?" She brought the Silex from the kitchenette.

Roy glanced at his huge watch. "One more, then I got to be going. Barb gets itchy when I get home so late. Hey, why don't you both come out to the Island and see us for a change? We only got one extra bedroom, but . . ."

"Fine with me." Casey beamed.

"You could make a weekend of it." Roy leered.

"And break Brother Daniel's vow of celibacy? Oh, the shame of it!"

"Attempting to contribute to the delinquency of a near minor," Dan said. "And you a cop."

"Let him talk," Casey countered, her voice rising over the jangling of the phone. "I like his ideas."

Dan held out the receiver. "For you, Roy."

Roy shook his massive head. "Like a frigging doctor, leaving them the number wherever I go. Yeah?" he said into the phone.

Then his jawline went slack. His eyes rose from the tan wall-to-wall carpeting to focus on Dan's.

"Damn!" he said. "When?"

The phone squawked in his ear. "Yeah," Roy said. "I'll come right back."

He dropped the receiver in its cradle, chewing on his lower lip. "Looks like my night's not over. There's been another one, Dan. This time it's Pennsylvania."

"Anything?" Charlie Lovett's voice was a hard rasp this morning.

"Yeah, Charlie. Somebody is killing the geezers of America. And the forces of law and order are haggling over jurisdiction. NYPD has the Helmsgaard killing. The Baltimore County Police are investigating the murder of Bernard Latza. And the Walter Rose thing—"

"The jeweler?"

"Right. That's in the hands of the Pennsylvania State Police. How's that for a bucket of snakes?"

Charlie leaned his bulk against the doorjamb, thereby making the cubicle feel smaller that a phone booth. "Where's the angle?"

" 'Where's the angle?' You mean the *NewScope* angle, the sin, sex, and sleaze? Hell, Charlie, all three of the victims were in their sixties."

"People still screw in their sixties.'

"You, too?" Dan said in mock dismay. "I'll tell you something. Homicide doesn't believe it. Baltimore County doesn't believe it. As far as I know, the State of Pennsylvania—"

"It's a commonwealth."

"A who?"

"The Commonwealth of Pennsylvania. It doesn't call itself a state."

"For God's sake, Charlie. All right, Roy tells me he doesn't think the Commonwealth of Pennsylvania believes it either. And of course Roy doesn't believe anything that isn't attested to in triplicate. But I believe there is a connection among all three murders."

"Based on what?"

"Based on gut feeling. Instinct."

Lovett shifted his weight to the other side of the doorway. "Based on the need to produce copy, I'd say."

"All of that."

"So what do you want from me?"

"I want to cover this thing."

"You are covering it."

"Oh, hell, Charlie. I'm rewriting press-wire copy and PI handouts. Hack rehashes. What kind of coverage is that?"

"That's the kind we pay for."

"Damn it, wouldn't it be worth the effort just once to have *NewScope break* a story—a real story? Not the crap that the free-lancers pour in here: 'Woman Wins Malpractice Award for Off-Center Belly Button.' "

"When did we run that one?"

"In August, as a matter of fact. I'm talking about *coverage*, Charlie, not rewrite. Don't you get conscience twinges running this recycling plant?"

"You don't seem to have a conscience about cashing the paychecks."

"If you didn't pay me, I wouldn't come near this place. Listen, Charlie, I'm talking about a couple of hundred bucks' expenses for a story that could sell a couple hundred thousand extra copies."

Charlie shuffled his shoes—big, scuffed wing-tips broken down on the inside. Like a lot of heavy men, Charlie was knock-kneed.

"The cops don't have evidence of a connection. I don't see a connection."

"There's a connection, all right. There are too many similarities not to be."

"No dice. You signed on to turn out crime rewrite. Do it."

Dan forced his eyes from Charlie Lovett's retreating backside and faced the pile of wire-service copy sheets on his desk.

"Well, I couldn't help overhearing!" Jonathan Blauvelt wore a blinding hot-pink shirt and blue plaid pants cut sausage-tight.

"I'll bet. Jonathan, what in hell are you advertising?"

"Guess, sweetie. Anyway, he'll never let you out of here. Charlie gets nervous if everyone of us isn't in his or her cell, grubbing away like a good little monk or nun. Turning press-wire pap into juicy gems for the checkout set."

He paused, his bird-bright little eyes following Melody Matso's ripe little butt past the cubicle door.

"I'm onto you, Jonathan."

Blauvelt's blow-dried coiffure swung back in. "Oh, her?"

"By Christmas. I have a bet with Harriss."

Blauvelt's thin eyebrows arched. "I haven't the slightest idea what you're talking about, you wicked man."

"Ho, ho, ho. She'll be your Christmas chicken."

"I didn't come here to be insulted." Eyes and voice gave him away. He glanced along the corridor, then moved into Dan's cubicle. "You actually think by Christmas?" He cleared his throat. "Since you appear to be a betting man, I'll put up ten bucks that Charlie will never parole any of his prisoners to cover anything worth anything outside. We're custodians of a literary landfill here, each of us frantically manning his own little trash compactor. Ten bucks."

"You're on."

And that was before Dan got the call from Cousin Roy.

"I don't know why I'm so good to you," the big detective rumbled.

"Because blood is thicker," Dan said. Why the curiously subdued tone of Roy's voice?

"Just got word from Pennsylvania State—"

"It's a commonwealth." Was this going to be yet another reinforcement of Roy's insistence on "no connection"?

"What?"

"Never mind, Roy. Tell my why the Pennsylvania killing hasn't a thing to do with the other two."

"That's the problem. It does. It was done with the same gun."

Ah, so! "But you said the guns were different. Ballistics in Baltimore—"

"Yeah, the Baltimore and Manhattan jobs were with different guns. But the slugs in the Pennsylvania hit—'

"Now it's a hit?"

"Whatever. The Pennsylvania slugs are a fair match with the Baltimore slugs. Not a hundred percent, because there's a lot of distortion. But they found the shell casings, too. An automatic leaves its own trademark on ejected shells. Obviously the guy didn't wait around to pick them up. The ejector and the firing pin marks, too, match pretty well. It's just about a sure thing that it was the same gun."

How about *that!* On his way back from Charlie's office, Dan detoured to stick his head in Blauvelt's cubicle.

"You lose," he said.

The apartment building was a walk-up, four floors. Lenora Helmsgaard lived on the fourth. She opened the door to the limit of a brass chain that stretched taut just below her chin.

"Another reporter? At least you don't have a camera."

She must have been a fine-looking woman once, short and no doubt dainty before the years had put on their poundage. Her gray-streaked brown hair was in a loose bun. Her mouth was still pretty. Her eyes would have been, too, but they hadn't recovered from the shock and strangeness of it all.

"So many questions. First the police, then the papers and TV. The TV people are the worst."

"I know. Camera in your face. All they want is reaction." He was fine one to talk, Dan thought. "I'm Dan Forrest, *NewScope*."

She nodded solemnly. Then the crack closed. He heard the chain rattle. The door swung wide.

"You can come in. *Newsweek* can come in. Would you like coffee? I was having coffee when you came."

The cup she handed him had a small chip at the rim. The apartment was furnished with the kind of stuff renters of beach cottages supplied their by-the-week tenants who couldn't care less. But the place was scrupulously scrubbed and vacuumed.

"It's not usually so neat." Lenora Helmsgaard had followed his glance. "When a woman has trouble, she cleans, Mr.— I'm sorry."

"Forrest. Dan Forrest," he told her again. "I apologize for the intrusion."

"But *Newsweek* wants a story anyway."

"It's not *Newsweek*, Mrs. Helmsgaard." Would that it were. "I work for *NewScope*."

Her strangely delicate eyebrows bent in a frown of concentration. "The thing I see in the A and P? You want to do *that* kind of story?" Then she laughed.

He didn't know how to react.

"It's crazy. I mean, Phil in a paper like that. The only thing he ever did in his life was draw and drink. He was a draftsman. I guess you know that already from the other papers or the TV. He was good, too, before the booze got him. After that, for almost twenty years . . ."

Abruptly her eyes filled. She pulled a rumpled tissue from the pocket of her peach-colored slacks.

"I'm sorry. You don't know what those twenty years were like."

"Yes, I do," Dan said softly.

She peered at him. "You, too?"

"Not for the past five years. But before that."

"So." She dabbed her eyes again. "So that's why it's *NewScope*."

Smart woman. Had Helmsgaard realized how smart?

"I'm sorry," she said again. "I'm crying for the wasted years more than for what happened, I think. Phil hated what he was doing. He came out of the army so eager to be somebody."

"You knew him then?"

"We were married then. The start of thirty-nine years married. I was eighteen. We were going to knock the world on its ear. Two know-nothings. You see how it came out. I guess it comes out like this a lot."

"You mean the way he was? The way he died?"

"No, not that. I mean you start out with such hope and joy, then you get worn down. He doesn't get the big job that would make all the difference. A baby is born dead. Then—" She saw his reaction. "Oh, yes, that happened. I was a long time getting over it. Something about Rh blood. I never did understand it all. But I knew we had to be so careful not to make me pregnant again. Always worrying about mechanics. Phil hated that. He was a Catholic." Her cheeks flared crimson. "Oh, please God. You wouldn't put that in your story!"

"Mrs. Helmsgaard, I'm not doing a story on you and Phil. I'm wondering if there's a bigger story. There have been two more elderly men killed the same way."

"Two more? There's somebody going around New York shooting sixty-year-old men?"

"Phil was the first I know about. Then a man near Baltimore. The third one lived in northeastern Pennsylvania. The same gun was used on those two."

"The same gun as on Phil, God rest his soul?"

"No, the gun here was different. They found it near the Candler Building, but it didn't tell them anything. No prints and untraceable."

She picked up her cup, not noticing it was empty. "Where's the connection with Phil, then?"

"The only real connection is the gun with the other two. With your husband—well, that's why I'm here. Same kind of gun, used the same way. Phil was about the same age as the others. Did he ever speak of a Bernard Latza or a Walter Rose? Latza was a retired engineer from some kind of defense work. Rose was a jeweler in Scranton."

"They're the ones?"

He nodded.

Now she saw her cup was empty, his half-empty, "Here, let me warm that up for you." The coffee had been several times reheated and was rank, but she appeared to need the break.

"No," she said as he took back the cup and saucer in both hands. "I never heard Phil mention either one. You think he was mixed up in some kind of middle-aged thing with those people?"

" 'Thing'?"

"You know, like something crooked?"

"Was Phil that kind of guy?"

"I didn't think so, Mr. Woods, but I never thought he was the kind of guy who gets murdered, either."

"Did he ever talk about who might want to . . ."

"Kill him? Never. Phil was a nice . . . drunk. Most drunks are nice people, Mr. Woods."

"Forrest."

"Oh, I'm sorry. Mr. Forrest. AA would tell you that." Abruptly she looked aghast. "I . . . I apologize for that."

"No need. You're right. AA did tell me that. I was a wonderful guy when I was squiffed. And for a year after I dried out, I was a terrible pain in the . . ."

"Yes, exactly there. That was Phil. Twice—no, three times—he stopped cold duck. I could hardly live with him. I hate to say it, but it was a relief when he went back to it, as long as he didn't get sloppy. Just a glow, you know? But a glow all the time. His work would get messy, and they'd fire him. They all fired him, except the guard service. As long as he shows up and makes his rounds—"

She broke off and stared at her hands. "I'm sorry. I'm talking like he'll come through that door while we're sitting here."

"Was he a gambler, Mrs. Helmsgaard?"

"With what? You know what we own? You're looking at all of it. Would you give credit for any of this?"

"Nothing else you can think of that he might have been involved in?"

"Nothing. We lived simple. When you don't have any money, that makes you live uncomplicated. The big thing in Phil's life was next year he'd be sixty-two."

"Why that?"

"Because that's when you can get early Social Security."

Dan got nothing more. She laughed a second time when he suggested the possibility of another woman and a jealous husband or lover. Really fishing at that point.

"Phil? He wouldn't know what to do with another woman. Lately he hardly knew what to do with me." She flushed a second time. "You wouldn't print that, Mr.—"

"Dan."

"You wouldn't, Dan."

"I wouldn't, Mrs. Helmsgaard. I'm looking for a killer, not bedroom stuff."

"That's a change." She looked sheepish. "I read *New-Scope* once. When Elvis died. You don't work for a nice paper, Dan. But you're a nice man."

He had to get out of there after that. He ran into Roy on the third-floor landing. The big detective was wheezing already. The young, worried-looking plainclothes cop with him seemed annoyed.

"Second time around, Roy? Just to make a better case for 'no connection'?"

"It's that frigging Baltimore-Scranton gun. This is Clyde Williams, Homicide. Clyde, Dan Forrest. Your wife read *NewScope*? Dan writes that crap."

"Thanks, Roy."

"You learn anything in there?" Roy pulled out a blue handkerchief and mopped his forehead.

"You want me to do your legwork for you, Cousin?"

"Just as long as I don't have to do yours. This whole thing is getting more complicated, Dan. The gun was carried interstate from Maryland to Pennsylvania. Now the FBI is making jurisdictional noises. Can you imagine the paperwork?" He leaned close. "What'd she tell you?"

"I don't think she told me a damned thing, Roy. I could have saved the time."

He thought he could have saved the time later that afternoon with Harry Gardelis, too, at Aaron Alert Security. Its most imposing feature was the frosted-glass door on the fifth floor of a soot-black granite building on Fifty-seventh.

"Mr. Aaron? There isn't no Mr. Aaron. I'm him. Like, I mean, Gardelis won't get you up front in the Yellow Page listings, so that's why Aaron. Still got beat out by AAAA Security. What can I do for you?"

A long, almost black cigar no thicker than a pencil jounced in the corner of his mouth. Harry Gardelis also chewed gum. Not incidentally, he would have weighed in

68

at three hundred easy. And he sweated the whole time Dan was in his birch-and-brown-formica office.

"Phillip Helmsgaard."

"You a cop?"

"Reporter."

"It's Aaron with two *A*s. Gardelis with one *l*. You don't take notes?"

"In my head. I found a notebook shakes people up almost as much as a tape recorder."

"Shakes me up when they don't take notes." He shoved a memo pad across the desk. "You take notes."

The logo used oversized *A*s. It came out "AA-ron," then "A-lert," all in the inevitable red ink of a cut-rate printer. His address was a lot better than his stationery.

"Tell me about Helmsgaard," Dan prompted.

"What's to tell? He needed a job. I can always use guys with clean records who'll work the hours we need for the bread we pay. He would. He checked out, so we took him on. Been with us a couple years, I think."

"What's checking him out mean?"

"Running him for raps."

"You got access to that kind of information?"

"You kidding?"

"You've got a file on him?"

Working his lips and tongue, Gardelis rolled his unlit pencil cigar to the other side of his mouth. He hadn't taken it out once. He raised his head in a defiant reflex, and Dan saw a brown bow tie under the chins. Nice complement to his tentlike tan shirt.

"Why should I show it to you?"

"Aaron with two *A*s, Gardelis with one *l*. I can be a lousy speller."

Gardelis grunted deep laughter. "A new one. That's good. Okay, just remember how cooperative I am."

He swiveled around like a chairbound sea lion and

pulled a manila folder from the filing cabinet behind him. Employment application, physical exam results, five AAron Alert semiannual evaluations, all five with "satisfactory" squares checked straight down the line.

"Not excellent or good. Just satisfactory."

"That was Phil. No unsatisfactories, either."

"It doesn't say anywhere in here that he was a drunk."

"Look, Forrest, the Candler job wasn't a big deal. That's why we gave it to him. All he had to do was walk the main floor five times a shift and clock in at the check stations. He did that fine. Anyway, who'd break into a building that has a big glass entrance like that?"

"Somebody did it. And killed him."

Gardelis folded huge, remarkably short arms. "Yeah, poor bastard." He wasn't exactly dripping with sympathy, more like regret over the paperwork.

"Who'd want to?"

"Beats the hell out of me."

"Nobody had it in for him?"

"Nobody I know of. Our people barely see each other, 'less they're on jobs together. They come here for an interview and to sign on. From then on they report straight to their assignments. We mail the checks. You see a squad room here?"

"Damn it, Gardelis, one of your men was shot on the job. Doesn't that shake you up a little?"

"Sure. Sure, it does. I feel sorry for the guy, and I hate to lose a man. But you gotta realize what kind of a city this is. All kinds of people out there. A nut gets hold of a gun, hates uniforms, and takes out his grief on the first badge he sees. No difference to him that I buy the badge from a specialty house in Des Moines."

"You're all heart, Gardelis."

"I'm all business, and that includes the insurance you'd see listed there if you'd looked far enough."

Dan opened the file folder again. Fifty thousand if death was employment-connected. Lenora Helmsgaard hadn't mentioned this. But Dan hadn't known enough to ask her.

He looked across the littered desk with new interest. "The law requires you to do this?"

"I got a good deal on group rates." The hard voice suddenly went soft. "This is the end of the line for the old ones, know what I mean?"

"It was for Helmsgaard. But he's worth a hell of a lot more now."

"That's for sure." Then Gardelis had the same thought that had hit Dan. "You're not saying he had some son of a bitch plug him so's his widow would get the money!"

"That's as good as anything I've come up with." Which was nothing. "Did you tell all this to Detective Forrest?"

"You know he was here?" Gardelis's mammoth face widened even further into what was supposed to be a grin. "I get it. Forrest and Forrest. A brother act."

"Not quite, but tell him."

New York was turning into a dry hole, unless the unlikely insurance angle had a glimmer of validity. Maybe Maryland would be a better gamble for Charlie Lovett's expense money.

SIX

ARBALESTA'S PLAN WAS TO STRIKE SWIFTLY, then move on without delay. *Battere e fuggire*. Hit and run, leaving the police to their ponderous investigations, procedures and form-filing. America, he was convinced, was once an efficient new nation, but now, like the long-established nations of Europe, it had grown overly fond of records, forms, procedures. Italy's centuries-old legal complexities were manifold. Surely it was becoming the same here, and that very cumbersomeness would shield him.

If America's police were only twice as efficient as Italy's *polizie*, he would have no trouble keeping literally ahead of them. America was in love with travel, a huge nation where you could cross thousands of miles and the borders of dozens of state jurisdictions without a single permission required.

As the United 737 climbed above the Maryland haze, Arbalesta pressed the button on the armrest and lay back in the seat. He closed his eyes. Two details he could have handled better, he reflected. But just two. A different weapon in Pennsylvania, though the risk of obtaining one would have had to be weighed against the improbability of the police in Pennsylvania matching the bullets with the Latza bullets promptly enough to cause a problem. He thought not. The small town—Dalton, had it been?—could not possibly boast a police department worthy of the name. A constable, perhaps. Or a sheriff, as in the American Western movies. No doubt an untrained, political appointee.

The other detail that still niggled at him was the matter of sequence. Perhaps he should have attended to Rose first, then Latza. As it was, he had returned to where he had already stirred up hornets. He had read a story on the killing in a copy of *The Baltimore News American* at the airport. But there was no police efficiency on earth that could have tied Victorio Literri to the execution behind the Free State Motor Inn.

Only the weapon connected the second and third executions. And there was nothing to relate the weapon to the rented car. That was why Arbalesta had not left the Buick at the Scranton–Wilkes-Barre Airport and begun his Phoenix connection there. Some genius, if there were any in this confused nation's police ranks, might have put together the coincidence of a Baltimore-Scranton weapon and a Baltimore rental vehicle left in the Scranton area.

So he had returned the car to Baltimore-Washington International Airport, where he had rented it. He could have chosen Philadelphia International or even Washington National. But it gave him satisfaction to return to the very airport where he had rented the Skylark. An act of defiance. Or disdain for Americans. Or even cockiness. The old reflexes were sharpening.

He would have to watch that. But the Literri trail was

74

severed at BWI. He had paid cash for the Phoenix fare and used the name Luigi Volpe. That seemed appropriate. *Volpe* in English was fox.

Dan registered at the Free State Motor Inn at 1:30 P.M., driving a rented mud-colored Toyota.

"Mileage will be reimbursed at twenty cents per," Charlie Lovett had told him. "That's what the government says you can operate a car for."

"What mileage? I'm from Manhattan, remember? I don't own a car. A license, sure, but no car. Where would I park the damned thing, in New Jersey?"

Lovett's face had turned somber. "You telling me you got to *rent* a car?"

"I'm telling you."

"A small one. For a goose chase, you get something Japanese."

"I'm going to goose a story out of this, damn it. Give me something decent to chase it in."

He got the Toyota. "Come back with the goods," Quince had cracked, "and maybe next time he'll let you rent a Realota." The car was better than he'd expected. Quick steering, in and out of New York traffic like a whiz. But on the Jersey Turnpike, then on 95 through Delaware and into Maryland, its tight springs certainly didn't make for any luxury ride.

At 1:45, he called Beechglade from his motel room, got a courteous woman with a peach of a Deep South accent but the hard head of a Yankee.

"Anyone at all who knew Mr. Latza will help."

"Mr. Forrest, you must understand that since that horrifying tragedy, we have tightened security considerably, And it was already substantial. Beyond that, there is the matter of privacy for our residents. Surely you realize they are at an age where personal security becomes a major concern. That is one of the prime reasons they have chosen Beechglade for their retirement years."

Quite a speech. It boiled down to "no."

"Mrs. Kenyon—it is Kenyon, isn't it?—I've driven here from New York to try to establish a connection among three murders. The other two have aspects similar to Mr. Latza's. No one knows what's behind these killings. There may be more." He was speculating on that, but who knew? "I'm sure your residents would want to help in any way they can." He could made a speech, too.

"Three murders?" The silky Georgia voice was silent a moment. Then Mrs. Kenyon said, "Our residents have helped, Mr. Forrest. A dozen of them have been interviewed by Detective Constanz, Baltimore County Police. They've told her everything they knew about poor Mr. Latza."

Charlie would kill him if he came out of here with an empty bag.

"Would you do this, Mrs. Kenyon? Would you ask who knew Mr. Latza best if they would talk with me? Let them decide for themselves? You can reach me here at the Free State."

She called back in twenty minutes. "Mrs. Fogelson will talk with you. Anytime this afternoon." Kenyon's voice had lost some of its sorghum and had taken on grits. "Check with gate security. I'll have you cleared."

The guard was a young, slicked-back blonde with a green uniform and a steel clipboard. "Unit Twenty-seven on Harmony, sir. That's the drive to the right."

The macadam wound through white pines, then autumn-flamed maples. The units were in groups of five with staggered entrances to avoid the rowhouse onus. Brick and dark-stained wood. Not a bad place to die.

The door to Unit Twenty-seven opened as he strode up the brick walk.

"Mr. Forrest?"

She was chubby, a sexagenarian Shirley Temple with saucy short hair dyed a vivid gold.

"Mrs. Kenyon asked you to talk with me about Bernard Latza."

"No," she said. "I insisted. I cut my visit to Bal Harbour short to come back for poor Bernie's funeral, may God have mercy on a nice man, and I'll talk with anybody who's trying to do something about it. You'll come in?"

The condo was cool and crammed with antique pieces that looked even more jammed in the light streaming through the broad picture window in the rear.

"The patio, I think. It's a warm day." She already had a wine carafe and glasses on a green-painted wrought-iron table out there. The late-afternoon sun filtering through the maples washed the patio in an odd reddish light. It struck her hair as she sat and turned it to flame.

"You are from what paper? The *Sun* or *News American*?"

"Neither, Mrs. Fogelson."

"You'll call me Myra. And you are—?"

"Dan, from *NewScope*. Do you know it?"

"Know it! Such baloney! I eat it up. But if that's what you want to do with Bernie, why come here? You could write *NewScope* schtick with your ears shut."

She was a perceptive woman.

"You'll have some wine."

He held up a hand. "Thanks, but I'd rather not."

"Not take wine? Would you rather iced tea, then?"

"No, nothing, thanks. This story's not the usual *NewScope* stuff, Mrs.—"

"Myra."

"You know about the shooting near Scranton?" he asked.

"No. Somebody was shot there like Bernie was shot?"

"Two bullets, same gun. A man of sixty-two. And in

New York, a Phillip Helmsgaard. Two bullets, different gun. But he was in his sixties also."

"Him I read about someplace. Maybe in *NewScope*. Your story? I remember the name because once I had a beau named Helmsgaard."

For a fleeting instant, Dan felt electricity. Was it possible?

"Not Phillip Helmsgaard!"

"No, Edgar." The electric current fizzled.

"How well did you know Mr. Latza?"

She flicked him a glance. Her eyes had a saucy crinkle. "You wouldn't quote me in your terrible paper?"

"You can trust me."

"Ha! A laugh. But what's to lose. You mind if I?" She gestured at the wine carafe.

"Enjoy," he said.

She poured herself a full tumbler and sank back in her chair with it. "I knew him better than anyone here knew him. Need I say more?"

He got it, all right. Mrs. Fogelson was a rouette and proud of it.

"Did he ever mention Helmsgaard or a Walter Rose?"

"Not that I remember."

"Or any specific relationship with Scranton or New York?"

"He had a stockbroker in New York."

"He talked with you about his investments?"

"We talked about a lot of things. Investments, health, memories. When you get to our ages, that's what you do." She winked then, actually winked. "That doesn't have to be *all* you do, of course."

If she were thirty years younger, Dan decided, we would already be on the floor.

"Did he talk about insurance?"

"You're sure you won't take some wine? I like a touch of

white wine this time of day. Helps keep me together, if you know what I mean."

"Mrs. Fogelson—"

"Myra."

"Myra, a touch of wine would be like a match to a fuse, if you know what I mean."

She studied him. "Oh, I'm so sorry. I didn't mean to press. Here, let me get iced tea."

"No, really, nothing at all. About the insurance, Myra?"

She crossed her chunky legs beneath the pleated Irish-wool skirt. "Oh, he said he had only his army insurance—you know, ten thousand worth—until a couple years before Terri, she was his wife, died. He bought—I think he said a hundred thousand term. For the inevitable, you know. Only the inevitable happened to her first, not him."

"So who's the beneficiary now?"

"He never said. It wasn't my business."

Neither was the rest of it, Dan thought. But she seemed to be pretty well versed in Bernie Latza's affairs.

"You're thinking none of it was my business."

"You read minds?"

"I read eyes, Dan. You're also wondering if I seduced poor Bernie so he would change his insurance, then hired somebody to finish him so I would get the money. I can tell you that's crazy because I already have some money. You can't live here on just charm and Bran Buds, you know. What Bernie and I had was something you definitely don't get from conniving for a man's insurance."

She took a long drag on the wine. "Maybe you should quote that," she suggested. "I thought I put it pretty good."

Dan stood. "You're a remarkable woman, Myra."

"But I haven't been any help."

"Yes, you have."

She looked startled. "I've told you something?"

"You've made me less afraid of growing old."

He located Detective Wilhelmina Constanz at Baltimore County Police Headquarters on a side street in Towson. The building was low, flat-roofed, and blue-paneled with a gigantic silver-painted plaster police shield in the lobby facing the glass entrance doors. She was in conference, the youthful officer behind the information window told Dan.

He cooled his heels in the small red-carpeted lobby for ten minutes. Then a tall woman with hair as black as a crow's wing walked out of the office corridor with a stride like a man's. She wore a rust-colored knit dress nipped in at the waist with a narrow tan sash tied at the right hip. Not much over thirty, Dan guessed.

"Don't get up. I'll sit." Her voice was low-pitched. Dan imagined that when she said "Halt!" they halted. "I'm Detective Constanz." The hand she offered was dry and cool. Like its owner.

"Dan Forrest. *NewScope*."

"They told me. National interest, such as it is?"

"You read *NewScope*?"

" 'Siamese Twins in Love Triangle' isn't exactly hard news. I read it sometimes for laughs."

He didn't think she laughed much.

"What possible angle brought you here?" Cool gaze from a cool face.

"I'm taking a flyer on this one."

"The twenty-two-caliber killings? Detective Forrest is your brother?"

"You're a perceptive cop. He's a cousin."

"With that kind of pipeline, I doubt there's anything I can tell you that you don't already have."

"Any known enemies? Isn't that the way they put it?"

Her eyes were an unnerving emerald green. "Not anyone we know about." Her left eyebrow raised a tad, giving her a speculative look. "Shouldn't you be talking to Arnold Snyder, our PIO?"

"I already talked to him." Dan saw no need to tell Detective Constanz that particular conversation had taken place days ago.

"What else are you looking for? Somebody mugged the man behind the Free State Motor Inn, got rattled, shot him, then panicked and ran. The deceased still had his wallet and watch and a diamond pinkie ring."

The deceased? "And the perpetrator got the hell off the premises?" She missed the little vernacular jab—or decided to overlook it. "And did the same thing in Pennsylvania?" he added.

"That does bother us. The gun may have been disposed of, then picked up by somebody else."

"Who used it the same way two hundred miles north? Come on!"

"That does bother us," she repeated.

"What about the insurance?"

"Insurance?"

"If I found out Latza had a hundred-thousand policy, so did you, Detective Constanz. Who's the beneficiary?"

She didn't answer, but her green eyes never left his.

"Myra Fogelson?"

The corners of Willy Constanz's wide mouth twitched. "You talked to her?"

"Long enough to decide that she and Latza were more than poolside partners."

"Isn't that remarkable? She's pushing sixty, and he'd just turned sixty-five."

"You know what the eighty-year-old man said when his doctor told him to be careful about marrying an eighteen-year-old girl."

Now both eyebrows went up.

" 'If she dies, she dies,' " Dan said.

Detective Constanz appeared to fight a grin, then she gave in to it. "Hadn't heard that one." She looked at the nobby red wall-to wall carpet. A pair of uniforms went by. "Hi, Sammy," she said to the rusty-haired one. Then she said to Dan, "The insurance goes to a Mrs. Emily C. High-tower in Kahului, Maui. That's in Hawaii."

"I could have guessed. Who's she?"

"His daughter."

"You checked her out?"

"As best we could. She flew here for the funeral, then flew right back. I spent about forty-five minutes with her. She seemed genuinely shocked and saddened. Her husband is with a real-estate development company on Maui. Makes a staggering salary. Maui County Police checked him out for us. No big debts. No apparent motive, if that's what you were thinking."

"You were."

"Yes, we were."

Charlie Lovett would have an instantaneous fiscal seizure if Dan asked for expenses to cover a quick trip to Maui.

"I'll take your word for it. No Hightower connection." God, if he only did work for *Newsweek*! He was trying to cover a Cadillac beat on a moped.

"The case is frustrating, Mr. Forrest. As best I can determine, Bernard Latza was a very nice man, highly regarded at Beechglade and by former business associates. And if you're looking for another kind of motive, Myra Fogelson was widowed and had no lovers except Mr. Latza."

"No crazed son who'd just escaped from the asylum in demented craftiness to avenge the latter-day loss of his widowed mother's virtue?"

The smooth coral lips, and they were quite lovely,

twitched again. "You certainly *do* write for *NewScope*. No, no such relative. Only the sister in Florida, a woman of sixty-eight with a hip problem."

"You're very thorough."

"We try to be, Mr. Forrest."

"So we have an aging man whom everybody loved. And we have no reason for anyone to kill him. but we have a big problem. Somebody put two bullets in his brain."

She crossed her legs demurely at the ankles, smoothed the rust-colored skirt, and leaned toward him. "Let me give you a little background. A few years ago, this department cleared ninety percent of its homicide cases. That was before the bodies really began to pile up. This is a big county. It surrounds Baltimore City on three sides. We're getting a lot of city spillover. Drug-associated, mostly. And some other unsavory body counts. Now we clear only seventy percent of county homicides. The chances of clearing the Latza case aren't good. It's listed as a 'stranger killing'—murder by a stranger to the victim. Those are the worst."

She opened her leather purse and fished out a pack of Virginia Slims. "Cigarette?"

Smoking, Dan had discovered, only increased the appetite for a drink. He was off tobacco, too. He shook his head.

She lit up, took a long drag, and blew the smoke straight up. "It was a mugger, Mr. Forrest."

"It was more than that, Mr. Sheen."

She was too young to get it. "The Pennsylvania incident, Detective Constanz."

"A copycat."

"With the same gun?"

"That does complicate the theory."

At Sky Harbor International Airport, Arbalesta used

his Victorio Literri credentials to rent a blue Ford LTD, this time through Hertz. Avis in Baltimore, and other companies were scheduled at the final two locations. Rollo had cautioned him that if he were to use the same automobile-rental agency throughout, it would not take genius on the part of the police—were they able to coordinate—to run a check of car-rental agencies at the six sites. The name Victorio Literri would pop up at five of them.

All that would take time, and not much more time would elapse before Arbalesta had carried out his sworn vengeance. Three were dead. Three remained.

He drove north on Twenty-fourth Street in moderate traffic and the unexpected heat of Phoenix, spotted Indian School Road readily enough, and followed it westward until he found himself in an area of run-down commercial establishments. He located the place quickly, parked along the crumbling curb, and stepped from the air-conditioned LTD into a wash of Arizona warmth.

The one-story cement-block building was painted pastel green. Above the dusty display windows flanking the entrance, black letters fading to gray spelled out ROBBIE'S AUTO PARTS. Arbalesta didn't like this part of the operation. Rollo had originally suggested that the weapons be deposited in airport lockers with the keys at a pickup point in each terminal. Too risky, Arbalesta told him. He was not sure of the preciseness of his schedule. Weren't the lockers checked periodically? And the key pickup procedure could involve more "outside" people in the already intricate plan. So Arbalesta made the weapons pickups directly from the sources.

The man in the tipped-back chair behind the dingy counter had a face carved of mahogany and coarse, shoulder-length black hair.

"Mr. Robbinet?"

He frowned over his newspaper. "Out back. Through there."

The rear door opened into a sandy workyard enclosed by a fence of sunbaked boards. The secluded area was strewn with engine and body components and a half-dozen automobiles in various stages of dismantling.

"Mr. Robbinet?"

The slightly built man in greasy coveralls pulled his upper body from beneath the hood of a battered brown Lincoln Continental and brushed hair out of his eyes with the back of his wrist. It left an oily smear.

"Yeah?"

"You have a package for Victorio Literri?"

"You him?"

"Yes."

"You prove it?"

Arbalesta showed him the Literri driver's license. He had weighed the value of using a different identification at each of these delivery points. Then he realized the people involved were as incriminated as he and most unlikely to be cooperative with any probing authorities. Moreover, he was striking fast and moving fast, confident that he was leaving a wake of abundant police confusion if, indeed, the many jurisdictions involved were able to piece together anything at all.

Robbinet placed his big open-end wrench on the Continental's fender, shambled to a gray plastic trash can, and lifted its cover. He pulled out a piece of cotton waste and wiped his hands.

Then he glanced at the back door of the building. Arbalesta had closed it behind him. Robbinet plunged his arm into the cotton waste up to his shoulder and came up with a small parcel wrapped in newspaper secured with red rubber bands. He stood there, apparently waiting for something.

"You have already been paid." The incredible heat bouncing off the yard's packed sand made Arbalesta irritable. That and the man's arrogant pettiness.

"Don't I get a tip?"

"You get to continue in business," Arbalesta said in a toneless voice. He stripped off one of the rubber bands.

"Cheest! Don't unwrap it here!"

"If it's not what was ordered, you will receive another visit but not another chance."

"*Yes, sir!*"

The man's insolence was uncalled for, but Arbalesta let it pass. He had what he needed.

He opened the oil-stained parcel in his room at the Desert Hills Inn on the north side of Lincoln Drive in Paradise Valley, northeast of the city. Lincoln Drive ran east-west between Mummy Mountain, a grayish escarpment that rose steeply behind the hotel, and the rounded crags of Camelback to the south, across the highway. Arbalesta had regretfully closed the drapes on a breathtaking view of the sun's last orange light painting Camelback's exposed faces oxblood red.

The pistol was a little American-made Jennings J-22, not quite five inches overall. Its six-shot magazine was loaded with .22 long-rifle cartridges. Walnut grips. Satin chrome finish marred only by the crude slot where the serial number had been routed out.

He worked the slide action and dry-fired. He'd hate to throw this one away, too. With regret, he had tossed the TP-70 over the roof of the Buick as it crossed a deep ravine near McAdoo in the Poconos on his return trip down 81 from Scranton. The little automatic had made a long arc as it cleared the bridge railing at the same speed as the car, then dropped out of sight into the woods below the interstate.

He slipped the Jennings in the breast pocket of the lightest sports jacket he'd brought with him, a brown shantung with nubby metallic-bronze underweave. He liked the weather here in Paradise Valley. Warm and dry. He was almost sorry his purpose required such a brief stay.

SEVEN

MICKEY JOSAITIS SPENT THE FINAL HOURS of his life with no premonition whatever of onrushing disaster. Quite the contrary. He enjoyed a growing sense of elation. At sixty-one, he was about to close the biggest deal of his life. It sure looked like McCorkle was going to sign.

The old Kelleher estate tucked up there on the backside of Mummy Mountain had been empty since Mabel Kelleher had finally "cashed in," as she would have put it herself, in 1980. Five years of neglect hadn't helped the big ramble of natural desert stone any, but five years of development in the flat miles all the way to Carefree sure had improved the view. At least from Leo J. McCorkle's standpoint.

"Like a valley of diamonds!" McCorkle ("Say, call me 'L. J.,' would you?") had told Josaitis when Mickey had carried through his inspiration to drive L. J. up there at night. "I like looking out at something, Mickey. Can I call you Mickey? Lotsa folks want to look out at nothing but cactus and scrub. I saw enough of that in the Panhandle."

McCorkle was a retired land speculator from Amarillo with a startlingly young wife who preferred to sun beside the Arizona Biltmore pool while L. J. tramped the countryside looking for a place to "spend my waning years. Know what I mean, Mickey?" He had nudged Josaitis with a granite elbow on that one.

"You seen the missus," L. J. explained, in case Josaitis was incredibly dense.

"Beautiful woman."

"You ain't just a bird turdin', pardner. A firecracker. My third." He'd said that proudly, as if using up baby-faced women was a special accomplishment.

They had crunched around in the dust of the Kelleher mansion's multilevels three times. "How much land did you say goes with this?" L. J. had asked the first time around.

"Forty acres. From the crest of the rise behind the house all the way down to the bend in the road." It looked like miles down the slope, an illusion of height.

"Forty acres . . ." The hefty old land speculator wasn't quite out of it yet, Josaitis thought. McCorkle bounded off somewhere into the dank recesses of the big rock pile. Josaitis leaned back on the sill of a broken picture window that overlooked twenty miles of Arizona desert; fifty when the copper mines weren't working and the air became clear as well water.

Sally Voss at Sun State Realty had told him not to waste his time on this place because everybody else who had handled it had gotten nowhere. The price was low enough, but only a McCorkle would want to lay on the wampum (he'd said that, too) needed to bring five years of decay and vandalism back into the twentieth century.

When L. J. asked to go back a fourth time, after Josaitis's inspired night ride up Mummy Mountain's north side, Mickey was gripped by an elation such as he hadn't felt since surviving his thirteenth combat mission. Not even his marriage to Stephanie Cowart had done that for him, a foreshadow of the horrific divorce that was to follow a dozen years of anguish later. She and every other Cowart had wanted him to "get a decent desk job." But he was a salesman. That was all he knew. Wholesale giftware through Illinois for a New York house. Then women's sweaters to Midwest boutiques. Pet supplies. Even electric organs for a while. A regular Willy Loman, and too much for Steph. She left, and he left, too. Came back to Phoenix to live with his older brother.

Mickey and professional bachelor Cal had made a hell of a thing out of all that freedom; years of wining and wenching with enough sales work to keep them solvent and sinful. Cal hadn't slowed down until five years ago when he turned sixty-four. Now he was right on the bottom edge of seventy, and the emphysema wasn't any help. Emphysema, for God's sake, in the place where people came to cure asthma!

That meant Mickey, lean, silver-crested, and fit contrasted to Cal's skinny, bald, and dying, had to work for both of them now. It wasn't getting any easier. Sale of the Kelleher monstrosity would do a lot besides proving to Sal Voss that there was juice in the old whangeroo yet.

He guided his four-year-old Chevy down the rutted road from Mummy Mountain's northern crest and sneaked a glance sideways at McCorkle's florid face.

"You see how far we've come from the house, and we're still on the property."

"Don't push me, pardner," McCorkle rumbled. "I'll let you know tomorrow."

"I'd be glad to take Mrs. McCorkle up there with you, if you'd like her to see it."

"Hell with that! Only place she's got inspiration is in bed. She ain't going to see nothing 'til it's rebuilt."

At that moment, Josaitis was sure he had the sale. It was all he could do to keep from shouting.

Dan's timing was terrible. He approached the Roses' home past a surprising volume of traffic going in the opposite direction on the narrow county blacktop. It came from the house. Some sort of get-together was breaking up. Then he realized it had to be the postfuneral luncheon, or whatever they had up here in the northern Pennsylvania hills.

He was half-inclined to turn around, find a coffee house somewhere, and cool it for a while. But what kind of reporter did that?

The house was two-story white clapboard with lots of windows and green shutters, imposing on its rise of ground with a fieldstone wall enclosing a terrace that ran across the entire front. Only two cars remained in the wide, blacktopped drive. Dan parked the Toyota near a towering spruce, walked up the flagstone steps through the terrace wall, and pushed the front door's mother-of-pearl chime button.

The big Dutch door swung open just a foot and a half. "Yes?" She was the color of black coffee; short, in a buff-colored maid's uniform with a white apron.

"I realize this is a bad time."

"Worst possible," the black woman said.

"Would you ask Mrs. Rose if she might see me for just a few minutes? I'm Dan Forrest from New York." It seemed a good idea not to pitch the *NewScope* connection at the moment. "I called earlier."

"It's all right, Mrs. Thompson." The voice from beyond a doorway to his right sounded remarkably composed, an even contralto.

The Dutch door swung wide. He found himself in a narrow entrance hall. The black woman nodded toward a room at its near end.

It was big, multiwindowed with exposed beams. Floor-to-ceiling fieldstone dominated one wall to form a huge fireplace flanked by bookcases and framing a snapping oak and beech log fire.

"Mr. Forrest, I'm Adele Rose." She was slender, three inches taller than the man standing beside her. She wore a plum-colored suit with a gold lapel pin, a daisy with a diamond dewdrop winking on one of its petals. Her salt-and-pepper hair was combed back in a tight bun. She was not the kind of Adele you called Addie.

"This is Walter's partner, Peter McClay." The guy in funeral gray was short, but he had a long face. His hand was moist and cold.

"We just came from the cemetery, you realize," he said.

"I know this isn't a good time."

"No time is good for this sort of thing," Adele Rose said. "I just want to get all the necessities over with as soon as possible, though I'm having a hard time convincing myself that your visit is a necessity."

Like her, the room was decorator cold. Everything was coordinated in beiges and blues, but there wasn't a whole lot of it. Hardly any personal touches, except for a photo of a young Walter Rose, Dan assumed, that stood in its silver frame on the piano in the far corner. The round-faced boy in the photo wore a pair of wings on his tunic. Outside of that, the room felt as impersonally formal as Adele Rose herself. One guess as to who'd been in charge of the decorating.

She motioned toward the sofas that flanked the fireplace. "Please. Sit, both of you. The caterer's about to leave. I'll be back in just a moment."

McClay perched primly, hands folded in his lap. "You're with some New York paper, Adele told me."

"*NewScope*, Mr. McClay."

The high narrow brow furrowed. "I don't know that one."

"A biweekly tabloid."

"Oh." That finished that.

"I was Walt's partner," McClay said into his own silence.

"So Mrs. Rose said."

"Tragic thing. Tragic thing. A man isn't safe in his driveway. Dreadful what people will do for just a few dollars."

"Was he robbed?"

"No. Apparently whoever it was got scared off before he could take anything. That makes it all the more senseless, doesn't it?"

That pattern again. Dan had heard it from Roy, from Detective Willy Constanz, and now from Peter McClay. Robbery was the motive, but nothing had been missing. "Scared off."

Mrs. Rose reappeared carrying a sterling tray laden with three small snifters and a cut-glass decanter.

"Courvoisier, Mr. Forrest?"

"Thank you, but nothing for me."

McClay accepted quickly enough, and she poured herself a stiff one.

"Now," Adele Rose said, sitting next to McClay on the small sofa facing Dan, "what could you possibly want of me?"

"I find myself supporting a not very popular cause, Mrs. Rose. In the past week, three men in their sixties have been shot, all in the same way with twenty-two-caliber handguns. One in New York, one near Baltimore, and the third was Mr. Rose."

Her steel-gray eyes held his. "And you're looking for a relationship."

94

"There is one between your husband's death and the Baltimore murder. They were done with the same gun."

"But that's ridiculous! Walter had no Baltimore connections at all. No social ones, and I don't believe any business connections, either. Peter?"

McClay shifted his feet. "No, we dealt with New York suppliers and a few in Philadelphia and Los Angeles. Nobody in Baltimore. What do the police think about all this?"

Dan compressed his lips. "That's why I called this an unpopular cause. New York Homicide seems to think the killing there is unrelated. Baltimore County is still thinking muggers. And I don't know what they think up here."

"It's under state police jurisdiction. Dunmore Barracks in Scranton. Sergeant Crowley told me they're working on the robbery theory. Whoever did it ran off when I came out of the house." Adele Rose stared at her hands.

"Did you see whoever it was?"

"I saw only his car. Just a glimpse as he raced north. Then the trees got in the way. The car was dark blue or gray. That's all I can tell you. That's what I told the state police."

"The driver was a man?" Maybe he could trigger some subsconscious retention.

"I'm quite sure. Would a woman do something like this?"

"The overcoat," McClay said unexpectedly. "Tell him about the overcoat. I'm sure your paper can make something out of that, Forrest. It is one of those checkout counter things, isn't it?"

"I'm afraid that's what *NewScope* is, Mr. McClay, but I'm covering this thing straight. I don't often get a chance to do that, but I'm trying hard. What about the overcoat, Mrs. Rose?"

95

"Walter mentioned it Friday night, the night before he was—" Her icy control unraveled without any warning at all. She speared a handkerchief from a pocket in the straight skirt. "I'm sorry," she managed. "I thought I'd finished with that."

Private school, Dan decided. That was where they turned out women for whom self-control was way up there on the highly-desirable-traits list.

McClay took up the slack. "Walt thought he saw somebody—somebody in a black coat—watching the store that Friday. We'd been broken into twice and robbed at gunpoint once. He was understandably leery about anyone who appeared to be casing the place. But this time he seemed more convinced that usual."

"He'd been suspicious of people before?"

"Couple of times. This time he told me—he always told me—*and* Adele about it. He really must have been worried about that particular guy."

"A tall man." Mrs. Rose had recaptured her composure, though she was a bit red-eyed. Not such a tower of ice, after all. "Well-dressed, Walter said, with a black coat."

"Would the man driving the car fit that description?"

"I told you, Mr. Forrest, I had only a glimpse of the driver. Only an impression."

"Anything else at all?" Dan prompted.

"That's what Sergeant Crowley asked. And I've tried hard to remember anything that might help."

He was, Dan realized, talking with the only known witness available for three killings, if the theory he was pushing proved out. Why in hell hadn't she run down the drive or rushed past the trees or done something other than just stand there transfixed for the couple of seconds it had taken the guy to get out of there! Then he wondered what he would have done in like circumstances. What anyone would had done.

"What happens to the store?" he asked.

"No effective changes in ownership," McClay said. "Adele and Walt together owned half. Now that half is entirely hers. I plan to keep the place going. You're obviously free to do whatever you want with your share," he said to Adele Rose. This was apparently the first time they'd talked about it.

"I think Walter would want me to keep the Rose name on the window."

So much for a motive rooted in business maneuvers. It was going to be as if Walt were still on board. This was a bitch of a case, where potential motives faded away like fog in the sun.

On the other hand, the dearth of local motives could be proving something. Yes, damn it, these *had* to be serial killings—somebody moving fast, hitting fast. Hitting at random? No, hitting three aging men. That was the general connection. And the use of .22-caliber pistols seemed a more specific one. But neither was the key connection. What in hell was it?

"I'm afraid I haven't been very helpful," Adele Rose said into his reverie. "But I just don't have anything more to tell you."

Cue accepted. Dan stood, thanked them. At the door she glanced back toward the living room and kept her voice low.

"I do read your paper, Mr. Forrest."

That was a surprise. "It's not a sin, Mrs. Rose."

"It may be sinful to admit that I enjoy it, but please, please don't let them make something tawdry out of this. Walter was a good man."

Somebody had pumped two slugs into that good man. Dan said, "I'm only looking for the . . . truth." He'd damned near said, "the facts, ma'am." That would have been cute.

"I called you earlier, Mr. Josaitis." The man was tall, blade-slim. He wore Gucci shoes that shone in the unremitting Arizona sun, tan slacks, and a bronze nubby-weave silk jacket. He had an accent, not a heavy one, but it was there. Mickey Josaitis had noticed it on the phone this morning.

"I don't want to drive all the way into Scottsdale, Mr. Josaitis." The voice had said his name was DeAngelis, Frank DeAngelis. "Might you meet me at the southwest corner of Lincoln and Scottsdale Road? There is a large market and a parking area. We could drive together from there."

That would be fine. The voice wanted to see properties that were remote, something with space and privacy. "The price is not a prime consideration."

Jumping junipers! If the guy really did have the inclination and the bucks, everything could finally be coming up desert roses!

DeAngelis was standing beside a blue Ford LTD when Josaitis drove into the supermarket parking area and nosed into an adjacent space. Money? Yes, indeed, Josaitis had decided as DeAngelis introduced himself. McCorkle and now DeAngelis. Big buckaroos, back to back. By God, he'd close them both!

"I've got a couple of dandies lined up to show you," he announced. "We'll take my car."

"I would rather we use mine," DeAngelis said. "I don't often have a chance to drive myself. In *Firenze*—Florence—I find it necessary to employ a *cocchiere*—a driver. The traffic, you understand."

Aha, an Eyetie with *multo lire*. "What business are you in, Mr. DeAngelis?"

"Chemicals. Shall we go?" He was already sliding into the driver's seat. Josaitis trotted around to the passenger side. He would have preferred to drive his own car, because the driver was psychologically the guy in charge. But DeAngelis had left him no choice.

"Take Scottsdale Road north for about nine miles."

They passed the oasislike McCormick Ranch, a vast housing-retail development, then the Scottsdale Municipal Airport. The road was arrow-straight, flanked by new development that sprawled into the recently civilized desert. Then the hopeful new condo and house construction became sparse, faded out. They traversed cactus and scrub that reached for flat miles on either side of the road toward distant haze-blue mountains.

"Take a right," Josaitis directed as they neared a crossroad nearly ten miles out. DeAngelis slowed the LTD and swung into the narrow dirt strip; the jouncing car began to kick a dust plume into the still air.

The place was a mile in, a pseudo hacienda crouching around an immense courtyard that could have benefited from some attention to the snakeweed growing in its cracked concrete.

They parked in there at Josaitis's direction. DeAngelis took a perfunctory look around. He seemed put off by the proximity of another estate a quarter-mile up the road and visible through one of the courtyard's decorative archways.

"Someone lives there now?"

Josaitis shaded his eyes. "Yeah, I see a car in the garage. Looks like a Jaguar."

It didn't look much like a Jag, but he was trying to tone up the neighborhood.

"But I prefer more solitude, Mr. Josaitis. Some place where neighbors are much more distant."

"Of course. I just wanted to show you a range of avail-abilities so's you could focus in better on the potentials."

A crock, but how would this foreigner know?

The second place was four miles farther north on Scottsdale Road, then a bone-joggling three miles west on one of those damned Arizona dirt paths that changed contours every time rain rushed out of the mountains. To Josaitis's dismay, at the end of the rocky drive was a squatter. A house trailer was pulled up in the shade of the empty two-story stone-and-frame that was now on the market for a mere three hundred fifty Gs. In a camp chair beneath a striped canopy extended from the trailer's side sprawled a spindly-legged man in shorts. He peered at them from under an incredible lion's mane of dun-colored hair, nodded, then returned to his midafternoon desert coma.

Josaitis felt his guts shrink. Again DeAngelis didn't get out of the car. "I am sorry, Mr. Josaitis, but you are not showing me solitude. Here we find a man who appears to be a *vagabondo* living in a house on wheels. Why do you bring me to a place like this?"

The day was not shaping up well. DeAngelis swung the Ford around angrily. They bounced the three miles back to the main road. Sweat that had begun to darken Josaitis's natty gray western shirt wasn't all from the heat.

He needed something breathtaking to salvage this fast-souring sales opportunity. The Kelleher place!

Wait a minute. Was that a good idea? He was sure McCorkle was going to pop for it . . . almost sure. It wouldn't hurt, though, to have a second offer in the wings. If he did this right, he could play one against the other and maybe even get the price up. Like an auction.

The LTD bounced across a dusty swale at the end of the lane. "Hang right," Josaitis said. They rolled onto the smooth pavement of Scottsdale Road and headed south again, toward Mummy Mountain.

The climb up the time-battered macadam of the hillside trail to the Kelleher mansion was impressive. Two hairpin turns and a double switchback, then the hard, straight ascent to the level parking area beside the big vandal-gutted stone house.

"*Eccellente!*" DeAngelis exclaimed. "Precisely what I had in mind."

Josaitis had become less taken with his prospective buyer as the hours had worn on. For one thing, the guy had discouraged all of Josaitis's attempts at small talk. He drove with his deep-set eyes locked straight ahead, didn't seem to give a damn about the local highlights Josaitis pointed out, and, frankly, the guy looked a little ominous. Thin face, long knife blade of a nose, kind of whitish upper lip in an otherwise tanned face. Cheekbones like that English actor—what was his name? Peter Cushing. Yeah, cheekbones of a skull.

What the hell? If the guy had the bucks, he could be Bela Lugosi, for all Josaitis cared.

They stood on the edge of the parapeted parking space and gazed across twenty miles of desert to the north. Ten-foot-high saguaro cacti were dark dots from up here. Among them were scattered the tiny white boxes of recently built homes, none closer than five miles. The late-afternoon sun felt benign on Josaitis's bare arms. He remembered not to fold them. Bad body language for sales.

"Might I see the inside?" DeAngelis's voice was oddly soft.

Josaitis had brought the key to the temporary door the realty company had installed. He'd lived with the key since he'd met McCorkle. The door was for effect, to show clients that somebody cared. Anyone could climb through any number of broken windows.

They stood in the grit of the flagstoned entrance hall.

"Used to have some great parties up here," Josaitis said, working the past glories angle. "The Kellehers made their money in Los Angeles real estate, and they knew the big Hollywood names. Norma Shearer, Valentino—Marion Davies when she wasn't romping around San Simeon. They all were here." He didn't know if any of them had been here, but neither would DeAngelis.

"What is that far out there to the . . . ah, north, is it?" He followed Josaitis to one of the ravaged windows flanking the front entrance.

Josaitis leaned on the dusty stone sill, careful not to brush against the broken glass that still filled the bottom half of the frame. DeAngelis moved close behind him.

"Where? You mean that little white building way off there to the left?"

"No, that way."

Josaitis thought the sudden pressure against his ear was some piece of jewelry on DeAngelis's wrist as he pointed over Josaitis's shoulder. That thought lasted only a fraction of a second. The rest of that final second was filled with two sledgehammer blows.

Josaitis was dead as he jackknifed over the raw edge of the broken plate glass. Arbalesta grabbed the back of his shirt and pulled him back inside, dropping the body in the floor dust.

In the parking area, he wiped the little JP-22 with his handkerchief, then threw it in a high arc into a tangle of mesquite that choked a gulley far below.

He got back in the LTD and drove down the winding entrance lane, down Scottsdale to Lincoln to Twenty-fourth and into Sky Harbor's access drive. There he took a United flight to Los Angeles International.

The girl drifted toward Tony Lavella's desk in sinuous ripples that began at her ankles, undulated up through thighs that her satin slacks didn't conceal a muscle of, churned her hips, then brought her shoulders into the act.

"Tony, baby, you got to get me more notice."

Behind the desk, Lavella spread his hands and pasted on a grin. "Sherry, you're in *Peeper* this month, full-page coverage. Three shots, one of them toes to topknot."

"Yeah, and with nothing on in between. I mean, like stark. I don't mean that kinda notice, Tony. Not skin books. Real stuff."

"Like *The New York Times*, for God's sake?"

She leaned over the desk, placed her palms flat on either side of his scuffed leather blotter pad. The scoop neck of her knit T-shirt gave him a panoramic view straight down silicone valley. Burgundy-tipped, they even held their rigid roundness inverted. Her snubby nose stopped just three inches from his eagle's beak.

"I'd settle for, like *People* magazine, Tony. Just a photo and cap."

"I've tried that, sweet stuff. That's a Time-Life book. You don't get in there just by sending in glossies. You got to accomplish something first."

Maybe a little earwash would quiet her down until he could think up the next gimmick to keep her on retainer. "Look, honey buns, I got a couple of high concepts in mind. Nothing I can specific in real time yet. But they'll develop topspin for you. Lotta topspin, believe me."

She pulled back and up, folding her bare arms below the jut of her mammarial escarpment. She really wasn't bad-looking, but she didn't have anything in the attic but brute determination to "get into the movies." Unfortunately there wasn't an up-front market for bimbos anymore. He didn't tell her she was forty years behind the times; couldn't afford to tell her. He needed the green folding of her retainer. He didn't know how she earned it, didn't care just as long as she delivered his monthly fee. That was what he lived on. Monthly retainers from any hopeful he could sucker into his stable.

Sherry Credence—née Hazel Baumgartner from Moline—gave him a disdainful flick of her shoulder. "You're putting a hold on my career, Tony. Honest to John, it's got to be you. I've had the boobs pumped, my tush jacked up, teeth capped, nose regraded. I've done my parts. Now it's agents that are holding me back. Morey and you. He says he can't land me anything decent until I get some real publicity. That lays it all on you, Tony."

Her voice had a plaintive wheedle, and he felt almost sorry for her. "How in the hell did you afford all that medical reconstruction? Those guys don't sell cheap cuts."

"Trade-outs."

Of course.

"That's the trouble with you, Tony. No trade-outs."

"I can't live on that kinda diet, sugar tart."

"What if they were bonuses? How many more column inches a month could that get me. A spread for a spread?"

"It doesn't work that way. You got to do something."

"I'm talking about doing something. Anything. Anything you want."

"Do something startling," he grumbled. How many of these idiots was a press rep expected to uncle through the byways of Tinseltown in a lifetime? "Learn to act."

She flounced out, banging the front office door. He winced. If she'd broken the frosted glass, he would have heard plenty from Ike Lance, the independent producer who let Lavella have this spare office for far less than the going rate per square foot in this ritzy Century City office tower. Without Ike's cut-rate rental, Anthony T. Lavella, Press Representative to the Stars, would be conducting business in some cinder-block trap out in Culver City or Burbank—or, God forbid, even out of his dinky apartment in the pink stucco walk-up on the low income end of Santa Monica Boulevard.

He pushed back from the desk and swiveled his chair around to gaze out the mini–picture window at the Atlantis-like rise of Beverly Hills, pushing into the northwest smog almost close enough to touch. So damned close. But he knew he'd never make it there. Not now. He might have once, right after the war when he'd first hit L.A. like a small whirlwind. Fast-talked Clint Hazen into being his first client. Anybody could have been a press success hanging on to the tail of Hazen's comet. One of the Big Three: Roy Rogers, Gene Autry, and Clint Hazen. Then had come the others, thirty-seven . . . no, thirty-eight at the peak. Mostly featured players, the faces people instantly recognized but didn't know the names to go with them. Lavella's job was to keep the names in front of casting directors, not necessarily the public.

Once he'd nearly landed Gary Cooper, or so he preferred to think. That would have bumped Anthony T. Lavella up more than a couple of notches, but it began and ended in the same ninety minutes, a lunch of not much more than "yups" and "nopes" on Cooper's part. The closing word was a "nope." Then Cooper paid the check and walked out of Lavella's grasp into such top billing that no Tony Lavella could hope to make a pitch to him ever again. Clint Hazen had changed press reps right after the Cooper lunch. Lavella had wondered how well they'd known each other.

Now he had barely a dozen clients. Five pathetic hopefuls à la Sherry Credence, girls barely out of their teens who were convinced that a cookie-cutter Marilyn Monroe could still make it; two wispy guys not long out of pimples who were devoted to the "art"—one of them actually called it "aht"—of acting; one hunk who hankered to do barbarian films like Schwarzenegger but was only five-three; and a handful of veteran bit players left over from the golden days.

From that unlikely cadre, Tony Lavella managed to extract a grand total of $1,240 per month. To that, he fairly often managed to add another $500 to $700 for nude photos sold to various skin mags, certainly neglecting to inform his cooperating clients that he was doing such traffic with the stills he'd cajoled them into coyly stripping for. Ike Lance's still-photo subcontractor would never tell. He'd never tell even Ike, and he worked comfortably cheap. Another erstwhile income source was Marve Drucker's medico schlock promo copy.

There was a noncash fringe benefit, too. Despite Sherry's protests to the contrary, Lavella did indeed work "trade-outs." He just didn't want to work one with Sherry. That would have been like laying down on one of those life-sized rubber dolls. Lavella's current arrangement was with a dark-haired twenty-two-year-old Oklahoman, not perfectly built, but at least it all was real. Cora Carson, her real name, had come to L.A. knowing nothing. Lavella was patiently teaching her. She had to be patient, because Tony Lavella was fifty-nine. They were up to shower-stall variations by now.

Still darkly handsome with his hook nose somehow enhancing the heavily-browed Mediterranean eyes and wide, generously-lipped mouth, he was beginning to broaden at the waist and rump. It had to be age; it sure wasn't a rich diet, not on less than twenty thou a year in this particular city. He was on Whoppers and Egg McMuffins, not steak and eggs Benedict. Come to think of it, maybe it was the diet.

Anyway, today would offer a change. He had an appointment with Marvin Drucker for late lunch at the Century Plaza, an easy walk through the ABC Entertainment Center plaza, then through the underpass beneath the Avenue of the Stars. Marve didn't get out of the sack until eleven, then he ate his first real meal around four. "Lupper," he called it. Lavella didn't care what Marve called it because Marve could always be counted on to pick up the check. Dr. Marvin Drucker ran a private clinic up in Glendale, and Tony Lavella wrote the ad copy for his miraculous "Diet of the Superstars," which Marve sold by mail order. For this, Lavella had access to a number of other clinic services. He'd never used the abortion facilities, but Marve had treated him for a bothersome infection Lavella had picked up from an all too willing female client. And Marve supplied Lavella with a vitamin regimen and periodic B-12 shots. Talk about trade-outs.

Marve also regularly brought Lavella a stack of back issues of various publications the clinic subscribed to for its clientele's diversion while they waited to be pummeled, prodded, and pierced. Many of these periodicals were those to which Lavella mailed out a continuous stream of hyped press releases, client glossies, and such other hoopla as he could extract from his clattering Royal. He did try, he really did. The problem was that the materials he had to work with just weren't Mad. Ave. capable. So it took a lot of poring through the reams of news- and pulp print that Marve delivered to find a Lavella-placed paragraph here and a Lavella-generated pic there. But he did find enough to keep the monthly retainers dribbling in.

At 3:45, Lavella draped a plastic cover over his typewriter, picked up his empty briefcase, and shut his office door behind him.

"Have a nice evening," he said to the impassive middle-aged receptionist flanking the Lance-Lavella main door. He emerged in the empty ninth-floor corridor. The elevator took him to the lobby level, from which he walked across the paved area between the twin office towers, then through the lower level of the ABC Entertainment Center shopping arcade, next beneath the afternoon traffic and the noisy fountain of the Avenue of the Stars. He found Marve Drucker already in residence at an umbrellaed table in the below-street-level outdoor dining patio of the Century Plaza Hotel.

A four-inch-high stack of tabloids and magazines was in the chair beside the shimmery-suited Dr. Marve. Lavella slid into the chair opposite, opened his briefcase, stuffed in the ragged pack of periodicals, and snapped it shut.

"I thank you kindly, sir."

Drucker folded his paper and set it aside. He had a peculiarly dished-in face with a button nose, closely set hamster eyes, and a tiny mouth—like somebody had scrunched his features all together and left a lot of sun-tinted margin.

"How's it hanging, Tony?" Marve Drucker said.

"More'n I can handle, Doc. More'n I can handle. How's by you?"

"Moving forward. Always moving forward."

A waiter appeared, and they ordered. Lobster salad for Drucker, and—what the hell—a club steak for Lavella.

Drucker reached in the breast pocket of his beige silk suitcoat. "Got something new here." He handed Lavella a folded sheet of typing paper. "Little addition to the line. Ought to pull in some bucks."

Lavella flattened the sheet and held it at arm's length. The old eyes were beginning to give him trouble when the light wasn't just right. He looked up at Drucker. "Potency pills?"

"Well, we won't call them that, of course. It'll be up to you to work out the copy that'll get the idea across without actually guaranteeing anything."

"You mean like 'Stand up and be counted. Come to feel like your old, hard-to-resist self'?"

Drucker grinned. "That's my copywriter! Give it your best shot, will you?"

"What's in the stuff?"

"Ah, you're interested. Couple of high-potency vitamins, a tap of testosterone, a touch of powdered alfalfa for color, all in a secret extender base."

"What secret? I don't think the Food and Drug Administration goes for secrets."

Drucker leaned forward with bemusement on his flattish face. "It's freeze-dried mothers' milk." His little beads of eyes blinked rapidly.

"I won't even ask how you get that. This stuff isn't going to poison anybody, is it?"

"Oh, hell, no, Tony. It's completely harmless."

"Does it do anything?"

"Tried it on myself. Never felt better."

"But does it work?"

"It's the ad copy that works with this kind of product. Convince a guy that he's taking something that will put ink back in the old ballpoint, and damned if that isn't exactly what will happen."

"But it's him, not the product."

"Do we care? If he doesn't use the product, he won't get the effect. Whatever produces it, right?" The gleamy little eyes narrowed. Drucker was over fifty, but when his broad face hardened, he looked a dangerous forty.

"You going purist on me, Tony?"

"What? Oh, no. Hell, no. I'm just trying to get a focus on the copy possibilities."

"That's my boy. You having any problems I can help you with?"

"Doing fine, Doc."

"You still keeping company with that little lady you told me about?"

"Still plugging along."

"You just let me know when you need another B-twelve goose, anything like that, you hear?"

"I hear."

"Have my copy ready Thursday, okay?"

"Do my best."

Their luppers arrived, and the conversation turned to the depressing reliability of the smog that currently left the area only an hour of clear sunlight per day, usually in the morning when Marve Drucker wasn't abroad to see it.

He paid the check, and they climbed the steps to street level to claim his car, a silver Alfa Romeo. He dropped Lavella off at the corner of the Avenue of the Stars and Santa Monica Boulevard, then turned right toward Rodeo Drive and Wilshire. Fifteen minutes went by before a westbound bus hissed its doors open. Tony Lavella climbed aboard, hoping as he always hoped that no client would happen by to see him taking a bus.

He climbed the two flights of worn rubber treads to arrive at his apartment door at 5:51 P.M. At that moment he thought he had some major worries. He couldn't scratch out quite enough money to keep the bills from eefing up a notch here and a squidge there; a financial ratchet. The times with Cora just weren't what such times used to be. Could Doc Drucker really help with that? Money and women: a man's two big problems.

He sank into a lumpy overstuffed chair by the living-room window and stared down into the alley between the apartment building and the blank green concrete-block wall of an office-supply wholesaler next door. The glory and glamour of Southern California.

Then he snapped open his scuffed leather briefcase and

lifted out the leavings of Marve Drucker's waiting room. Lavella had joked with him about doctors subsidizing a printing house that published old magazines, but Drucker's stuff was never more than a month out of date. Newer than that for the *National Enquirer, The Star, NewScope,* and the other tabloids.

He found a paragraph on one of his more recent clients, a Brooke Shields look-alike named Thea Bedlow, in the *Enquirer.* The look-alike angle had sold the photo. And he clipped out a paragraph on the stumpy hunk. The latent barbarian had won a pepperoni-lifting contest Lavella had staged at a Sunset Strip pizzeria, mainly accomplished by jollying the owner in Italian.

At 6:00 P.M., Tony Lavella began to leaf through the most recent copy of *NewScope.* It wasn't on the stands in L.A., but Drucker got his by subscription. At 6:13, a headline on page five caught Lavella's eye. It eyebrowed a story by somebody name Forrest. He read idly at first. Then the familiarity of the name Phillip Helmsgaard hit him like a contract cancellation. And Bernard Latza. His heart shoved right up his throat, choking him. His eyes raced down the page.

His chest thudded hard, just behind the rib cage where the thumping pumped sweat right through his shirt. He forced himself to read the story again, slower. Tried to concentrate. His mind jumped track to Helmsgaard and Latza. Both of them shot dead. Both the same way. Surely no coincidence. God Almighty, no coincidence. A . . . a vendetta!

His impulse was to dive for the phone. But he couldn't tell the police. They'd want to know why. They'd want to know it all.

Warn the others? Walt Rose, Mickey Josaitis, and Eddie Connell? He had no idea where they were now.

III

❧

They'd never kept in touch, any of them. They hadn't wanted to.

Lavella hunched forward in his rump-sprung chair like a man ready to take a hard blow. The pages of *NewScope* slid off his knees into a jumble on the floor. He began to tremble, a reaction he'd never before experienced.

Then he shoved out of the chair and rushed to the bathroom on legs that threatened to pitch him into the calcimined living-room wall. He barely made it there before he bent double and vomited.

EIGHT

C HARLIE, I'VE JUST DRIVEN over six hundred miles, spent two not really nifty nights in cut-a-buck motels, eaten God knows how many gas-fired hamburgers. And I just had no fun at all trying to convince the car-rental agency girl that she should accept your AARP discount on my charge."

"Did she?" Charlie was unmoved.

"No. You've let it run out."

"Damn!" Charlie Lovett slapped his desk. "I thought I renewed that sucker. You mean she hit you with full freight?"

"Full freight," Dan assured him, not without satisfaction. "And this'll make your day: I still don't have anything conclusive."

"Holy sweet damn! You're—"

"But I do have notes."

"Notes."

"New departure." Dan pulled a little blue-covered spiral-bound notebook from his hip pocket. "The things's getting too complex, or I'm getting too old. Had to pick this up and start putting it all down in B and W."

He flipped the notebook open. "Look, right here. See the similarities?" He moved around the end of the desk to peer over Lovett's shoulder.

"Well, they're all old . . . older guys," Lovett said hesitantly. "Helmsgaard, sixty-one. Latza, sixty-five." He flipped the page over. "And Rose, here, sixty-two. All plugged with a twenty-two, two of them with the same gun. Hell, Dan, we knew this much before you took the joy ride. And that's where the thing falls apart. What else did you find out that means anything? One was a watchman, one a retired engineer. And this third guy was a jeweler. Nothing the three had in common there that I can see."

"All three were married, or had been."

"Yeah, and I'll bet all three married to women. You're trying to sell me smoke, Dan."

"That's what we sell to the public."

Lovett tossed back the notebook. "You already pumped all the smoke out of this one there is to pump. Forget it. Find a nice chain-saw job on the ticker, buy the AP's photos and run with that. Be good for you. It'll clear this nonstory out of your attic."

They both looked doorward at Jonathan Blauvelt's discreet rap on the glass. Today he wore a cerise sateen shirt with the top three buttons open.

"Watch yourself at all times," Lovett muttered.

Blauvelt opened the door and jutted his head in. "Phone for you, Danny boy." At *NewScope*, whoever was nearest covered a jangling phone. That saved on secretarial help.

"Go on," Lovett grumped. "I think we were finished before we started."

Back in his cell, Dan found Cousin Roy on the line, not altogether calm. "Thought you would want to know, Dan. There's been another."

Dan thought he could hear his own pulse banging in the receiver. "Another?"

"Yep. Guy sixty-one, out in Arizona. Two shots in the head. Came over the NCIC computer line just a couple minutes ago."

"I gather I'm no longer the only guy in this great United States who thinks there's a link somewhere?"

"I've been thinking, Cousin." Another surprise. "I'm thinking at the moment that the choice of weapons may be the only link. But I'm keeping my options open. So I put in a standing request to NCIC for anything the Center gets on men in or near their sixties who are hit with twenty-twos. And the Arizona thing just came through. Good news and bad news."

"The good news is—?"

"The good news is that the longer a serial killer—"

"Ah, so. Now you're thinking serial killer."

"Maybe. A perpetrator who travels cross-country through various jurisdictions killing as he goes. The longer he keeps at it, the more likely he is to get nailed. That's the good news."

"Except for the people he does it to," Dan pointed out. "What's the bad?"

"The bad news is that now we got an Arizona sheriff's office, the Pennsylvania State Police, the Baltimore County Police, and NYPD in the act. And the FBI more than ever wants to jump in and make it easy for all of us. I remember something you told me once."

Dan went for it. "What's that, Roy?"

"That one of the great American lies is 'I'm from the government, and I'm here to help you.' It's turning into a real kettle of stew."

"I did pick up a little something in Pennsylvania you might find interesting."

"Like for instance?"

"A sort of description of some guy Rose noticed the day before he got it. A tall man, well-dressed in a black top-coat."

"You kidding? I don't want to take the starch out of your sails, but that's only a step away from a tall, short, thin, fat man. Cuts possibilities down to maybe fifty million American males. And a fat lot of good a black-overcoat search would have been in Phoenix. It's in the eighties out there."

Dan studied the calendar over his desk. Next deadline was days away. Charlie would have apoplexy—if anybody had that antiquated sort of thing these days, it would be Charlie, but this was getting too hot for Charlie to cut him out of just to squeeze a few dimes. If it came down to this last-ditch job against a real live reporter-style story, then he'd just have to chance it. If the whole thing turned into a handful of sand, maybe Casey could get him a job lugging around Fiscal Processing Systems computerware. A terminal job. Damn, the story possibilities were worth the risk.

"Looks like I'm the only free agent in this," he told Roy. "I'm going west."

"You fill me in on anything you dig up that might be of interest, you hear? And don't fiddle-faddle if you get anything. I just found my name on the Compro list."

"What the hell is that?"

"Computer proficiency. They're sending a bunch of us to computer seminars on a rotating basis. It could happen any day."

"What happens to the Helmsgaard case then?"

"You tell me. So if you get anything, buzz me pronto, buddy."

The way Roy came right in with that made Dan wonder if that was what Roy'd had in mind all along. Not the brightest cop in the city, maybe, but not so near the bottom either, Cousin.

Charlie wasn't going to be nearly so easy to sell.

"*Phoenix!*" he exploded. "That's hundreds of dollars before you're even on the ground, *plus* car rental, *plus* meals, and a ho—motel to boot! Give me back the charge card, Forrest. I mean now!"

"Chance of a lifetime, Charlie. I'm going to crack this thing, and *NewScope*'ll have headlines that will make the *Enquirer* cry. Your mother will be proud."

"Haven't got a mother. Give me the damned card!"

"Charlie, Charlie, I'm going to make this rag into something it's never been. A real paper. All it takes is this little piece of plastic."

Charlie lunged across the desk, missed, then fell back in his chair in wheezing resignation.

"I'm telling you, Dan, if you come up dry on this, I'll flay your butt. I swear it! You'll pay back every cent, or it'll be out the door."

Dan was already out the door. He snared his London Fog on the way past his cubicle and left a fuddled Quince Harriss in his wake.

Quince jerked his head in that holdover teen reflex to flip his hair out of his eyes. "What's with him?"

Lovett stood in his office doorway and slowly shook his head. "Poor son of a bitch," he said to no one in particular. "He thinks he's still a reporter."

Tony Lavella was not having a good day. He'd managed only a glass of orange juice and a cup of reheated coffee for breakfast, had gagged on a scrambled egg, then scraped it into the plastic-lined trash can under the sink. He hadn't slept. Now he couldn't eat.

To think that one stupid incident could come back to haunt him—to *threaten* him—after all this time. And he was the one who had tried to stop it, for God's sake! Who the hell had talked? And to whom? Who would get torn up about it at this late date? It didn't make sense.

But now somebody in addition to the six of them knew about it, that was for sure. Somebody who had already blown away Phil and Bernie. That left Walt, Mickey, Eddie—and him. Who in hell could be doing this horror?

He crumpled into a hard chair by the kitchen table and stared into the alley without seeing anything. If it really *was* a vendetta . . . He shuddered. He had a Sicilian uncle, Zio Alfonzo. Those people took that kind of thing right into their souls and had no peace until the wrong was avenged.

Lavella held out his hands, palms down, and spread his fingers. Damn, just look at that. The fingers trembled. This was nuts, insane. Some kind of grisly coincidence.

He dragged the copy of *NewScope* across the table and forced himself to restudy the article. Maybe this guy Forrest made the thing up. Lavella knew how these stories were written. A fact here, a fact there for springboards. Then an adept writer without a conscience would fill in the blanks with spicy speculation.

He tossed the paper on the floor and stood to stare into the uninspiring alley vista three floors below. Come on, Tony baby. The guy could make up those two names? The guy could make up the part about the .22 slugs in the ears? It *happened*, you poor slob. And it could happen to you.

Unless . . . No, not the police, for God's sake! What could they do? At best, put a man with him for a couple of days, if they could spare anybody. Then what? They wouldn't play bodyguard forever. They might not play at all, lacking a threatening letter or some sort of evidence that he was in real danger. He could tell them he'd gotten a phone threat.

No, no! What in hell was he thinking of! They'd want the background, the whole damned story. He'd never give them that. The L.A. columnists with their ears in every police HQ would gobble it up and him with it. His life wouldn't be worth cold vermicelli.

Lavella's brain raced like a trapped rabbit. Give the cops an anonymous tip? "Come on," he said aloud. That would break the thing wide open, too. He'd be dragged in surer than hell.

A private dick? He was so close to the edge now, where would he get the money for even a day's worth, let alone an extended tour?

Run. That sure would make it hard for whoever was tracking them down with his lousy little .22. But running would take money, too. Lavella had exactly three hundred fifty-four bucks in his First Western account. But he did have valid credit cards. They could give him a month, maybe two, before the overdue payments choked off further credit.

Not a bad move. If he made himself scarce enough, whoever was after the six of them would have to go after the other three first. You shoot five guys, something is bound to go wrong. The law somehow would catch up.

But getting out of here clean was going to be some job. He couldn't just pack and bug out. Some of his dozen clients were going to be highly pissed, or maybe even worried enough to go to Missing Persons. Then he'd have the law after him, too.

It had to look like a vacation. He just wouldn't tell anyone where he was going. Where *was* he going? Somewhere pretty damned far away. East Coast? Why punish himself? Hawaii? Too frigging expensive. Mexico? Not bad. A foreign country, and he wouldn't need a passport. He could really lose himself in some Mex backwater for a while. And cheap.

So okay, now he had a plan. Half-assed, maybe, but it sure beat waiting around to get blown away. Step one would be to make reservations on a flight to Mexico City. No, first he'd better notify his clients . . . Damn! There was that ad copy for Marve Drucker. Well, he could mail that along the way. No, he didn't want to leave a postmark trail. He'd have to write the lousy copy or come up with some kind of sidestep Marve would accept.

Then there was Cora. He sure would miss her tight little butt and her eagerness. She had some kind of drive, that kid. Best student the old teach ever had. Shame, but no way around it. Or maybe take her with him? There was a thought.

This was getting complicated. Better get some kind of organization going. He rummaged in the kitchen-table drawer for pencil and paper.

Number 1: Get clients off back.
Number 2: Something to keep Drucker happy.
Number 3: Cora?
Number 4: Tickets and pack.

Oh, and there was Mrs. Murfine. Had to tell her he'd be out of town for some weeks. She'd want the rent in advance for November, no doubt.

And Ike Lance. He'd have to let Ike know that he'd be out of the office. God Almighty, this was a damned complex situation. His list of notes grew.

Let's see. Maybe find out about flight connections first, then work from there. And a place to stay in Mex City. Where the hell would he stay?

Tony Lavella tore the top sheet off the little note pad, crumpled it, and began again.

Number 1: Air reserv., hotel.
Number 2: Pack.

Or should he pack first so's he'd be ready to skip quick, no matter what else needed to be done?

Now that he'd gotten some planning underway, he felt a little better. Besides, wouldn't it take the killer—Lavella shuddered a little when he thought the word—a while to find him? Lavella himself didn't have any idea where the others were or had been. How could some stranger find him without a hell of a search?

Rollo Scorza had found, assessed, and photographed Tony Lavella weeks ago with the resources to which he had access through the U.S. connections of Esportatore Varieta. The search for the six targeted Americans had been conducted quietly through legitimate data sources and through some computer nets that American business and government did not know existed. It continued through on-site recon teams conducting "soft hits" which included unobserved photography with 200mm lenses through one-way-glass–equipped vans.

The distillation of that extensive operation was in the notebook in Vincenzo Arbalesta's pocket. He already knew Lavella's home and business addresses along with such addresses of the other five. Discreet phone calls placed by Rollo had ascertained the presence of Lavella and the others at these locations during a period in October, the two weeks that Arbalesta necessarily scheduled for the fulfillment of his sworn vengeance.

While Lavella ran through his emotional chain-dance of stunned disbelief, fear, confusion, then just a touch of misguided confidence, Arbalesta never departed from his tight schedule. He didn't have to. He had not lost so much as a half-day anywhere, and that much variance had been incorporated in the itinerary.

In his room at the Century Plaza Hotel, Arbalesta unwrapped the compact parcel he had picked up at a particular pawn shop in West L.A. on the drive here from Los Angeles International Airport. The formula remained totally efficient: rent a car at the airport, pick up the weapon at the prearranged "safe site," exact the the revenge within the fewest hours possible, dispose of the weapon as soon as practicable, and leave with minimum delay. What was the American expression? Charming work? No, works like a charm. That was it.

The charm was at work again. His rented Pontiac was on call at the hotel garage. The weapon he had just taken from the string-tied pink tissue in the brown paper bag was another smooth-action Beretta, a model 950, its clip loaded with .22 shorts. This time the target was almost to come to him, according to the notebook. "Habitually takes lunch at any of several restaurants in shopping area one block west Ave. of Stars, noon–2:00 P.M., except when periodically meets unidentified white male at Century Plaza lower level restaurant."

Lavella would come to him from the Century Plaza Tower, where he had his office. But now that Arbalesta had surveyed the layout from his balcony of his fifth-floor room, he knew he could not terminate Lavella in this area. Too open. Too many people. There had to be a way to isolate the target from this openness with its many witnesses.

But the man possessed no automobile. To get him somewhere isolated would require a taxi or bus—potential risks in the inevitable investigation. With Latza, the matter of separating him from his secure surroundings had been simple because Latza had an automobile. And Josaitis had offered an even more efficient opportunity.

But Lavella was a greater challenge. He moved in a restricted pattern: apartment building to bus to high-rise office to crowded sidewalks for the short stroll to his shopping-center lunch, then back to high rise, then along highly visible sidewalks to bus and back to his apartment on heavily traveled Santa Monica Boulevard. The apartment building was a small one, only three stories with every tenant in that not exciting neighborhood undoubtedly overly interested in his or her neighbors' visitors.

Despite his fancy office address, Lavella appeared to be one of the least successful yet the most protected of the six. There had to be a way to move him out of the narrow routine that shielded him so well. Arbalesta slipped the Beretta into his suitcoat pocket, hung the coat in the room's closet, and eased into the chair that faced the sliding-glass door that accessed his balcony. He sank low in the chair, made a tent of his fingers, and rested his chin on their tips. A way to remove the man from all these potential witnesses. Or the witnesses from the man.

Ah! He had the way.

Cal Josaitis looked like a wizened desert prospector gone respectable. He stood in the doorway of the one-story stucco rancher on the south side of Camelback Road as Dan parked out front. The quarter-acre lawn was remarkably green and edged all around with a raised, sodded berm.

Josaitis caught his look. "It's for the watering. Every Thursday. City lets you flood the lawn couple inches deep. Really for the half-dozen lemon and orange trees I got out back. This is one of the few places in the country where a man can raise a cash crop in his suburban backyard. You're Mr. Forrest, I take it?"

"Dan." He stuck out his hand.

Josaitis's grip was bony and weak. "Just call me Cal. Pity you have to be out here on this kind of sad affair." He wheezed for breath. "We—I don't get to see a lot of folks. Be even fewer, I reckon, with Mickey gone. 'Casionally he brought 'round a prospect for a drink. But I don't do nothing like that now. I'm just plain outta business. Social Security and a pension. Hey, come on in, Dan. Get outta the sun."

With the sunside shades drawn, the house was dark after

the brightness outside. The air conditioning felt good. Its compressor, though, had a serious-sounding buzz when it cut in. Kind of like Cal himself.

"Take that chair there, the good one." He disappeared, then called from what Dan assumed was the kitchen. "You take a drink with me?"

"Soft stuff. Maybe a Coke if you got one."

"Off the alky, uh? I oughtta be, but what the hell. Be seventy next month. What am I saving myself for?" His voice had an unhealthy gaspiness. "Goddamn emphysema! And I give up smoking ten years ago."

The place was a man's, all right. Or men's, until a few days back. A Winchester 30.06 and a Remington 12-gauge pump hung on a rack over the sofa. A pair of Rocky Mountain bighorns curled over the fireplace. The furniture was angular and in solid, not really compatible browns, blues, and murks. The end table hadn't been dusted for a while. There wasn't a frill in sight. The brightest touch was the beautifully woven, colorful Navajo rug on the center of the living room's scuffed hardwood flooring.

Cal Josaitis returned with a glass of Coke for Dan, a can of Coors for himself. "Sad business, this. I figured Mickey'd be putting me under 'fore too much longer. Never thought it'd come out the other way 'round." He slumped on the sofa with a grunt and took a long pull at the beer.

"Damn!" he said. "He was a pretty good boy, that Mickey. Who'd wanta put a bullet in him?"

The Coke tasted good after the drive through Phoenix traffic. "That's what I was about to ask you."

"Took him way to hell and gone up there on the backside of Mummy Mountain," Josaitis said as if he hadn't heard Dan. "Plugged him and didn't take so much as his wristwatch. What kind of sense does that make?"

"No more sense than the others."

Josaitis's high, age-spotted forehead wrinkled. He had a

fringe of wispy white hair that could have stood a trim. "What others?"

"You ever hear your brother mention a Phillip Helmsgaard or Bernard Latza or Walter Rose?"

Josaitis rolled his beer can between his palms. Dan heard his labored breathing until outside the near wall the air conditioner compressor cut in again.

"Nope. Can't say I ever did."

"They were the others. All killed the same way in New York, Baltimore, and northeastern Pennsylvania. Two small-caliber bullets in the head, nothing taken. Police in three states—four now—are talking botched muggings."

"That's what Sheriff Culhane thinks. You talk with him?"

"I did, and he does. He wasn't any more help than Sergeant Crowley, Pennsylvania State Police. They both seemed hung up on muggings."

"But you're not."

"What could have interrupted a robbery up there on the mountain?"

"Got a point there," Cal agreed. "Got a theory to go with it? Or are you just stabbing around hoping for something sensational for that grocery-store rag you said on the phone you work for?"

"Both. It's a serial killing. Has to be."

"You mean some nut traveling state to state, knocking people off at random? I read about those guys."

Dan set his glass on an out-of-date *Field and Stream* on the dusty end table. "Like that, but there's got to be some connection here. All four victims have been men in their sixties."

"Mickey was fifty-nine."

"Close enough. Lived here with you how long?"

"More'n twenty-five, maybe twenty-six years. Divorced that Stephanie bitch and kinda helled around for a while after that. Then he came out here from Illinois—that's where he'd met her, and that's where they lived 'til the breakup. Come back to Phoenix in . . . lessee, nineteen sixty, sixty-one, if the old memory cells are still working for me. We both was born here. Phoenix wasn't much more'n a crossroads then, still dreaming stagecoaches and Indian uprisings. Now it's high-rises, condos, and Sun City for the burned-out set. There's a goddamn housing development of them cheap little one-story boxes smack across the rise where we had our horse ranch."

He stopped talking, panted, and stared at the rug. When he had his breath back, he looked up at Dan and snorted. "Hell, why am I knocking progress? I ended up living in a house just like those damn things. We're sitting in it."

"When did your brother leave Phoenix?"

"Left for the war. We both did. I picked the navy. He went into the air corps. Both saw action, then I came back to a tumbledown ranch, both parents dead. Got a job with the power company. Sold out the ranch and sent Mickey half the money. He'd met this gal, you see, in Chicago, where he'd gone to tech school. Married her when he got back from Europe. Ten, twelve years of hell, he told me. Don't know how he took it so long, her getting tired of waiting for him to hit it big and sneaking back to the sassiety men she'd knowed before."

Cal stopped, panted, took a noisy suck from the can. "He shucked her finally, helled around the Midwest for a while, then come to Arizona, moved in with me, and we helled around together. I like to tell you, we went through women like they was going off the market. Mickey was the wildest, making up for all them lost years married to that Illinois iceberg."

"What was he doing for money?"

"Selling. He could sell hair dye to Kojak, that brother of

mine." Josaitis fell silent, then chuckled at some old memory and took another pull at his Coors.

Again, Dan thought, no apparent connection. The four dead men had nothing in common but an age bracket. Charlie Lovett was going to be livid.

"Where'd Mickey go to school?" It had just struck Dan that all four had to have been in school about the same time.

"Went through high school here."

"College?" Maybe it was some kind of stupid fraternity thing. Talk about straws . . .

"Come out of high school in forty-three and went right into the service. When he got out, he tried Northwestern, think it was, in Chicago under the G.I. Bill. But then he got married, and that ended the college."

Now Dan had the notebook out. This was an angle he hadn't checked on the others. When he got back to the Holiday Inn on Scottsdale Road, his phone bill was going to give Charlie a twinge on top of the airline tickets, car rental, and a wad of room-and-boards that were piling up nicely on this story that might not be a story.

Yes, it was, damn it! But where in God's name was the key?

"One of these men was a night watchman who'd been a sheet-metal draftsman. Another was retired from electrical engineering. The third was a jeweler." He watched Cal's face. "Anything there? Anything at all that seems to tie in to your brother?"

"Maybe the service," Josaitis said. Then he began to cough, pulled a soiled red bandanna out of his hip pocket, and covered his mouth. When he stuffed it back in his pocket, his voice was hoarser than before. "Were they all in the service?"

The hairs on the back of Dan's neck seemed to realign themselves. "You said Mickey was in World War Two?"

"We both was. Him in the air corps, me in the navy. How 'bout them other guys?"

Dan had seen Walt Rose's wild-blue-yonder photo on the piano. Air force for him. Latza and Helmsgaard? Hadn't Lenora Helmsgaard said she and Phil had married just after he'd gotten out of the army? Damn, why hadn't he begun taking notes earlier instead of relying on a memory that too soon had become bogged by the ever-increasing mass of details on the growing list of victims?

"Rose was a flier." The wings in the photo had told him that. "Helmsgaard was in the army. I don't know about Latza, but I'll find out. What did your brother do?"

"On a bomber. Twenty-nine missions. He was a gunner."

A tie to Walt Rose? The use of the same .22 had tied Rose to Latza, and here might be another link—but such a wildly different one! A war that had taken place more than forty years ago?

"Another Coke?" That wasn't a hint to end this. Cal Josaitis looked as if he was ready to settle in for the rest of the afternoon.

"I appreciate your time, Cal. But I think we've done it here. If you come up with anything at all that might be some kind of a link among these four people, give me a call at the Holiday Inn anytime up to early tomorrow. After that, you can reach me in New York." He gave Josaitis his *NewScope* number on a page torn out of his notebook. Cheap Charlie had seen no reason to invest in business cards for his cadre of rewriters.

" 'Preciate your coming out," Josaitis said at Dan's car. He'd followed him down the narrow walk as if this had been a neighborly chat. Poor lonely old gaffer.

"You take care," Dan offered.

"Sure will, sure will," the old man wheezed, "though I don't know why, now." A hacking attack shook him, and the bandanna came back out. Then he grinned weakly. "They say it's not the cough that carries you off, it's the coffin they carry you off in."

Spunky old bastard. On impulse, Dan laid a hand on the bird-boned shoulder. "The police are going in circles on this one, but I'm going to do my best to get the son of a bitch who killed your brother."

Cal Josaitis looked down, kicked some loose gravel with his clunky workboot. When he looked back up, tears had filled the squinty gray eyes. "I'll 'preciate that, Dan. I truly will."

"How good is that machine of yours, Casey?"

"Now, Daniel." Her voice was low and suggestive. "If we're going to get that personal, we'll just have to try it out, won't we?"

"I'm talking about the damned computer terminal, Case."

"I was afraid of that. It's top-notch, and so is the operator."

"Don't play. This phone call on top of the others I've made out here is going to set Charlie on his parsimonious ear, but maybe we can put all that gear of yours into the act."

Four o'clock in Phoenix, but already six in New York.

"I guess you can't do much with it today, but hit it as soon as you can, will you? There may be a lot riding on this."

"Daniel, it really would help if you'd tell me what in hell you want."

"That's part of the problem. Overall, I'm looking for the link that ties the four victims together. Specifically, all I have is a welter of details." He paused. "You know something? It's nice to hear your voice." Without the visual impact of her consistently oddball garb, she sounded, well, more woman and less kook.

"It's nice to hear you, too, Daniel." Very little smartass in that. Distance made the difference?

"Got pencil and paper?"

"Who uses a pencil? Got a ballpoint and paper. Reel it off."

"Okay, your column headings are Helmsgaard, Latza, Rose, and Josaitis. That's J-o-s-a-i-t-i-s."

"Got it."

"Now here's what I have." For five minutes he gave her every note he'd taken on all four: work history, marital status, schooling, military. The last two categories he'd filled in just minutes before with calls to Lenora Helmsgaard in Queens and to Detective Willy Constanz in Baltimore County.

"Yes, Phil had been in the army. I thought I already told you that, Mr. Forrest." Lenora Helmsgaard's voice had had a brittleness that told him she was getting thoroughly tired of questions. Didn't blame her.

"What did he do in the army?"

"He never talked about it. Didn't I tell you that too?"

"Sorry. How about schools?"

"High school in the South Bronx, before it turned into a battlefield. Then he started at City College, I think. Dropped out because the war came along."

Not much out of her, and Detective Constanz hadn't been any big step upward either. "Mr. Latza, according to my notes, was in the army from nineteen forty-three to nineteen forty-five. We found his military records in his personal effects."

"How about school?"

"You are grabbing at whatever, aren't you? Poly—that's a technical high school in Baltimore City, then a degree in engineering at the University of Maryland on the G.I. Bill after the war. You really should be talking to Mr. Snyder about this case, you know."

"I'll never tell."

Adele Rose hadn't answered and Sergeant Crowley was elsewhere. So he'd had to go with what he already had on Walter, plus the piano photo. The mutual-schooling idea was shot apart already, but the photo kept the military possibility open.

So now his notes were better, but the link sure hadn't dropped out in his lap. It had to be in here somewhere, damn it. Somewhere in this welter of personal histories was the key to four murders. And now he was grabbing at another whatever, as Willy Constanz had so aptly put it: Casey's access terminal. Maybe that was a ludicrous idea, but it was better than stewing here in Scottsdale until plane time tomorrow.

"Got it, got it," Casey said, her voice fade telling him she was juggling phone, notebook, and ballpoint pen frantically as he finished pouring out his stream of facts and fragments. "Got it all down in nice little boxes. Did you try this, too? Only the age bracket and the fact that they all were in World War Two mesh. Oh, and they all were or had been married. And they all were men, if you're really fishing."

"Worse. I'm trawling. Thought old Cal had given me a lead when he got on the military-service angle. But two were in the air force, two were in the army. Anyway, see what you can do, will you?"

"Garbage in, garbage out, Daniel. You've heard that. There aren't any miracles in microchips, just dog work. That's what we're down to, isn't it?"

"I'll be back in New York tomorrow. Drop by."

"That's an order?"

"That's maybe the last gasp."

"I could take a sick-leave day tomorrow. FPS is pretty

liberal about that. This thing's probably going to give me mental cramps anyway. I'll only have to lie a little."

"That's a good girl. If I think of anything else, I'll call."

Fat chance of that. He'd given her everything, every remote fact he'd managed to track down.

He had a quick supper in the motel coffee shop, showered, then lay naked on his back on the queen-size bed, hands cradling his head. The answer wasn't on the acoustical tile ceiling, but it was a comfortably neutral background for thinking.

Age, marriages, military service. Three threads. The only threads stringing four killings together. Useless threads? How may sixtyish men weren't or hadn't been married? How many men in or near their sixties had not served in World War II? The way Dan had heard it, just about the whole country had served in that one. It would be more of a revelation if the four of them had not been in the service.

Two in the army, two in the air force. "Air corps," Cal had called it. Quaint Cal.

Then it hit him. A realization that began hot under the cool skin of his belly, then turned into a chill along his backbone.

Air *corps*. When had it become the air force? Not until . . . He'd done a military background piece for the *Times* twenty— God, that far back? Twenty years ago, had it been?

The air corps hadn't become the United States Air Force until nineteen forty . . . When the hell had it been? Forty-seven? After the big war, for sure. Before that, it had been the U.S. Army Air Corps and the U.S. Army Air Forces— part of the army.

Was it possible?

He called Casey a second time.

"Daniel? You sound newly fired up."

"It just hit me. Two in the air force, two in the army. That's what I gave you."

"That's what my chart says."

"Check that out first. The air force back then was part of the army."

"You mean—"

"I mean. A long shot, but that's about the only shot left, Case."

"You're putting me to a lot of work, Daniel. If anything comes of this, I want a reward."

"You mean—"

"What do you think I mean, you bozo? Have a nice evening."

He left an undercurrent of excitement that didn't fade after he'd hung up. Maybe that was because he might have just opened up what he'd thought was a dead end. And maybe some of it was because he'd realized how much he liked the sound of Casey's voice.

NINE

Wouldn't you know? Tony Lavella thought. Along with his problems had come opportunity. He'd never heard of Angelo Bellino, but they'd just had a wonderful conversation in Italian, from *com es ta?* to *ciao, paisan* with an agreement between that Lavella would hang around the office until eight when Bellino would finally be free to show up.

"It is *complicato*, this tour," he had said. "Two groups in different parts of the U.S. at one time. And me having to fly between them." Lavella had never heard of either group, but that wasn't surprising. Rock groups came and rock groups went, and only the luckiest—or best publicized—lasted much more than a year.

"Have you had experience in such a field?"

He'd lied only a little to Bellino. But surely press coverage for a gaggle of rock-and-rollers couldn't be any more difficult than scratching out column inches for the Sherry Credences of this noisy side of show biz.

He'd wanted to get into the music bag anyway. A fair

hunk of Beverly Hills was now rock-rented if not -owned. The public wasn't aware of it, but the collapse of the old studios and their star system had sent a financial shudder through BH real estate. Behind more than a few of the wrought-iron fences, security TV circuits, and AKC-registered Dobermans and Rottweilers up there, a gaggle of astoundingly affluent string pluckers had replaced some of the biggest names of yesteryear, as they say. Lavella had long hankered to expand his limping stable with a couple or more latent Boy Georges or Earth, Sand and Stars or whatever they called themselves. The times, they were a-changin'. Maybe this Bellino paisan could have helped Lavella change with them. Two European groups, he'd said, in need of a West Coast press rep. A four-figure monthly retainer. Four figures!

A futile dream, of course. The situation had forced Tony Lavella to work out quite a different angle. He had watched the luminescence that was the sun behind three thousand feet of smog sink and fade, nodded good night to blimpish Ike Lance who had made one of his rare office appearances today, wished their crotchety shared receptionist a good evening, and listened to the corridor's home-bound scurry.

Now the hum and oily roll of the elevators had ended. The building was empty. At least the ninth floor seemed to be. The only sound Lavella could hear was an occasional muted auto horn nearly a hundred feet down as the last of Century City's wage-slave traffic worked into the main-stream of Santa Monica Boulevard.

Lavella paced the carpeted reception area, absently began to pluck a leaf from the potted ficus, then remembered it was plastic. He returned to the swivel chair behind his desk. His stomach growled. He'd given up supper, such as it would have been, for this Bellino character.

The turmoil in his stomach wasn't only the result of a

skipped supper. Tony Lavella was about to operate a con, the first true con of his career. He realized that some of his clients might have argued that he had been conning them for decades, but that wouldn't have been accurate. He had at least tried to grab some column inches for every one of them. Sometimes it worked, sometimes it didn't. But he tried. At this late hour, though, he had no thought of working out in services the sizable hunk of "initial retainer" he was going to exact from Signore Bellino.

The man had talked rich and had talked a novice showbiz line. A pigeon for the plucking. Getaway money on the hoof. Lavella was going to nail Bellino for enough scratch to take him to Mex City and beyond without using the plastic. That could delay the credit wolf howl for maybe another whole month. Beautiful! Talk about topspin! Nailing down a real R-and-R promo contract would have been a dream come home, but a man had to go with the flow. Life had just dealt him a kit to split.

Lavella crossed his ankles on the windowsill and laced his fingers behind his head. Interesting how a guy could relax when he knew that every door downstairs, except the main entrance, was locked by now. And that one was under the eyes of building security with a sign-in sheet. Only way you could get in here was to have an appointment that had been prelisted on the night guard's visitor sheet. Lavella had logged in Bellino when he'd ducked out for a quick sandwich at noon.

So for the moment, Lavella was secure here nine floors above the groomed plaza lawn. No one could get to him except Bellino.

Then his heart thumped, a single hard bang in the center of his chest like somebody'd whammed him there with a rubber mallet. He froze.

Except Bellino! And Bellino was only a voice on the phone. Anybody could be a voice on the phone. Anybody could say he was a big R-and-R googamooga. Anybody. Even the anybody who had put out the lights for Phil and Bernie.

Holy Mother, had he opened a path through the building's security system for his own assassin!

At the precise instant that realization hit him, the phone on his desk jangled. He jumped. Then he snatched the receiver with a damp hand.

"Lav . . ." He cleared his throat. "Lavella."

"Mr. Lavella, Bud French here, security desk. Your guy's in the lobby. An Angelo Bellino."

"I can't see him," Lavella blurted. "Tell him I can't see him. Got a sudden call."

Not very convincing, he feared, but Bud French wouldn't have to worry about that.

"Sorry, Mr. Lavella. He's already at the elevators around the corner."

"Stop him! For God's sake, stop him!" Lavella's tongue stuck to the roof of his mouth. He worked his throat uselessly. Then he slammed down the receiver. He had to get out of here. Fast. He grabbed his powder-blue linen suitcoat off the hook on the back of his office door, snapped out the lights, and bolted. To hell with locking up.

Out in the hall, the rows of numbers above the twin elevators both showed a light on 1. Lavella punched the Down button frantically.

The 1 square on the left elevator blinked out. The 2 lit up. Then the elevator on the right began to move.

They came up together.

Lavella had an inspiration. He dashed back into Lance-Lavella and stabbed the light button on. Then he ran down the corridor past the elevator bank and yanked open the door to the emergency stairs. With the toe of his Docksider, he held it ajar just the fraction of an inch he needed to squint through. Brother, this would take timing!

But at first it seemed to take forever. He heard the thudding of his pulse louder than the elevator machinery on the other side of the stairwell wall. Maybe he should go on down the stairwell. No, that would be too slow—and he would be too exposed.

Sweat beaded his forehead, the sweat of fear and, he realized, the sweat of anxiety over what an ass he was making of himself if Bellino was on the level.

Yet he couldn't take that chance now that he'd realized what could be happening here. Phil and Bernie. The names kept coming at him. Both killed the same way.

One of the elevators stopped. He heard the roll of its opening doors. Then quiet footsteps. A man moved into the portion of the hallway Lavella could see through the cracked door. A tall man who wore tan slacks and some sort of nobby-weave sports jacket. Lavella couldn't see his face. The guy appeared to be maybe in his forties, his slicked-back hair speckled with gray.

The tall man crossed the corridor in four long strides. Then Lavella heard the second elevator's doors open. The guy looked back. Now Lavella saw his face and wished he hadn't. A long, mean face with bony edges. Sunken cheeks, sunken eyes. Like a skull with a mouth that looked like it never smiled. The eyes, dark glitters in their shadowed sockets, swept to the stairwell door. Paused there? Moved on.

Then the man turned back to the entrance to the lighted office. He grasped the polished knob, turned it, pushed, and slid inside. His shadow glided across the frosted glass.

Lavella swung open the stairwell door and curdled at its squeak, a whisper that sounded like a shout in the empty corridor. Both elevators gaped wide. He stabbed an arm inside the far one, punched the top button, then turned and slipped into the other car.

Come on, come on! He jabbed the lobby button frantically. He heard the door of the first elevator begin to close.

Then the gaunt man burst out of the office. His death's head glared at the elevator bank, speared straight into Lavella's eyes. One hell of a chilling stare. Lavella's gut churned. He was paralyzed, finger frozen to the lobby button.

The elevator doors began to close.

The guy leaped across the hallway. His right foot shot forward, neatly inserted itself between the closing panels.

Lavella came to life. He drew back his Docksider and swung at the polished Gucci. All his weight was behind it, and the man in the hall was off balance.

Lavella's desperate kick banged the expensive shoe aside. As he yanked his bruised foot back in, the rubber bumpers grazed the shoe's toe. Then the doors closed. The other elevator was already on its way up another dozen floors. Lavella's car began to sink.

He fell against the car's wall and kept from sagging right on down only by hooking his elbows over the waist-high wooden rail that ran around three sides of the car. He was soaked clear through. It was only by the grace of not having gone for supper and something to drink that he hadn't wet himself. He could remember only one other time when he'd been so scared. Well, a couple times, but they'd all been the same kind of threat: the terror of being blasted out of the sky by flak or fighters.

That had been impersonal, though. This had been personal, all right. The death's-head bastard had been after him specifically. And no doubt still was! That had been just a delay up there on the ninth floor. A few seconds' delay.

In the lobby, the elevator door opened on a totally frightened man. Tony Lavella quaked out of the car on legs that felt like he didn't have a muscle left in them. He managed only a few steps before he had to hug the wall.

Then he heard the other elevator descending in its shaft. He threw his head back to stare above the door. The 8 glared bright yellow, flicked out. The 7 flashed.

Panic gave him sudden strength. He shoved away from the wall, rushed down the corridor, and ran into the lobby. Bud French, his visored cap thrust back on his wiry black hair, swung around at his desk.

"Mugger!" Lavella shouted. "Coming down the elevator. Stop him!" He tore past as the burly black security guard leaped up. His chair crashed to the floor behind him.

Lavella threw himself against the entrance door's panic bar. The big glass panel swung outward.

"Hey, Mr. Lavella, hold on! I'll need—"

The rest of French's cry was caught behind the closing door. Lavella dashed into the plaza between the twin office towers. The sun had set only minutes before, but the murkiness of the Los Angeles air accelerated darkness. The night was close and still, more like July than October. Lavella stripped off his coat and threw it over his shoulder. His shirt was sodden. His undershirt clung to his chest like a suffocating bandage.

God, that had been close! He'd been so hungry for getaway bucks that he'd missed the Italian connection like a mark caught in a slick con. There was no doubt in his mind now that "Bellino" had been no rock-band manager, not that evil-looking son of a bitch. Bud French no doubt had him in custody now. That would delay him long enough for Lavella to get the hell out of town. Obviously, that had to be done tonight, sooner than he'd planned, but he already had a bag packed and waiting at the apartment.

Lavella slowed to a fast walk. His whole body vibrated.

Please God there would be a bus along quickly when he got to Santa Monica Boulevard, just a little over two blocks distant.

How long would French be able to hold the guy without Lavella there to make specific charges? Could French make an arrest for trespassing? Could he make an arrest at all? He was a rent-a-cop. Could he hold someone on the strength of a blurted accusation from a building tenant who didn't stay around to see it through?

Then Lavella was gripped by a new wash of frigid sweat. How stupid could he be? That one chilling look at the guy up there in the ninth-floor hallway should have told him right on the spot. That was no ordinary hood. Add to that the deaths of two men without witnesses, and Tony Lavella had just been hit with the realization that the man with the death mask wouldn't stop at the lobby floor to rush into Bud French's waiting arms. Hell no! He'd get that elevator back, hit the lobby button, then let it run on down by itself to a confused French while he dashed down the fire stairs to the street-level exit. The exit doors were locked from the outside, but fire laws made them operable the other way.

The new jolt of fear made Tony Lavella jerk a reflex glance over his shoulder.

Mother of God!

In the hazy half-light of the open plaza, a distant figure cast a long finger of shadow toward him, a tall figure thin as a stiletto. And it kept pace with him.

A taxi! That was what he desperately needed now. No two-block trot to the boulevard. No time for that, not with the skull-faced man a hundred yards behind him. He'd grab a taxi on the Avenue of the Stars.

Lavella stretched his stride. The entrance to the ABC Entertainment Center shopping arcade was two hundred feet distant. Then he began to run. Behind him, the tall man quickened his pace.

Lavella dashed the final hundred feet into the shopping complex, swung up stairs to his right, took them two at a time to street level, and emerged behind the Shubert Theatre to race around it on the upper promenade.

At the curb of the service road that paralleled the broad Avenue of the Stars, he fought for breath. Surely the guy wouldn't try anything here in view of a dozen potential witnesses. Surely Lavella had outmaneuvered him long enough to grab a cab unobserved. Yet when a taxi finally did respond to his flailing arms and pulled into the service lane, Lavella was panting with icy terror.

"Santa Monica and . . ." He forced himself to slow his tumble of words and managed to blurt out his cross street. Then he sank back into the seat cushions. A respite. He sure needed it. He twisted around to watch the sidewalk he'd just left grow smaller as the cab rolled down the gentle slope toward the boulevard.

The tall man did not appear. Lavella decided he'd lost him in the dash into the shopping mall, then up the stairway.

Good! That would give Lavella time to grab his two-suiter and shove off for the airport. The guy wouldn't have such an easy time finding the apartment. To confine his business aggravations to his office, Lavella had an unlisted home phone number. Finding his apartment sure wasn't going to be a simple matter of checking the phone book. All Lavella had to do now was stay just one step ahead of that eerie bastard until he was safely aboard a Mexico-bound plane. He'd already withdrawn all the cash he had. It would be enough to buy a one-way shot, and he'd do that in a phony name. That would cut the trail clean.

He was sorry that he wouldn't have time to do anything about Marve Drucker's ad copy or make some arrangement with Cora. They both would have to be just plain out of luck.

Lavella found himself able to grin, a weak one, but it sure beat the hell out of what he'd just gone through. He'd show that creepy Italian skeleton a thing or two about evaporating.

On his way up in the office-tower elevator, Arbalesta had marveled at the naiveté of Americans. Like children. Not only had Lavella eaten his ridiculous story that had set up their appointment, he'd even gone along with the odd hour Arbalesta had requested, and Lavella had conveniently cleared him past the only potential threat in the plan: the armed guard at the building's entrance.

Then Arbalesta had been set back on his expensive heels. Lavella had actually shown a flash of intelligence. Arbalesta had himself been duped by the light in the office and the unlocked door. He'd been stunned when he'd heard the quick footsteps in the supposedly deserted hallway and the elevator doors closing.

Where had Lavella come from? Ah, the fire-stair door, of course. Arbalesta had noted that it was slightly ajar, but had thought nothing of that in his growing contempt for the innocence of his victims and the ease of carrying out his dead mother's sacred charge.

A temporary setback. No more than that. In fact, he emerged from the ground-level outside door in time to follow the man. Logically, given the childlike American behavior patterns, Lavella was bolting for home. After that, though, he could be out of reach. He showed all the symptoms of a man in panic: the slack stare between the closing doors of the elevator, the juvenile but effective kick at Arbalesta's shoe that had left an irritatingly deep scuff, the quick looks over the shoulder, the fast walk then trot then dead run as Lavella reached the shopping-center steps. All giveaways.

Lavella would continue to run. That could destroy the efficiency of Arbalesta's carefully timed plan. He had to finish the man tonight. If that involved yet more risk, that was risk he must face. He was already in some degree of jeopardy from the security man who had admitted him to the office tower. The man had been half-asleep, a not overly observant-looking attendant who had barely glanced up as Arbalesta signed the space beside the hand-printed entry A. BELLINO. And the departing Lavella had been in the lobby barely long enough to blurt out more than a couple of words, if he'd had the voice to say anything at all. So the risk of the guard could be considered minimal.

From the rear of the street-level portion of the shopping arcade, he had watched Lavella hail the taxi. Arbalesta immediately changed direction, strode out a side exit, and reached his rented car in less than seventy seconds. He had parked it along the north curb of nearby Constellation Boulevard headed toward the Avenue of the Stars for easy departure after his planned termination of Lavella in the office tower close by. Now it was no less convenient for a change in that plan.

He caught up to the taxi easily at the Santa Monica Boulevard traffic light. When the cab turned left into Santa Monica, Arbalesta cut inside its wide sweep. Then he drew a block ahead, two blocks. Lavella had fooled him once, but now the man was as predictable as rainwater seeking a low spot. He would not escape vengeance again.

Tony Lavella felt almost buoyant as his taxi neared the cross street that flanked the entrance to his apartment building. He'd shaken the guy for sure. Even if skull-face had stashed a car somewhere in the Century City complex, he had obviously lost the trail. Lavella had asked the driver to take it slow, but not a single car had hung behind them all the way here.

One quick call to the airlines, then he was off. He could even ask the taxi to wait. No, the hell with that. Why should he pay for a meter to keep running while he worked out an airline reservation? He'd call another.

The cab pulled into the side street. Lavella paid and got out. The taxi glided away and left him in a deserted block. Well, almost deserted. There was a single car parked near the apartment entrance. A Pontiac, was it? Lavella walked past, his fingers digging in his pocket for his key.

Then he heard a groan. What the hell?

He stopped. Was it coming from that car? He heard it again, a hoarse moan. He took a step toward the car and bent down. In the weak glow from the corner streetlight, he couldn't see anybody in there.

"Oh, my God!" a strained voice said. "I shut my hand in the door. I've broken it."

A voice sick with pain. Now Lavella could see the hunched-over figure of someone rocking in agony. He walked to the car and stuck his head in the open window.

"Can I—"

He never finished his offer to help. An arm snaked around his neck. Something cold and hard pressed against his forehead, and the night blew into a thousand blinding pieces.

"I've got something," Casey said. Her matter-of-fact tone failed to mask her excitement. Dan could feel it like something he could have reached out and touched.

"Come in, come in, for God's sake! What is it?"

"You got coffee?"

"You're going to hold me up for coffee? What in hell

have you dug out of that electronic marvel of yours?" He closed the door behind her. "I'll get the coffee.

She sat cross-legged on the sofa, fingers tapping a sheaf of longhand notes. The coffee mug rattled on the side table when she put it down.

"You're all twitchy, Case."

"I found the link, Daniel. I really did."

"You kidding?"

"No kidding."

"Let's have it, then. My God, let's have it!"

"I don't have a printer yet, so I copied all this off the CRT in longhand." She waved the notes at him. "They all were World War Two veterans."

"Casey, we already know that. I hope to hell you've got more than that."

"Hope to tell you, Daniel. All five of them were in the U.S. Army Air Forces."

"Bingo?"

"Bingo! All five were in the Fifteenth Air Force, to be specific. To be even more specific, they were in the same bomber group—that was like a division, I think. And in the same squadron, which was part of a group. And to be still more specific, they all were on the same bomber crew. The pilot was named Brice. Captain Rolland W. Brice."

He stared at her. "Damn! You're really something, Casey. How'd you do that?"

"Through the most convoluted, immoral, certainly illegal combination of stolen entry codes and relays the computer world has ever seen. I could go to jail, Dan, if certain of my inquiries could be traced."

"Can they?"

"I don't think so. I sure hope not. Army records in St. Louis and the Veterans Administration in a lot of places have been most helpful, though they don't know it. I imag-

147

ine I've committed some sort of federal crime right from my little old apartment."

"How many men were on those bombers? Did you find that out?

"Of course I found that out. The group these people were in used B-twenty-fours, four-engined things called 'Liberators.' There were ten on the crew—four officers and six enlisted men. Except near the end of the war, they stopped using bombardiers on most crews. So that cut those crews to nine."

"You got all this out of that keyboard of yours?"

"Please. It's an on-line data inquiry terminal. Yeah, I got all that through it. I'm wired to the world, Daniel, including the New York Public Library research data bank for the general stuff. Here's more—maybe pretty important. Helmsgaard, Latza, Rose, and Josaitis all were enlisted men on Captain Brice's crew. I'd guess that whoever's doing this is after the enlisted men."

"Or is hitting them first. Or just found those four first. You said there were six enlisted men on a crew. You find out who the other two were?"

"Anthony T. Lavella and Edward R. Connell. Lavella's an L.A. press agent. Found him through VA records and confirmed it through Los Angeles Information. Connell is in New Orleans." She handed Dan a sheet of her notes. "Here are their phone numbers and addresses. That's Lavella's office number and address. His home phone is unlisted, and I couldn't figure a way to crack through that."

"You're incredible!" Electricity coursed through him. He grabbed his phone.

"Dan, it's after midnight!"

"Casey, somebody seems to be systematically knocking off the enlisted men who served on that old aircrew. There

148

are two of them left. I don't think there's any time to spare." He dialed Roy's home number.

" 'Lo?" Barbara Forrest's voice was fogged with sleep. Dan could picture her, eyes still shut in the darkness, taffy hair spilling across her heavy shoulders.

"It's Dan, Barb. Sorry about the hour, but this is important. Put Roy on, will you?"

"Can't. He's up in Kingston. That computer seminar they're sending the detective twos and threes to. His turn came."

"Damn! How long?"

"He left this afternoon. He'll be there until next Monday. His desk is being handled by Fred Dowling."

Dan had met Detective Frederick Dowling just once, but he remembered him, a by-the-book unimaginative plodder. There was a lot of Roy in him, but Dan could make Roy listen.

"Can I reach Roy up in Kingston?"

"I guess so, through a message board. He called me after he got there and told me they won't take calls to him, but they'll put them on a message board."

"You think there's any chance of getting him sprung out of there? This is pretty damned crucial."

"Dan, that computer school is one of the chief's sacred bulls." She was mellowing now. Probably had the light on and was coming awake. "Roy'll have to tell you to work with Fred Dowling."

Great. Somebody stalked the country with a deadly little .22, and Roy was back in school.

"Sorry, Dan," Barbara said into his silence.

"Science marches on. Go back to sleep, Barb. And thanks."

He hung up, staring blackly at Casey. Then he grabbed the paper she'd give him and began to dial again.

"Dan, what—"

"With that unlisted phone number, Lavella's out of reach for the moment. But maybe I can get to Connell. You think he's going to hate me for waking him up to save his life?"

"He is if this whole theory turns out to be ridiculous."

"I'll take the chance."

The phone was picked up on the fourth ring. "Mrs. Edward R. Connell?"

"Yes?" The voice in New Orleans was wan and choked with apprehension. Dan realized that nothing good comes from a midnight phone call.

"Is Mr. Connell the same Connell who served on a bomber crew in the Fifteenth Air Force?" That, Dan realized too late, was a perfectly lousy opener. But desperation was setting in.

"I beg your pardon?" She had a grand Deep South accent. "Who is this?"

"Dan Forrest, Mrs. Connell. I'm with *NewScope*, a newspaper in New York. Please let me speak to your husband."

Silence. Then, "A New York paper calling at this ridiculous time of night? It's almost midnight, Mr. Forrest, and close to one A.M. where you are."

Why was she stalling? He had to get past her. "Mrs. Connell, this is vitally important. Please put Mr. Connell on the line."

"I'm afraid I simply do not understand, Mr. Forrest."

All right, lady. Shock treatment. "If your husband is the same Edward Connell who was a member of Captain Rolland Brice's bomber crew in World War Two, we have reason to believe that his life is in danger. That's Brice—B-r-i-c-e. Does that sound familiar?"

"He never talks about it."

"But is he that Edward Connell?"

"Well, he was in the air force in Italy. Yes, on a bomber."

"Let me speak to him, Mrs. Connell."

"You can't speak to him."

What was this? "I don't understand."

"He's at a conference that he told me was called un-expectedly. He's in insurance, and he's at a sales confer-ence."

Dan's knuckles showed white. Here he apparently had the key to four murders, and the intended victims for two more, and the world was going to meetings.

"*Where*, for God's sake?"

"In Denver."

Dan rolled his eyes at Casey. "Do you have a number where he can be reached?"

"The Denver Hilton." She gave him the phone number. "Ask for Mr. James Lawson's room. They're sharing ex-penses." There was an odd tone in her voice.

"Thank you very much, Mrs. Connell. And don't worry. Everything will be fine." He sounded like a doctor reas-suring a terminal patient.

"I thought everything was fine before you called, Mr. . . . I apologize. You've rattled me a bit, I'm afraid."

"Forrest. With *NewScope*."

"I'll never get back to sleep now."

"I'm sorry." He dropped the receiver into its cradle with a bang. "He's at an insurance conference in Denver, for God's sake! Told his wife to contact him through a James Lawson. They're sharing a room."

Casey frowned. "Isn't that a little odd?"

"Odd?"

"I mean, they'd both have to register, so why should callers have to go through Lawson to reach Connell?"

"Including Connell's wife." He recalled the shading in her voice when she'd told him that setup.

They stared at each other. "Especially the wife," Casey said. "Are you thinking what I'm thinking?"

He was already dialing the Denver Hilton.

Lawson didn't sound tired at all, but it was only 10:45 in Denver. "Forrest, you say? You the Forrest with Inter-state Eastern I met in Las Vegas last year?"

"Afraid not. Dan Forrest, *NewScope* in New York. It's urgent that I talk with Edward Connell, Mr. Lawson."

"Hell, man, call me Jim."

"Is Connell there?"

"He's down at the bar, Dan. It is Dan, isn't it? Down there, suckin' it up, as they say in Honolulu. You ever been there, Dan?" Evidently Jim had sucked up a few himself.

"Get him."

"I can't do that, Dan. It's seven floors down, and I don't know exactly where—"

"His life can depend on your getting him to this phone, Lawson."

The voice in Denver took on an apprehensive edge. "This some kind of threat?"

"No, damn it, that's what I'm trying to save him from."

"You kidding?"

"Lawson, four people have already died. All of them served on Connell's old bomber crew. Apparently there's some maniac traveling the country trying to exterminate the men who served on that crew —or the six enlisted men who were on it. Your friend is one of the only two left alive. I'm trying to save his ass, and you don't seem to want to help." The receiver was slippery in Dan's grip. "Just where the hell is he, Lawson?"

"How . . . How do I know you're not the guy who's after him?" Lawson's voice had lost its salesman's boom.

"You can call my editor at *NewScope* first thing tomor-row. I won't give you the number. Call information in New York to make sure you're not being conned. If that isn't good enough, I've got a cousin in the police department here. Manhattan Homicide. Ask for Roy Forrest." Dan hoped Lawson wouldn't follow through on that. He'd get Dowling, and God knew what Dowling would say. "If that still doesn't do it—"

"Okay, okay. I'll take the chance. But for God's sake, don't tell his wife."

"Tell her what, Lawson?"

"Don't tell her that Eddie isn't here."

"You're covering for him?" Dan nodded at Casey. "That's why she's supposed to ask for you if she calls him, right?"

Lawson's voice was subdued. "That's it. If she ever found out . . ."

"I think she already knows, Lawson. It was in her voice."

Silence.

"Lawson?"

"Honest to God, he didn't tell me where he really was going. I'm supposed to stall anybody who tries to reach him here. Like say he's in the bar or in a seminar or something. Say I'll relay messages, then come up with some sort of phony reply from him. That's it. That's all of it. I don't know where the hell the guy really is. But he's sure not here."

"He's played this little game before?"

"Couple times."

"You're leveling with me, Lawson?"

"Yes, I am." The bluster and banter were gone. "You really think he's in trouble?"

"I really do. If you come up with anything, anything at all that might help, call me first." Dan gave him his number. "Or," he added, "if I'm not here, call my assistant, Miss Pickett." And he gave Lawson Casey's work and home numbers, then hung up.

"I've been promoted," Casey said. "From neighbor to assistant. That's nice." Then she frowned. "Dead end, right?"

"For the moment."

She held up her notes. "Should we give all this to Dowling?"

"I'm afraid so. First thing tomorrow." He took the notes from her, laid them on the end table, and bounced to his feet.

"In the meantime, Katherine Claudia Pickett, you will be perfectly justified in pointing out that you have performed admirably. Astoundingly, in fact. And that's your side of the agreement. If you want to collect the other—"

He was astonished to see the blood drain from her face, leaving her scared-looking.

"What hit you?"

"You don't have to," she whispered. "I was . . . I was . . ."

He reached for her hands. They were surprisingly cold. "Casey, what is it? Ever since you moved into this old pile, you've been chirping about your sadly neglected body. And I've manfully resisted temptation."

She looked up at him. "You have?"

"I have. You're too young for me."

"It's not much of a body, Dan. You don't want it."

"I think at this point that I not only want it, I need it. And you're confusing the hell out of me, Casey. Up to now, you couldn't throw that body at me fast enough. Now that I'm ready to catch it, you're fading away on me."

She popped off the sofa. "I'm going back to my own apartment."

"Not until you straighten this out. What's with you,

Case? Are you turning me down after all that big, brave talk of yours? What's going on?"

"Nothing's going on. I'm leaving."

"I thought you lived in a state of constant frustration."

"I do."

"But now, when I—" He shrugged. "Forget it. Good night, Casey." He was baffled and, to be frank with himself, miffed.

She didn't move.

"Good night, Casey."

"That wasn't good-bye, was it?" Her voice was shaky.

"No, it's not good-bye. But I can't play emotional rollercoaster with you. I grew out of that in my teens."

She stood in the center of the living room and stared at him with wounded eyes. Then she shook her head slowly. "I built this trap for myself, didn't I? Oh, Dan, I'm so sorry. I'm such a fraud."

He extended his hands, palms up, at a loss for words. What the hell was she talking about?

"It's been a cover-up, Dan. Don't you see? All the big talk, all the challenge—it's a cover-up. I never really thought you'd—"

"A cover-up for *what*, Casey?" Her anguish made his throat dry. "For *what*?"

"Oh, God!" Her eyes glistened. Then her shoulders sagged. And all at once, she yanked the tassled serape over her head, threw it on the floor, and stripped off her rumpled white shirt. No bra. She stood naked to the waist in the bright living-room light, defiant now, her breasts those of a young girl.

"For Pete's sake, Casey! You're lucky. They'll never sag." He almost laughed at her.

"It's not that." Her face was a mask. She jerked down the zipper of her jeans, shoved them below her hips and kicked them away. Then, with her suddenly vulnerable eyes on his, she hooked her thumbs in the waistband of her white cotton briefs and slid them down.

He thought it was a bruise, a huge purple bruise that extended from her waistline to her thigh, painting the entire left side of her tight, little buttocks a deep magenta.

"You see that? It's called a portwine stain. A birthmark, a terrible birthmark that grew bigger and bigger as I grew. I hate it. I'm so ashamed of it! What man could want a woman with a thing like this, Dan? What man?"

Her eyes filled, and her shoulders began to shake with silent sobbing.

He took her in his arms, enfolding her nakedness against him. "This man," he whispered. "Now. Right now."

In the darkness of the bedroom, she was tense beside him, tense and silent. But not resisting. Not compliant, either, but in a trancelike limbo. Then he felt her begin to let go, to let bunched muscles loosen, finally to begin to be a part of it.

Her mouth found his. A long, sweet, gentle kiss that ever so slowly became demanding. Now she was supple, eyes closed, arms reaching up for him. Then her fingers gripped his shoulders. She trembled, seemed to resist, gasped a little kitten mew. Then she let it just happen.

Her arms locked around his neck, and her whisper was right in his ear. "Oh! Oh, wow!"

After a breathless moment she said, "That was nice. So nice!"

And just after that, he was gone, too. When he could speak, he said, "Yes, it really was, Casey."

Then she stunned him. She pulled his head down beside hers and burst into sobs. He held her tight until they passed.

"I think—" She swallowed and tried again. "You just

took me past one hell of an obstacle in my life, Daniel. If there's anything you ever want, call on me."

Twenty-four hours earlier, at 1:45 A.M. EDT, 12:45 Central, Arbalesta was in his New Orleans hotel room reassembling the Heckler & Koch HK-4 double-action pistol he had just field-stripped for inspection. He had taken delivery of the weapon just after midnight in the backroom office of a club on Bourbon Street.

The HK-4 was longer at 6³/₁₆ inches and heavier at 16½ ounces than he preferred. But its checkered black plastic stock fit his hand comfortably. The West German–made weapon would serve well enough.

One target remained. Then the vendetta would be fulfilled.

TEN

Dan's call to Detective Fred Dowling saved him a
call to Los Angeles. But it left him with a sick roiling in his empty stomach.

"Did you say Lavella?" Dowling sounded like a college
freshman, but Dan remembered him as a black Irishman
in his mid-thirties. Heavy brows that met over a snubbed
nose. Eyes bright pinpoints of emerald set close together in
a wide face of continuous suspicion. That kind of cop.
"Anthony T. Lavella?"

Dan licked suddenly dry lips. This didn't sound good.
"That's it, yeah."

"He's been offed. Night before last, with a twenty-two
outside his apartment in West Los Angeles. Came over the
NCIC readout just a couple minutes ago. That's the National Crime Information Center."

"I know what it is, Dowling. It sure took them long
enough."

"It's an imperfect system. When VICAP is set up, maybe
we'll do better on this sort of thing."

" 'VICAP' ?"

"Violent Criminal Apprehension Program, a federal computer system better than their NCIC project. That's what's behind the FBI's interest in this thing. VICAP is a Justice Department effort. NCIC isn't exactly programmed to pick up MO patterns. That's one of our problems with it."

Dowling sounded like he knew what he was talking about, but he also sounded like a confirmed procedurist. A desk man.

"Just listen a couple minutes, will you?" Dan laid the whole thing out for him. Which lengthy monologue was followed by a lengthy silence.

"You still there, Dowling?"

Roy's stand-in cleared his throat. "And they told me Kong's—Forrest's—caseload wasn't going to give me problems. Standard Manhattan fatals, they told me. Nothing like what you're talking about."

"Didn't you read his file on the Helmsgaard thing? It should be on top. He told me he was hanging in on it with the Baltimore County Police, the Pennsylvania State cops, an Arizona sheriff's department, and the FBI. Now it looks like you can add the LAPD, too, Dowling. You realize I shouldn't have to tell you all this? You should be telling me."

"Maybe I'd better bone up on this case."

"While you're boning, somebody's closing in on Connell."

"That's your theory, Forrest. I'm gonna have to sort all this out before I jump in with all four feet."

"That's a luxury you don't have, damn it. Issue an APB for Connell, and you just may save his butt."

"More likely I'll get my own in a sling. I can't just barrel into this and start firing APBs around the country. Connell's from New Orleans, not our jurisdiction."

"Damn it, Dowling! We're wasting a whole lot of time here. In ten days, whoever is after these six guys—"

"That's your theory."

"Whoever's after them has nailed five already. You think he's going to sit around while you study Roy's file?"

"Get off my back, Forrest. I got no jurisdiction in Louisiana, and you got no jurisdiction anywhere at all. I'll look into this, you hear me? When I've got all the facts straight, then I'll follow procedure."

"Wonderful."

"If you wasn't Roy Forrest's kin. I'd log this as a crank call."

Dan slammed down his office phone. His next call was going to have been to Lavella's office number, but now he knew he was more than a day late on that one. Zero. That's what he'd gotten out of Dowling, except for the news on Lavella. He jerked open his desk drawer and rummaged through four years of rubble. He found an old half-used roll of Tums, popped one in his mouth. Hadn't had to do that for a long time. but he'd never been into this kind of thing before.

He pushed back his chair and shut his office door. Hadn't done that in a long time either, but this took some concentration. Baltimore, Scranton, Phoenix. He'd been traipsing around the country in this guy's wake. But he'd damned near caught up with him in Los Angeles. He'd been *ahead* of him in New Orleans. If Connell had kept it in his pants and gone to Denver like he was supposed to, Dan would have been in time.

If . . . if. But Connell was holed up somewhere—fat, dumb, and happy with some willing woman while death by .22 closed in on him.

. . . Unless Dan could find him first. Obviously the .22 killer had had information on the other five. He could never have hit them on such a tight schedule if he hadn't.

So he must have data on Edward Connell, too. But did he yet know more than Jim Lawson—the beard who was covering for Connell?

He was in a race, Dan realized, a race with a ruthless, efficient killer who up to now had enjoyed all the advantages. Up to now. At this moment, Dan felt they were running neck and neck, one hell-bent to kill Edward Connell, the other trying to save him. Dan knew he couldn't afford to lose another damned minute. He grabbed his phone.

Mrs. Connell, who now sounded worried as hell, gave Dan her husband's office number. Dan dialed New Orleans again. Charlie was going to love the office phone bill this month. The hell with Charlie.

"Jarrett, Kaiser and Connell Insurance." A magnolia-blossom voice smiled through a thousand miles of wire.

"Mr. Connell's secretary, please." Dan hoped she might have been given an emergency number, some way to reach Connell in a life-or-death emergency. This qualified.

"I'm sorry, sir, but Miss Adair is on vacation. Was there someone else who could help you?"

"Did Mr. Connell leave word where he would be?"

"Why, he's in Denver, sir. You can reach him at the Denver Hilton. May I give you that number?"

He didn't relish blowing Connell's cover, but this was no time for niceties.

"He's not there, Ms.—"

"Miss Landstreet. Ginny Landstreet." Not so big on the "miz" game in bayou country?

"He's not in Denver, Miss Landstreet."

"But he said—"

"Ginny, listen to me. I'm Dan Forrest, a reporter for a New York newspaper." He figured *NewScope* might not be so big down there either. "We have information that

Mr. Connell's life is in danger, and we've got to reach him. You understand what I'm saying?"

"Oh, Lordy!" Then she fell silent.

"Ginny?"

"Mr. Forrest, I . . . I just don't know what to do."

"Then get somebody on the line who does, for God's sake."

"It isn't that." She sounded close to tears. "You're a reporter?"

"That's right."

"Can I tell you something off the record, something you can't ever print?"

What was this? "Yes, sure." He'd take any drib-drab of information any way he could get it. Come on, girl, come on!

"It's Sandy."

"What's sandy?" What in hell was she talking about?

"Sandy Adair. She's Mr. Connell's secretary."

It hit him. "By God, they're off together, aren't they?"

"She's a friend of mine, Mr. Forrest. A good friend. I don't want to hurt her."

"Tell me where they are, and you could be saving her life—along with his. You understand that?"

"Oh, my God!" She was crying now. "They're in Florida. On Sanibel Island."

Bingo! "You have a phone number?"

"There's no phones at the motel. Just a pay phone."

"What's the name of the place?"

"The Gulfpride Inn. But they always register under a different name, Sandy told me, and he pays cash."

"Maybe she'll call you."

"She never has."

Damn! On the other hand, would Connell believe such a wild phone conversation anyway? And warning him was only part of this. Dan was after the story behind the killings. Fat chance that would come over the phone. He needed to talk with Connell face to face—and quickly! He felt that at least he was one jump ahead of the fast-moving assassin.

"They do this often?" he asked Ginny Landstreet.

"Twice before, that I know about. When he was supposed to be at conferences."

The son of a bitch had a good thing going, but he could have outsmarted himself this time.

"Mr. Forrest, cross your heart you won't tell a soul about this?" A delightful girl with the engaging thought processes of a fifteen-year-old. She'd die right on her call director if she knew what kind of a paper he worked for. But he promised.

"If she calls in," he added, "or if he does, tell him to call Detective Fred Dowling, New York City Homicide." He gave her the number.

"Why can't he call you?"

"Because, sugar, I'm going to Sanibel Island just as fast as I can get there. And listen to me, Ginny, if anybody else calls you about this, anybody at all, you know nothing, you hear? Nothing!"

She solemnly promised.

"One more thing, Ginny. I need a description of both Mr. Connell and Sandy. If they registered under a phony name, I'm going to have to search them out."

"They're both tall."

"How tall?"

"He's about six feet. She's five-nine."

"That helps. What else? Is he fat, thin, what?"

"He's just a little . . . heavy around the middle. White hair." Her voice rose at the end of each sentence in questioning Southern style.

"Bald spot?"

"No, but he keeps his hair short. Real short. Everybody kids him about that."

"You mean like a crew cut? Know what that is?"

"Like in the old pictures of the forties? Yes, that short."

"How about your friend?"

"She's got long black hair and mostly wears it tied back in a ponytail. Oh, and she's got a real nice figure."

"How old is she?"

"Twenty-six. I sure do hope all this helps, Mr. Forrest."

"So do I, Ginny. So do I."

As he headed out, he couldn't resist sticking his head in Charlie Lovett's office.

"You ever heard of Sanibel Island, Charlie?"

Lovett's crested dome jerked up.

"It's in Florida," Dan tossed at him. "I'm on my way."

Lovett leaped toward the door, spilling his coffee across the desk blotter. "Jeez to mutiny, Dan! Maryland, Pennsylvania, Arizona, and now Florida! You think we're the Associated Press? Hey, I'm talking to you. Come back here!"

But Dan had already gone.

The leaching glare of the fluorescent fixture over the sink accentuated Arbalesta's pallor. The unremitting tightness of his schedule had begun to make its stamp on the drawn face. Jet lag hadn't helped. The eyes were sunken in fatigue-darkened sockets. He'd lost weight, and it showed in the sharpness of the cheekbones. Had the creases that flared from nostrils to the corners of his mouth deepened so much in such a short time?

He had thought his mission in juvenile, gullible, innocent America would be easy. As he intended, the five terminations had apparently not been linked, except possibly the Maryland and Pennsylvania strikes—if their ballistics experts somehow managed to compare findings. Even if they had, he was certain that he still was not at serious risk.

Yet the strains of travel, the acquisitions of weapons, the necessity to operate a punishingly tight schedule all had left their marks. Not the killings. Each had given him a sense of relief. Each had meant he was another step closer not only to completion of his sworn and sacred promise, but also to the freedom from the physical frustration that had clouded his life from his earliest humiliating encounter with a willing woman.

One final execution here in New Orleans, and he would be released from that terrible disability and from this vendetta that had begun to take such an unexpected and visible toll on him.

He checked his platinum Rolex. Barely 8:00 A.M. He would shave, take breakfast, then make the confirmation call. His distrust of hotel phones would make it necessary to find a public phone.

He made the call to Jarrett, Kaiser and Connell at 9:15, from a public phone on Canal Street. The hateful new public telephones on walls with separators that shielded only head and shoulders had forced him to walk several blocks before he found a suitably enclosed booth.

"I'm sorry, sir," the female voice said, "but Mr. Connell is out of the office."

"He has not yet arrived?"

"I mean he's not in town, sir."

Impossible! Had not Rollo's man in this city confirmed Connell's schedule? The Lavella incident had not gone quite according to plan because somehow the target had become suspicious. Of what, Arbalesta would never know. Somewhere a flaw had surfaced in the meticulous procedure. But he had managed that temporary setback in Los Angeles.

Here, the problem promised to be more serious. Connell

166

was not where he was supposed to be. Arbalesta forced himself to concentrate. He must manage this problem as well.

"Sir?"

He realized he had been silent too long. "When will he return?"

"Not for several days, sir. May I take a message?"

"Do you know where I can reach him?"

Now she was silent a few seconds too long herself. "Denver, sir. He's at a conference there. You can reach him through Mr. James Lawson. Would you like the number?"

In his career, first as a small-time *ladro* in Naples, next as what in American circles would be called an enforcer, then a narcotics subchief, and now a primarily Rome-based international supplier through his Esportatore Varieta, Arbalesta had developed a near-infallible ability to recognize a liar. It was a matter of eye movements, body signals, and voice stress. Here he had only the woman's voice as a reference. But he knew beyond a doubt that she was lying.

"Is there a message, sir?"

"No," he said. "No message."

He emerged onto the busy sidewalk. For the first time in this complex mission, the telephone had failed him. One final step to be taken, and the plan had come to an alarming standstill.

Arbalesta moved with the flow of the morning foot-traffic. He forced himself to concentrate, to improvise. Was it possible that the sixth and final man had somehow been warned? That he was at home behind locked doors or in some hastily reserved hotel suite, perhaps with a bodyguard in an adjoining room?

No. That was not possible. Each day, Arbalesta had carefully combed the newspapers in each city and had watched local and national telecasts. He had not read nor heard a single word about the possibility of a link among the killings. It was not a national story, as best he could determine. Therefore, it was highly improbable that Edward Connell had somehow been warned. No, there was some other reason for the receptionist's lie. To reach Connell, Arbalesta would have to get past that lie.

The problem was how to do that without putting himself in unreasonable jeopardy. He would have to improvise—and do it quickly. Every additional hour was an added risk. But such improvisation to repair the now fragmented final stage of the plan was a challenge he could meet. Abrupt revision had been one of his strongest assets in the old enforcer days. This was not so different. In fact, he found himself feeling a degree of anticipation, even exhilaration.

The first stage of the revised plan would necessarily be one of reconnaissance. He was certain the short-cropped blond woman—not really much more than a girl—at the receptionist's desk in the insurance agency's seventh-floor office suite did not notice his slow stroll past the wide plate-glass entrance doors. He needed only a glance to imprint her pale doll-like face in his brain. "Ginny Landstreet" announced the nameplate on her desk.

Back on the street, he made one more phone call to that office, a call to determine just one fact: closing time. Now with much of the day to kill, he strolled across Canal, then down Bourbon Street into the French Quarter. He was struck by its tawdriness, the window displays of tacky T-shirts imprinted with crude obscenities. So typically American, he thought, to disgrace the quaintness of the architecture, the oddly beguiling Old World *atmosfera* with such tasteless trash. Then he recalled certain streets in Rome. Small-time entrepreneurs were the same the world over.

He turned right on St. Peter Street and walked past Jackson Square's iron fence with its displays of sidewalk art. He found an empty bench on the levee overlooking the surprisingly wide and muddy Mississippi and remained there well into the afternoon. To a casual passerby, he was a distinguished-looking middle-aged man, a tourist of possible Slavic extraction with those prominent cheekbones: a man enjoying the steamy Louisiana sunlight. Certainly none of the informally dressed people ambling along the broad levee with their noisy children would suspect that he had shot five men to death in the eleven days since his arrival at Kennedy International and that he was here on the riverbank not as a tourist but as an executioner on a carefully structured schedule.

As the afternoon wore on, he removed his sports jacket and folded it carefully in his lap so that the bulge of the heavy HK-4 did not show.

In midafternoon, he rose from the hard bench and ambled down the elevated riverbank to seek out the Royal Orleans Hotel, which he had passed on his stroll down Bourbon Street. The Rib Room, an attractive salon with tall arched windows, offered beef specialties. He ordered prime ribs and was impressed. He lingered until the restaurant closed to prepare for the evening rush. In the hotel lobby, he bought a *Times-Picayune* and took an unobtrusive corner chair. At 4:10, he made his way out of the French Quarter to return to the glass-and-steel office tower.

He rode the elevator to the seventh floor and took up position midway along the corridor that fronted Jarrett, Kaiser and Connell's offices. There was a broad floor-to-ceiling window here that offered an impressive northward view of the city. He leaned against the waist-high varnished safety rail and unfolded his newspaper.

This was high-risk, he conceded, but it could not be

avoided. He appeared, he hoped, as a husband waiting for his wife to leave the insurance agency or any of the several other offices along this corridor.

At 4:33 the exodus began from the insurance office and two others down the hall. The receptionist with the short, pale-gold hair did not emerge until 4:37, a delay that had given Arbalesta a bad few moments. Gossiping, no doubt, or in the ladies' room?

Then she pushed through the glass doors talking with two other women, a black girl with a huge purse over her shoulder, and a mousy little woman wearing a depressing brown business suit.

He merged with the homebound employees from a publishing office at the far end of the hall. For anxious seconds he thought the elevator she had entered would fill up before he reached it. But he slid inside as the doors began to close and edged behind a taller and far broader man.

All of the car's occupants departed at the lobby level. Some walked to the front entrance, but most of them moved cattlelike to a wide door behind the elevator bank, the entrance to a street-level parking garage in the rear of the building. The receptionist was in this larger group, occupied with plucking lint from her fuzzy blue sweater, an activity he appreciated because the large man he was using for cover was now holding one of the front doors open for the little mousy woman in brown.

In the oppressive fume-laden heat of the garage, the black girl murmured something to the blonde and walked off to the right, reaching in her big bag for her keys. The receptionist walked straight up the line of parked cars on the left. Then she pulled her own keys out of her purse, moved into the line of cars, and bent down beside a red Datsun.

Arbalesta edged casually between a closely parked Cadillac and Buick and faked the unlocking of the Buick's door. Across the turtlelike row of intervening automobile roofs, he watched the four-door Datsun sedan back out of its numbered space in the darkened corner of the underground garage. *Eccellente.* Another day would be required, an additional day to his schedule. But it was necessary. This was the final link in the chain of vengeance.

Ginny Landstreet would never forget Friday, October 26, as long as she lived. But until exactly 4:43, the day had been like any other Friday—except for the terrible tension that had gripped her. The fact that the day signaled the beginning of the weekend helped a little. Maybe she would take Alan Polan up on his invitation to take the dinner cruise tomorrow on the old stern-wheeler *Natchez*. The cruise could be fun, but she knew she would end the day fending off Alan in her apartment. Or maybe she would finally give in this weekend. She knew she would eventually. She always did. And, well, he was a nice enough boy, wasn't he?

In between calls—why was there always such a lot of calls on Fridays?—she began to convince herself that not only did she want to go all the way with Alan Polan, she *needed* to, actually needed to do that. It was this awful nervous clutch in the pit of her stomach ever since that distressing call from Mr. Forrest day before yesterday. She'd taken a Valium at lunchtime and that helped for a while. Another in midafternoon had helped more. Now, at closing time, she was almost in a state of walking withdrawal from reality, her mind more and more on tomorrow night with Alan: his slender fingers drifting down her back, touching, gliding a zipper, slipping buttons. Warm and cuddly. Alan, honey, if you don't just plain blow it tomorrow, you and little old Ginny are going to have *some* kind of Saturday night!

Only the reflexes of three years' experience at this gentle drudgery saw her through the ritual of closing down the call director and her desk.

"You all right, honey?" Josie Caldwell asked in the elevator, her bittersweet-chocolate face screwed into real concern.

"I'm fine, just fine." Ginny struggled to put conviction in her fuzzy voice. Oh Lordy, she would have to drive extra special careful, the state she was in.

In the garage, she walked close to the line of car bumpers as a kind of reference to keep her from weaving. She knew Josie was watching her. She looked back. Josie turned away abruptly and walked to her own car.

I'm really all right, Ginny told herself. The Valium is wearing off, truly it is. She thrust her hand in her purse for her keys and moved between her Datsun and the blue car beside it.

"Do not turn around. Do not speak."

Her spine froze into a rigid column of ice.

The hard voice was right in her ear. Where on earth had the man come from!

"What—"

"Be silent." His voice was flat, without emphasis. It had a deadly impersonality that just plain scared the hell out of her. "Unlock the door. Then reach inside and unlock the rear door. Do not dare to look back."

He was so close behind her she could smell the coffee on his breath. Was this one of the men from the office, she suddenly wondered, pulling a joke? Larry Schubert was known for this kind of crazy trick, and he had been after her for a date. But could Larry disguise his voice like this?

172

Something hard like bunched fingers struck her just above her right kidney. She gasped.

"Do as I told you."

Not Larry. Oh God, she heard about strangers in parking garages, but it couldn't be happening to her!

With jittering fingers, she managed to get the driver's door open, bent her right hand around the doorpost, and pulled up the rear door's locking knob.

"Get inside."

She slid behind the wheel and heard and felt him get into the seat behind her. He shut the rear door.

"Move the mirror aside." The flat, purposeful voice chilled her anew. She stabbed the mirror askew with her right hand.

Then the man said, "I have a straight razor. A new one I bought today. It's the sharpest piece of steel I've ever seen."

"Oh my dear God!"

Through her panic, she realized he had some sort of accent, not heavy, but certainly there.

"If you do not do as I tell you, I can reach forward and slice through your carotid artery. That will not hurt much, but you will bleed to death in less than five minutes. Do you understand that?"

The Valium's afterglow drained into her legs, numbed them, then left her nerves naked to the paralyzing onset of terror. Her throat constricted. She could only nod.

"You will drive out of here to Claibourne Avenue, then to Swamp Elder Road east of the city."

She knew the road, a winding, deserted strip of pocked macadam that faded to a dirt lane beside a bayou.

"When we reach the end of that road, you will get out of the car and remove your clothes. *All* of your clothes."

"Oh, *God!*"

"Then we will play. We will play in many ways. Do you understand?"

A pervert. An evil, dangerous pervert with a *razor*! Why her? Dear Lord, why her? Ginny's head bobbed in panic. Agree with him and hope for a miracle. Hope for somebody to notice the two of them in the closed car in this shadowed corner of the garage. A forlorn hope, she knew. But that was all she had left. Cooperate and hope.

"If you do not comply in every way—in every way—first I will slice away your left earlobe. This is a new razor, extremely sharp, you remember. You will not feel much pain, but you will bleed. You will bleed much. If you do not then do exactly as I tell you, I will remove the *tetta*—the tip of your left breast."

She bit down on a scream. Beneath the clinging sweater she wore to ward off the frigid office air conditioning, perspiration burst in the hollow of her chest. She gagged.

"You do not like what I am going to do?"

What answer did this insane creep want? She was afraid to move.

"Ah," the sinister, soft voice said. "You do not like my demands."

She swam in sweat now. It trickled down between her breasts, slicked her forehead, glued her hair to the nape of her neck. Her lungs constricted. She panted for breath. And she had a terrible need to go to the bathroom. She thought she couldn't hold it much longer.

"I am a reasonable man. I will give you an alternative. We can play my games with the razor as referee. Or you need not do that at all. You may drive away from here as if nothing has happened. Because nothing will happen."

What was he saying? That he would not rape her, mutilate her on lonely Swamp Elder Road? If she would—what?

174

"Do you understand me? You will speak, Ginny."

God, he knew her name!

Her voice cracked. She swallowed, forced dry lips to shape words. "What . . . do you want?"

"Only information, Ginny. You know where Mr. Connell is, do you not?"

And now she recognized the voice. The man who had asked to speak to Mr. Connell yesterday morning.

"I asked you a question, Ginny. Either you answer it truthfully, or we drive." His fingers gripped her left shoulder like a hawk's talons, dug beneath her collarbone, and closed with such ferocity that her stomach churned.

Mr. Forrest had been right! This had to be the man he was talking about, the man who threatened Mr. Connell's life.

But now he was threatening hers. She'd never been faced with such a horrible decision. Could she endure rape and the threat of a razor's horribly intimate slices to protect a company executive she barely knew?

"Start the car," the voice behind her demanded.

"No!" Her loyalty washed away in uncontrollable dread. "He's on Sanibel Island. In Florida." The words came in a gush.

"Where on Sanibel Island?"

Shame eddied through her, but she could not stop herself. "A motel. The Gulfpride Inn.'

"He is alone there?"

She managed to hesitate. The talonlike fingers dug in. "He is alone?"

She cringed under his cruel grip. "There's . . . a woman with him. One of the girls in the office. Don't hurt her. Please, please don't hurt her!"

The hard grip released. The hand slid out of sight behind her. Then the man's right arm snaked around her throat, clamped her hard against the headrest.

"Listen to me. You will tell no one of this. No one. If you are so stupid to do so, I will hunt you down. You are easy to find, Ginny Landstreet. I will hunt you down, and I will kill you by many small slices where it will hurt and bleed the most. Do you understand?"

She tried frantically to nod in his crushing grip. This was grisly, horrible.

"That will indeed hurt, but it will be only the beginning. You again have a choice, Ginny Landstreet. Silence or death, a death so slow and unthinkable you will wish you never lived."

She had not ever felt so thoroughly scared and so totally helpless in her life. Her heart would surely burst from its wild racing. Her fingers clawed uselessly at his constricting arm. Her breath choked off. Through the windshield, the concrete of the garage wall was speckled with black dots that merged, then robbed her of vision. She grew dizzy, began to whirl into hollow black silence.

Then the arm slid away. She heard the rear door open, then close, heard his rapid footsteps fade.

She drew a ragged, stabbing breath. Her vision cleared. She managed a quick look through the line of car windows as the man rounded the partition at the end of the ramp. A tall man, dimly seen, wearing light-colored slacks and a darker sports coat. Then he was gone.

She had a terrible moment trying to fit the key into the ignition. Then she realized it was the wrong key, her apartment key. She sat back and looked in amazement at her hands. They twitched and jumped all by themselves.

Ginny Landstreet sat there a moment longer, staring at her uncontrollable hands. Then she collapsed over the steering wheel and burst into sobs of hysteria.

She didn't hear Arbalesta's rented Oldsmobile come to life on the other side of the garage wall behind her. He backed out carefully, then rolled the brown Cutlass to the exit.

No provisions had been made, obviously, for the safe acquisition of a sixth weapon. He would either have to pack the HK-4 in his suitcase and hope the airline would not spot-check the bag on a short flight to Florida, or he would drive the entire distance from here.

ELEVEN

THE TAKEOFF OF Eastern's 10:50 flight to Atlanta was delayed forty minutes at Kennedy, a routine matter of heavy system backup. That left Dan a nerve-tightening twelve minutes to catch the connecting Eastern flight to Fort Myers. He raced up the exit ramp into the tan-carpeted corridor of Eastern's Concourse A, searched frantically for a TV-screen readout of departures. Gate 17, Concourse B. Damn!

He danced through the foot traffic to the brick-floored crossover point, took the agonizingly lengthy and slowly descending escalator. Three steps below him two middle-aged women were conversationally locked in place. He fumed.

In the broad below-surface connecting corridor, he dashed onto the moving walkway and trotted along its black footway belt, adding its forward motion to his. Then he rode up the Concourse B escalator, fingers tapping impatiently on his leather overnighter.

At the top, he veered down the long pier, plunged

through the churn of arrivals and departures, and reached Gate 17 sweaty and short of breath, only to discover this second flight was to be held up nearly an hour for a new reason. A fast-developing low-pressure area in the Gulf of Mexico had spawned a flurry of nasty little squalls across the Florida peninsula. Flights to Miami, Orlando, and Fort Myers were being threaded through a changing pattern of storms, an exacting process that took time.

Finally aboard the DC-9, Dan agonized through the standard Atlanta takeoff backup. Fourteenth in line. A bloated DC-10 roared down the runway that paralleled the taxi strip. The DC-9 inched forward. Thirteenth. The afternoon wore on.

At last, long-delayed Flight 243 pivoted onto the runway, brakes howling. The engines screamed. The jet clawed into the Atlanta haze, then through a thin overcast to break into late-afternoon sunshine with blue everywhere but ahead. There the sky was smudged with dirty gray cloud buildups.

The turbulence began over the Georgia-Florida line, right after drinks had been served, of course. Quickest way to bring on rough air. Then the sunlight was blotted away by towering clumps of cotton-waste cumulus. The jet tore through an iron-gray squall that threw horizontal streaks along the cabin windows. The rain hit like coarse sand.

Then they were clear again, arrowing between hulking thunderheads. There was a tension in the cabin you could read in the forced smiles of the chunky blonde and the brown-bunned flight attendants, in the unremitting glare of the FASTEN SEAT BELTS sign, in the jawline of the iron-haired woman perspiring beside him. Everyone on board was earning wings today. Dan forced his attention back to his in-flight magazine and forged through a whole paragraph before he realized he'd already read it. Nice flight.

Then the jet began the rolling metal noises that told him

they had started down. Flaps extended, wing slots opened. The landing gear locked in place with a whir, a grind, and the final vital thump.

The DC-9 broke out of hard-riding fleece at two thousand. They were over Gulf Coast wetlands above Cape Coral, an expanse of sun-seared, flat greens and browns edged by the lead-hued water. Then the sprawling and mostly uninhabited road grid of Cape Coral slid past, next the Caloosahatchee River, then Fort Myers.

The jet clumped into Southwest Florida Regional Airport, moaned its engines into the thrust reversers, and taxied in. To the west, the sky was the color of an angry bruise.

The rental-car paperwork took ten minutes, long enough for a tropical deluge to plunge the airport into near darkness and to dump a Niagara of white water across the front of the terminal. The girl driver had the shuttle-bus door open for him. He put his head down and ran. But he was soaked when he leaped aboard the van. He'd toted his London Fog to sunbaked Phoenix, then left it home for this mess. Good planning, fella.

"Welcome to Florida," the driver offered. A freckled carrot-top, she drove the clumsy vehicle as though it were a motorcycle. The trip took six minutes from the terminal around the end of the public-parking section to a service road that edged the rental-car parking compounds. When he stepped out of the air-conditioned van, the squall had passed, leaving thick, moisture-laden air in its wake.

The car was white, another Toyota. He'd figured he could stretch Charlie just so far. He twirled the little import out of the lot, turned right into the service lane, then merged with the Fort Myers–bound traffic on Daniels Road.

Veils of vapor rose off the rain-cooled pavement of the dual-lane highway. The road ran straight as a spear through five miles of roadside mangroves, palmettos, and grassy marsh flats to Sumerlin Road, where a Sanibel sign took him hard left through more scrub, then the scattered commercialization of South Fort Myers.

The sky to the west was hard slate when Sumerlin made its westward sweep to join the south end of McGregor Boulevard. Occasional billboards blazed out the news of a new Sanibel condo development, but largely without fanfare the island suddenly appeared through a break in the roadside scrub on the left. Startlingly green in a chance wash of sunlight through the roiling thunderheads, Sanibel's low, fourteen-mile length lay three miles across the steel-gray water of San Carlos Bay. Then the wild tangle of tropical shrubbery closed out the view again.

Was he still a step ahead of the man who had brutally murdered Phil Helmsgaard and Bernie Latza and Mickey Josaitis and Tony Lavella? Dan hoped he had dead-ended the killer's transcontinental death run in New Orleans, but he knew that hope hung on the thin thread of a young woman's silence. Dan had gotten the information out of her easily enough. Would the murderer of five men find Ginny Landstreet any more of a problem . . . if he did find Ginny Landstreet? The other five appeared to have been in predictable locations. Connell wasn't. Yet Dan should be closing in on him now. Would a man who had pressed a pistol against the skulls of five men in ten days and mercilessly jerked the trigger have an insurmountable problem finding the sixth?

The killer would come here. Of that Dan was certain. But was he here yet? Not unless he realized that Ginny Landstreet was the key to Connell's whereabouts and forced her to break her promise of silence. Several imponderables there, Dan realized, but a man who could commit five murders and leave the police of five jurisdictions milling ineffectually behind him was a man you underestimated at your peril.

Thanks to Casey and her genius with her computer-access terminal, this was now a race to find Edward Connell—to warn him or to kill him, depending on who found him first.

Rain speckled the windshield again. Dan flicked on the wipers. The white Toyota rounded a curve, and ahead lay the Sanibel Causeway tollbooth. He paid the three-dollar toll and accelerated onto the causeway pavement. The tires rumbled along the metal grid of the boat-channel drawbridge, then he followed a gradual leftward bend the length of a long, man-made island, crossed another low bridge, then another island and bridge as milky veils of rain swept toward him across several low-lying islands in the bay.

Sanibel's boomeranglike arc lay mostly to his right. The causeway came ashore off the final bridge a mile and a half from the island's eastern tip. He hit a four-way stop where the causeway road intersected Periwinkle Way. Motels straight ahead and to the right, a sign near the intersection had told him.

He spotted a gas station a block down Periwinkle. Lightning flared. The pumps and station building glared bright against dark trees. He pulled across Periwinkle's glistening blacktop, and he felt the thunder's vibration in his stomach.

A wall of rain rolled out of the dark pines that arched over the road to the west. Dan pulled close to the station door and wound down his window. The rush of rain was louder than the Toyota's fast idle. The attendant stuck out a chubby, mustached face. He held a yellow slicker above his head with both hands.

"Gulfpride? Back to the intersection, turn right. Follow Lindgren to the Hilton, then swing left on East Gulf."

Wind tore at the little car as Dan guided it down the half-mile length of Lindgren Boulevard, a divided stretch flanked on both sides by low, expensive-looking homes. Their white stucco and plaster facades flared chalkily in blue-white lightning flashes. Thunder shook the Toyota. The wipers' frantic flip-flop failed to keep up with the torrent.

He almost missed the sharp left turn onto East Gulf. He ran the stop sign, spun the wheel late, and barely managed to avoid skidding into the Sanibel Hilton's rapidly flooding parking area. Then the shieldlike wooden sign of the Gulfpride Inn came up so fast he almost missed that, too, as it lay nearly flat in the rising gale. He pulled into the drive and parked in the welcome shelter of a portico at the office door.

He shut down the little Japanese car and dashed into the office, wind-driven rain pushing in with him. Behind the registration desk a sleepy-eyed youngish man in a beige T-shirt glanced up, then lay his paperback facedown on the desk. His face looked like he'd left it in the sun too long. The scaly pink of the burn ran right up through his thinning sand-colored hair.

"Welcome to the Gulfpride. Hope you're enjoying our fall weather."

"Not typical, I hope."

"What's typical in the hurricane season? This is the front edge of Dennis. Sounds odd, doesn't it? Using men's names? Not as convincing as Dora or Debby, for some reason. Damned thing isn't a hurricane yet, but it's sure cut down on business."

"I saw your Vacancy sign."

"Off-season anyway, then you throw in the storm threat, and what you got is a wide choice. How about an upstairs, gulf-front unit? One of our best."

"I'm looking for a fellow I met on the plane." Dan had concocted this little deception on the flight from Atlanta. Connell and friend were registered under fictitious names,

184

according to Ginny. Dan was going to have to use descriptions. He didn't want to spook the desk clerk with a blurt that he was looking for a guy who was about to be murdered, so he had come up with what he hoped would be a plausible story.

"He got me interested in some liability insurance, gave me his card, and I promptly lost the damned thing. All I remember is that he said he and his wife were staying here. Tall guy with short white hair, in his sixties. She's tall, too. Good-looking woman, black hair. Younger than he is."

"Sure, that'll be the Carrolls." The clerk leaned sideways in his chair to consult a room chart. "They're in unit twelve, the end unit in the Gulffront Building. I can put you in number seven at the other end. Living room, bedroom, kitchenette. Seventy a night. Or a unit in the Poolside or Court Buildings for sixty-two."

Dan took out the *NewScope* credit card. What the hell? "I'll take the big one."

He pocketed the key, got back in the dripping Toyota, drove around the rear of the Court Building to where the drive widened into parking spaces, and pulled to the diagonal section of concrete curbing marked 7. The rain hit in bursts, angling through the headlight beams. He twisted the switch. The parking area plunged into gunmetal blue. Lightning glared, three quick flashes. He grabbed his bag off the bucket seat beside him and ducked through the downpour.

The second-level access was a stucco-faced stairway that made a reverse turn halfway up. There the rain hit him full in the face, and thunder banged like cannonfire. All in all, this was a thoroughly rotten late afternoon.

The six upstairs units opened onto a balcony that ran the length of the building beneath the roof overhang. Its concrete floor was sopping. He gave the key a half-turn and opened the door into the air-conditioned clamminess of a narrow hall past the bedroom and bath. It led to a decently large living room with a maple sofa bed and several rattan chairs, a TV set on a metal stand, and a table and four ladder-back chairs near a stove and sink with birch cupboards above.

At its far end, the living room opened onto a screened porch through sliding-glass doors. The place had wall-to-wall green carpeting, the outdoor kind that resisted sand, sea, transient kids, and daily vacuuming. All in all, not a bad unit for the price.

He tossed his bag on the sofa, used the bathroom, dried his soaked head. Now for the reason he was here, more than a thousand miles from New York on a barrier island out in the Gulf of Mexico where a storm named Dennis was doing its best to put South Florida under. If he pulled a blank, he was going to be one scandal-sheet writer in big trouble. Like everybody else, Charlie Lovett had a breaking point.

He opened the door on a crash of thunder that vibrated the balcony, shut it quickly behind him, and walked down the row of unit entrances. The intensity of the storm had brought early dusk. Number 12 was at the balcony's far end, not a glimmer of light showing in its window. Not promising. There were four cars in the parking area in addition to his. The place wasn't deserted, but unit 12 certainly seemed to be.

He rapped the flush door's green-painted panel.

No response. Damn!

He knocked again, harder this time. A stab of lightning drilled into the beach not a hundred yards away, a giant flashbulb that seared his corneas with a snapshot of ghostly white sand, frothing breakers with black water beyond. The snapshot stayed there when he blinked. The near-simultaneous thunder crash hurt his eardrums.

Then a light flashed on in unit 12. The door opened. Barely three inches. The guy was big and squint-eyed, as though he'd been asleep. He clutched a terrycloth towel around his waist. Otherwise he was naked.

Silhouetted by the dim hallway backlighting, he wore a stumpy halo of a Mohawk-like haircut, a go-to-hell, out-of-date World War II crew cut. A "whiffle," had they called it then?

From the doorway to the right, the bedroom, came a woman's voice. A young, musical Southern drawl.

"What is it, honey?" It didn't take a genius to realize that whiffle-cut and honey-voice had been in the middle of a lot more than a late-afternoon nap.

"Are you Edward Connell?" Dan asked.

"Oh, shit," said Edward Connell.

Three hours out of New Orleans, Arbalesta had realized what a task he had set for himself, a *punizione* for a forty-five-year-old man who had been tired when he'd started. He had purchased a road atlas and had studied it hastily in the shopping-center parking lot. Only two states to cross, the narrow southern tips of Mississippi and Alabama. Not much more than a hundred miles. Then he would be in Florida, and Florida was his destination.

But the weather had begun to sour even before he had twisted the chocolate-brown Cutlass through the New Orleans rush-hour traffic to Interstate 10. The early-evening air had thickened into mist. Then a soft, persistent rain slowed traffic to a creep across the causeway at the eastern end of incredibly huge Lake Pontchartrain.

He was able to pick up the pace when Interstate 10 veered eastward north to the lake. The rain increased, too, the fringe effect of a "tropical depression" out in the Gulf, so said the radio. He wasn't sure what a tropical depression was, but it sounded menacing. He certainly could do without the rain, and the glare from oncoming headlights was bounced into his face by the slick pavement. Darkness had come prematurely as he pushed the Cutlass past sixty on the remarkably straight and flat highway.

He traversed miles of marshland before the lights of Biloxi flared out of the night and then fell behind. An hour later, the highway curved left around the lighted towers of Mobile then swung hard right to cross Mobile Bay's black waters. The interstate plunged eastward into the oppressive darkness of a rain-drenched southern flatlands night.

Arbalesta crossed the Alabama-Florida line a few minutes after nine, thanks to the excellent American highway system, but no thanks to its ludicrous fifty-five-mile-an-hour speed limit. In Europe he would not have been held back by his near-paranoid apprehension of a siren screaming behind him, blue and red lights flashing in the night.

A few minutes later, he began to pass the lighted Pensacola exits. At one of them, he pulled off the interstate into a gas station, filled the tank himself, then drove to the adjacent fast-food stop and ordered coffee and a detestable hamburger (Ham, he wondered? It looked like overcooked beef) and took his tray to an unpopulated section of the seating area.

The plastic bench was hard and cold from the overdone air conditioning. So much in this garish country was overdone. He would be relieved when he could finally free himself of this mission which was becoming a curse.

He was tired. His arms and back had begun to protest the tense miles. So many of them. He opened the road atlas he had brought with him from the automobile. In the New Orleans shopping-center bookstore, he had been concerned with leaving that city as quickly as possible. He believed that he had thoroughly terrorized the Landstreet girl, but who could ever be certain of a female's reaction to terror? Perhaps she would not talk, but perhaps she would. If she did tell of her garage encounter with a deviate madman, he doubted that she would do so for many hours—with luck, days.

He had played his role well, he thought. In truth, he had found himself enjoying it in a near-perverted manner. With his arm crushing her throat, he had felt a sudden rush of heat to his groin, an urgent fullness he had never before experienced. In retrospect, that had unsettled him. Had he unwittingly discovered a black facet of his character, a *need* to threaten, perhaps actually to maim?

No, no. He rejected the intrusive thought. The resolution of his physical disability had to be more honorable than that. He had avenged his mother's and his own honor five times. The completion of the vendetta demanded the sixth and final retribution. Here in Florida.

He studied the map. For the first time, he became aware of the immensity of Florida's land area. Four hundred miles in length, the distance from Rome to the Brenner Pass. And coming into the state on its long western finger, he must travel a distance greater than that. He had pushed two hundred miles through rain on treacherous pavement. He still had more than five hundred to drive—not kilometers, but lengthier miles.

Arbalesta bunched together the paper and plastic debris from his order, dropped it in the trash bin at the door as seemed to be the custom, and emerged again into the sticky night. Now the rain drifted through the glare of the elevated parking-area floodlights, for the moment as soft as a caress yet soaking his face and hair and rumpled coat. Five hundred miles yet to drive through this sodden tropical night. A young man would welcome such a challenge. He was no longer a young man, but he did have the impetus of urgency. At the end of these punishing miles lay release from this obsession that was making him old.

TWELVE

C HARLOTTE SENT YOU, didn't she?"
Edward Connell clutched the door with one hand,
the towel with the other. He looked absurd. A roll of fat
bulged over the towel. His eyes blazed with fury beneath
his spiky whiffle cut.

"Nobody sent me, Connell. I came here on my own to
save your ass."

"You got to be kidding! I don't know what the hell you're
talking about, buddy. Why don't you just get on about your
business and leave me and the missus—"

"Sandy Adair?"

Connell's iron-gray eyes fixed on Dan's. "You're hard to
read, mister. Just what is it you want?'

"Do the names Phillip Helmsgaard and Bernard Latza
mean anything to you? How about Walter Rose and Michael Josaitis? And Anthony Lavella?"

A change rolled over the heavy face, like colors fading
out of stained glass, to leave it blank and staring. Then the
contrasting black eyebrows furled into a frown.

"Where'd you get those names? That was forty years ago."

"They're dead, Connell. Every one of them. I'm here to try to keep you from being dead, too."

"If you're some son-of-a-bitching blackmailer—"

"I don't want anything but the story behind all this," Dan broke in. "Dan Forrest, *NewScope*."

"A damn reporter."

"One who's found out that you're a target for a madman racing around the country with a twenty-two pistol. Two shots in the head for all five of your old crew members, Connell. You're the only one of the six enlisted men left alive."

"This is nuts! What in the hell am I doing, talking with I don't know who, a guy who's got some lunatic story about people I knew forty years ago?"

Dan hadn't known what to expect when he confronted Connell. Surprise, certainly. Doubt, of course. Then probably fear. Eventually, with great good luck, maybe gratitude. But Connell was rapidly hardening into an arrogant pain in the butt. Somehow Dan had to get past the big man's anger.

"I'm sure it hasn't occurred to you," he said, "but you make one great target standing here in the open door with the light behind you."

Even that didn't do it. "Buddy," Connell said, "what guarantee do I have that you're not the guy you're talking about?"

"Because if I was, you'd already be flat on that rug in there with two bullets in your ear."

Connell's eyes held Dan's. Then he jerked his head back toward the living room. "Get in here . . . Forrest, was it? Go out on the porch. I'll be there in a minute." He stepped back to let Dan pass through the short entrance hall, then he disappeared in the dark bedroom.

Dan walked through the living room and opened the sliding door to the little screened porch under the broad beachside roof overhang. There were two metal chairs out here, flanking a small table. He sat in the far chair, recoiling at its unexpectedly cold wetness.

Connell reappeared barefoot in baggy ink-blue shorts and a sky-blue T-shirt emblazoned with a tan pelican in full flight across a huge orange sun.

"Forrest, what damned paper did you say you're with?"

"*NewScope.*"

"Never heard of it. Local rag somewhere?"

"National. In every supermarket east of California."

"Oh, God. One of those things frustrated housewives get off on. Why in hell should I be talking with you?"

"Because I know what's going on, Connell. I just don't know why."

"You're ahead of me."

"I'm not so sure about that."

"If those five guys are dead, how come I haven't read about it in the New Orleans papers or seen anything on TV?"

"You know what a serial killer is?"

"Wait a minute." Connell reached behind his chair, opened the sliding door, and shouted into the unit. "Get me some coffee, hon!" He turned back to Dan. "You want coffee?"

"Fine."

"Make it two," he called. Evidently Sandy Adair was willing to take brusque orders.

Connell sensed the thought. "Obvious what's going on here. You print it, and I'll bust your ass, buddy. What's so terrible? She offered to put out, I offered to help her career. Woman uses what's she's got, man returns the favor. She's a sweet kid, using me for all she's worth, but you see the equipment she's got for that, and it'll help you understand. If the wife doesn't know, what's the harm?"

Charlotte Connell did know, Dan believed, but why add that to the load he was dumping on Eddie Connell?

Wind sang through the porch screening and sprayed them with occasional bursts of fine rain. New lightning flared behind the distant lights of Fort Myers Beach across the mouth of San Carlos Bay, but the squall that had just drenched Sanibel had rolled inland behind them. Its thunder was now like muted cannon on a subsiding battlefield. The island air was thick with moisture. The glass doors, cooled by the unit's air conditioning, were opaque with condensation. Beyond the glass, Dan heard the girl clink dishware in the kitchenette.

"Now what was that you said? Something about a 'serial killer'?"

Dan gave it to him broadside, from New York to L.A., with Maryland, Pennsylvania, and Arizona death stops between. The Roy Forrest connection, Fred Dowling's bureaucratic diddling, Dan's realization that the whole thing had bogged down in jurisdictional turf protection and procedural channelization on an awesome scale. Nothing malevolent about any of that: it was just the way American law enforcement worked. But it had put Dan in the position of being the only free agent in possession of what he was sure somebody somewhere, and much too late, would call the big picture. Roy would surely use that if he weren't out of it, stuck up the Hudson in computer school.

"So what do you want out of this nutty story you're trying so hard to sell me?" Connell asked; quite blandly, Dan thought, for a man whose life could well be on a short line. "Something from me?"

"That's right, something from you."

The fogged sliding door vibrated from Ms. Adair's kick. Connell sprang up to yank it open. Even playing waitress

194

with the tray of mugs, sugar, cream, and a pot of steaming instant, she was something to see. Tall, supple, tied-back hair glossy black as polished coal, breasts jutting out her yellow silk robe. Naked beneath, Dan assumed. Deep tan under there, no doubt, like her bare forearms; the kind of toasted brown only dark-haired girls could properly achieve. He didn't know what or how Connell was paying her, but the guy surely was getting his money's worth.

"Sandra, this is Mr. Forrest. He'll be out of here soon, then we'll go on out to dinner at Chadwick's just like we planned, honey bear. You get dressed now, you hear?"

"Mr. Forrest," she acknowledged as she centered the tray on the table. Just three syllables, but they told Dan a lot. A wise young woman, compliant when it counted but nobody's permanent acquisition.

"You see what I meant about her?" Connell bragged when she had left them alone again.

"I saw." Dan could still feel her brief presence in uncivilized cells that vibrated with animal reaction.

"And you expect me to put my tail between my legs and run out of this setup because you have a wild theory about some nut serial killer?"

"I hope you'll give me some kind of clue on what might have caused all this mayhem. After that, I don't know what I expect. Maybe the motive will give me a goose. What do you think?"

"I think you're after a story for that shitsheet you work for. I don't for a minute think you give a damn for me."

"You're not making it easy to give a damn for you, Connell." Dan took a drag of coffee and burned his lip. It was scalding. Nothing was going right.

"I haven't gotten where I am by being popular on campus," Connell said. "You know any hot insurance agents you really love? It's a pushy business. It takes push to sell a product you and the customer both hope will never be used, and when it works out that way, then you've really sold him no more than a sheaf of paper for a fat price. That takes a salesman with drive. That's me, Forrest. A hard driver, and to hell with whoever gets in the way."

"Even if he's got two bullets with your name on them?"

"To hell with your lunatic—if there is one—and his damned little popgun. Twenty-twos are the kind of pearl-handled toys women carry around in their purses, then try to shoot their unfaithful lovers with. More often shoot themselves in the leg trying to get the damned thing out of the Kleenex and lipstick. You think I'm afraid of that?"

Dan took his coffee more gingerly this time. "It's also the kind of weapon the Mafia has taken to these days. Don't underestimate it. Some military rifles have calibers that small because when the slug hits the body, it tumbles and does a lot of internal gouging. And don't underestimate the guy carrying that twenty-two. He's killed five people since the fourteenth of this month, and nobody's laid a finger on him. The police of five states don't know what he looks like—except maybe he's tall and thin. That much came out of Pennsylvania. Five murders, Connell, and the guy's still roaming at will."

"So you say. But you also said the police are working on a coincidence theory."

"Some coincidence. Five of your old bomber crew."

The rain pelted straight down.

"I think you should—"

"You said all you got to say?" Connell cut in.

"You're a hard man to convince."

"Yeah. If you're through, I got to change into something respectable. The lady and I have dinner reservations."

Dan set his mug down hard. "Damn it, Connell! I've busted my butt to put this thing together. I missed on La-vella, but I got here in time for you. And you're more concerned about schmoozing with golden girl in there than you are about your own hide."

"Ain't that always the way?"

On his way back through the unit, Dan noticed a collection of seashells on the dinette table. He nodded toward the bedroom. "Hers?"

"You don't think I'd spend my time down here on a handful of shells?"

So she did have other interests than career enhancement. He liked her a little better after seeing the shells, but there was nothing visible to redeem Connell's bricklike impact. Yet Dan couldn't let it go, not after he'd come so far.

"You want to open up a little and maybe extend your actuarial statistics, I'll be in unit seven, other end of the balcony, through tomorrow." Surely Charlie Lovett wouldn't begrudge him just seventy more bucks . . . if Dan could get a mile and a half closer to Eddie Connell. So far that was like trying to share confidences with a grizzly.

Not until 2:00 A.M. did Arbalesta reach the intersection of eastbound Interstate 10 with southbound Interstate 75 near Lake City. In Tallahassee he had almost opted for a shorter-appearing route down 90 to 19-27, thence along the coast through Clearwater. But as best he could read his map, that route would take him through towns, not past them as would the interstate system. So he had raced through that Tallahassee interchange and headed grimly eastward toward 75.

His fingers clamped like talons on the sweaty wheel. The muscles of his right leg had bunched between ankle and knee and threatened to cramp. The small of his back was a knot of pain. His eyes felt as though they had sunken even deeper beneath the hooded lids, bloodshot with fatigue.

The approaching interchange northwest of Lake City jolted him to alertness. He slowed, threaded through the exit ramp, then accelerated off the ramp onto the divided pavement of southbound 75. A dozen miles later, he had slumped back into the dreary hunched posture of the long-distance interstate driver.

On a long stretch just north of Gainesville, he had the eerie feeling that the steering wheel was slowly rising toward him. Then he realized he had been close to sleep, his head drooping. He stabbed the radio on, let the inane twangy music blast him fully awake, and turned the air-conditioning outlets to drench his face in their icy wash.

An hour later, he stopped at an all-night food-and-fuel oasis adjacent to an isolated interchange below Ocala. He had the tank filled and bought a roll of caffeine tablets, took two on top of strong coffee and was jolted to jittery alertness. In the men's room, he was startled at his appearance in the rippled mirror over the sink. How had he lost so much weight? He saw a face drained of expression. He stared at a skull.

Arbalesta came out of the rest room with hatred burning even more intensely in his gut that it had after it had been kindled like an explosion in the dreary Sicilian bedroom where his mother had told him of the humiliation that had haunted her for forty years. She had tried for vengeance the day after it had happened, had walked angrily to the air base and reported the incident to the military police. She had only the name on the jackets to give them, but surely that would be enough. The base provost had listened to her, had even taken notes, but she realized later that had only been an act to mollify her, to keep her outrage contained.

Within two weeks, her own mother's health required her return to Sicily. Shortly after that, the war in Europe ended. When she had been able to return to Cerignola to press her case, she found only empty desolation: a broad mile-long strip of blacktop pavement rimmed with cracked taxiways and circular hardstands. Only concrete foundations marked the locations of the maintenance hangar, mess halls, officers' and enlisted men's clubs. She stood in the ruined orchard trembling with rage. Surely they had planned it this way, had wrapped her charges in self-protective bureaucratic delays until the group was evacuated beyond reach.

She had no means with which to press the case across thousands of miles of ocean. But she would exact her vengeance if that took the rest of her life. Ultimately, because she could not bring herself to bare her shame to people who knew her, she had turned to her son as death neared, had sworn him to the vendetta so long ago. . . . Only two months ago? Surely longer than that.

The vengeance had become his obsession. Six men had to die before he would be free of this terrible weight that had begun to crush him. He would not be absolved of his oath for revenge until all six were in their graves.

He returned to the car, wound back on the interstate, and accelerated past sixty-five. Around him in the rain-filled darkness, Central Florida slept. He encountered only an occasional other car. The rain came in dense bursts with unpredictable winds that sometimes threatened to veer the Cutlass into the parallel lane. Or was that the result of the heavy caffeine dosage? He was wide-eyed and felt alert, but his reflexes seemed curiously out of synchronization.

No matter. He need only guide the speeding Cutlass through the rain for another few hours, rest a minimum time, find the man, Connell, quickly eliminate him, then drive the hundred-odd miles from Fort Myers to Miami.

There he would turn in the car and book his return to Rome. All that surely could be accomplished in less than forty-eight hours. Perhaps less than twenty-four. So he was only a day from home as new rain battered the Cutlass near Tampa. All that remained between this miserable moment in the black predawn deluge and a crisply clean first-class seat on a Rome-bound Alitalia DC-10 was the last man he had sworn to kill. He would relish pushing the HK-4 against Edward Connell's head and pulling the trigger.

"Aren't you ever coming to bed, Eddie?"

He had been pacing and puttering since they had returned from the restaurant. And there he had fussed about the preparation of the lobster, which she had found to be just fine. He hadn't finished his. He'd seemed so preoccupied ever since that Forrest man had left. She was worried, not about Eddie Connell himself but about the fact that he had barely noticed her since that odd visit.

The idea was to have Eddie concentrate on her, to make him yearn for her when she was away from him on the beach, to make him want her all the time. To accomplish this, she had established a delicate balance. She rewarded him enough to keep him in control, but not so often that he became sated.

She liked this game. It paid off beautifully. Already she had risen from a nonentity status in the steno pool to the prestige and much higher pay of Eddie's administrative assistant, that promotion having followed the trips to Myrtle Beach and Louisville. Myrtle Beach in June had been fun. But Louisville . . . He'd had a business conference there, had taken her along, and it rained all three days. When he returned to their room after each all-day business session, there had been only one entertainment in which he was interested. That took every bit of originality she could muster to keep him hungry for more. That was where she'd made administrative assistant: from eleven thousand a year to seventeen thousand in one bedridden weekend.

But now something had gone wrong.

"Eddie?" She hated the wheedle that had crept into her voice.

"Huh?"

Why was he poking around out there?

"You know, honey," she called suggestively. "What we talked about this morning."

"Oh. Oh, yeah, that."

She pitched her voice low. "I promised you, baby. And I always keep my promises." That should get him.

It did, but he was still thinking about other things as he stripped off his shirt, slacks, and shorts in the small bedroom.

"I'd better shower first," he said unexpectedly. He was gone before she could think of a response. She lay nude on her back, her hair fanned across the pillow, long legs stretched out. She had achieved, she thought, a wonderfully exotic Indian look. A younger man would have instantly swan-dived on her with a roar of appreciation. Old men were weird.

He came out of the bathroom rubbing himself with a towel, then finally appeared to notice her. The hand with the towel fell to his side.

"You're beautiful, you know that?"

This was more like it. She raised her arms and beckoned with wiggling fingers. "Come here, Eddie."

She played him superbly, two gasps forward, one sigh back until she knew she had driven him to a feather-edge of control. Then she drove him up and over. He almost babbled with delight.

"I'll just bet you've never done it like that!" she said triumphantly.

His response was remote. She wanted to credit that to her irresistible techniques, but she knew he had begun to think about that Forrest man again.

Eddie Connell felt the insistent flutter of her fingertips, all right, but his mind kept drifting. He'd never before had such focusing trouble with her. That damned Forrest!

The guy's story had been incredible. No, that wasn't the right word. The story had been wild; crazy, maybe. But not quite incredible. All the names were horrifyingly accurate. Forrest hadn't asked for money, nothing like that. Could really be a reporter, just like he said. If that was it . . . God! It had finally caught up with him, with all of them. Forty years later. Who in hell would believe a thing like that? Forrest couldn't blame him for the way he'd reacted, could he?

"Eddie, honey? You still with me?"

"Sure, sweetstuff. Sure am."

So now what? He'd sleep on it, but that wasn't going to make it go away. Tomorrow he would . . . tomorrow he'd . . .

Her persistent ministrations suddenly broke through. Took over. Shattered his musings. He groaned, arched. Fell back.

Then he sat up and wrapped his arms around his naked knees. He felt old and foolish, as he always did for a few minutes afterward.

"There's not a whole lot for you in that particular game," he said.

"My fun is giving you fun, Eddie." A facile, even professional, riposte. "Just remember little things like this at Christmas-bonus time."

He turned to look down at her in the night-table lamp's glow and couldn't see past the dazzle of her even little teeth, satin-sheen lips, and eyes so startlingly blue that he'd thought for months they had to be tinted contacts.

"I'll remember," he said. Justifying her inflated bonus would be a rough one, but he'd figure something to placate the firm's business manager.

When he came out of the bathroom again, she had

slipped beneath the blanket and sheet, still naked. He hunkered in beside her. Sleep wouldn't come for him, but she sure didn't have any trouble. Her rhythmic little sigh was unsettling. He rolled his back to her.

Phil, Walt, Bernie, Mickey, and Tony. Especially Tony. He'd tried to stop it. If Forrest was telling a true story, Tony deserved a lot better than two bullets in the forehead.

Eddie Connell bumped over on his back and stared at the muted pattern thrown across the ceiling by a balcony safety light just beyond the bedroom window's venetian blind. Was the air-conditioning hum louder tonight? The monotonous drone should have brought on sleep, that and the endless downpour outside. Sometimes he'd had trouble staying awake in the old B-24 with its four Pratt & Whitneys rumbling a few feet behind his turret up there in the nose. Monotonous sounds usually did him in like taking a sleeping capsule.

Then the air conditioning *was* the roar of the P & Ws muted by leather helmet and rubber-clad earphones. He shuddered. Cold up here. Cold in the penthouse of hell, but they all had been sold on this. Rolly Brice, middle-aged at twenty-four in the pilot's seat. Hen Rigby, two years younger in the copilot's bucket on Brice's right. Heinie "Wrong Side" Voltz up here in the bomber's nose at his little navigation desk behind Eddie's turret. And the other five enlisted men, the "EM's," in position in the chunky, slab-sided fuselage. Damned strange way to make war— from ecstasy to shit-scared in hot milliseconds.

"FWs coming in seven o'clock level!" Tony's voice was squawky with the strain of trying to sound like everything was under control when he knew the soft blue was about to blow apart in his face.

Then the firing started. Eddie jolted awake. Had there really been a noise, maybe no louder than a .22? He lay rigid, eyes on the ceiling. He knew Brice had gone with an airline. American, wasn't it? No question about Rigby. Heinie Voltz, incredibly, had tried to give American Olympic bobsledding a whirl, failed at that, then wandered through semipro winter sports. The last Eddie had read in the sports pages, Heinie was managing a ski lodge in Colorado.

The rest of that nine-man aircrew of *Brice's Crisis*, the six EMs? A tacit understanding there. After the incident, after the crew was broken up for brief reassignments, then discharged on its U.S. return to Bradley Field in Connecticut in the summer of '45, they had gone six separate ways. With relief. None of them wanted any more of a reminder than his own sick memory. Eddie had never heard from— or of—any of the other five. Until today.

All of them dead? Was Forrest right about that? All five shot in the head? The incident had been ugly, shameful, but had any of them deserved that? Surely not Tony. Or any of them, damn it. All dead, those clean young men corrupted by war, then killed for that corruption four decades later?

The ceiling blurred as Eddie Connell's eyes filled. Was it because this was a limbo hour of very early morning, the time a man was weakest? Or had he just realized that he believed Forrest's horror story?

He tried to strangle the unexpected sob that clutched his throat, but it overwhelmed him. And woke Sandy. Her fingers brushed his arm.

"What . . .?"

He rolled ponderously to her, reached out, and gathered her nakedness close, seeking refuge or compassion or just the reassurance of her young warmth against his slack vein-streaked aging.

She nestled her head in the hollow of his shoulder. Her arms slipped around him, and she held him. For the first time since he'd started this thing in Myrtle Beach, Eddie

Connell did not feel like he was in bed with America's best-looking office call girl.

Had the rattle of wind-shaken palm fronds above the air conditioning's whisper made Dan sleep so poorly? Or had it been Connell's stunning rebuff? When colorless dawn finally seeped past the bedroom window's slatted blind, the wind and rain had lulled, but ominous gloom persisted. Dan groped out of the insomnia-tangled bed with flaming anger pounding behind his eyes. That son of a bitch!

After Connell had bounced him out into the rainy dark, Dan had gunned the Toyota down Periwinkle, found a deli where he had forced down a corned beef and coffee, then brought back instant coffee, sugar, and a bag of sweet rolls for the morning. Connell's arrogance had pretty well blown away his appetite, but he had to start the day with something.

Now, wearing only his shorts, Dan opened the drapes. To his amazement, people were already prowling the wide beach, peering down, stooping. He remembered one of the billboards on the way in: "Best shelling beach in America." Those nuts out there in the muggy dawn were shell collectors.

He showered, shaved, then dressed and put on a pan of water for coffee. Now what? He'd barreled in here like a white knight . . . Damn, the car *was* white, wasn't it! And the poor sucker he'd come to save hadn't wanted any.

All right, Connell, now it's Digger Dan the Scandal Man you're going to have to contend with. If Connell persisted in being such an arrogant idiot, Dan would *pry* the story out of him and run the thing just the way Charlie Lovett would like it best—warts, liver spots, and all.

Connell didn't want to talk? He'd *make* the smug bastard talk. Any way he could. And Connell sure was vulnerable with that tall, toasted groin-boiler sharing bed and board.

With his thumbnail, Dan broke the paper seal on the jar of instant, spooned a double dose into a mug from the cupboard over the stove, sugared it, and walked to the porch door, steaming mug stinging in his hand. He rolled open the glass panel. The air was soggy. Off to the left, behind the mainland shore, another squall was building, blue-black like a giant bruise. That was the Everglades back there behind the uneven bone-white stand of condos along the distant shore.

He set his mug on the porch table and stepped back into the unit for a towel to wipe the dripping chair. At that moment, he heard a tap at the unit's entrance.

Dan glanced at his watch. Who in the hell could that be at 6:10 A.M.? The manager, to tell him Charlie had rescinded *NewScope*'s American Express card?

He yanked open the door. Not the suncooked manager. Eddie Connell stood there on the wet balcony, his pelican T-shirt and baggy slacks hanging on a man who seemed to have shrunk, a stoop-shouldered old man with white stubble on his cheeks and chin.

"You got something to drink, Forrest?"

"You came to the wrong guy for that."

"Coffee, then?"

"I've got instant." Dan stood aside, and Connell shambled in.

"I don't think I slept ten minutes at a stretch," he muttered.

"That makes two of us." Dan ran more water in the saucepan and flipped on the electric burner.

Connell leaned against one of the chairs at the kitchen-ette table. "I'll tell you something, Forrest. It took a while, but you shook me good."

"You just seemed pissed to me."

"I was. I apologize for that. The thing didn't catch up until I stared at the ceiling for a couple hours."

Dan filled a mug with hot water from the saucepan, slid it across the table to Connell, and gestured toward the jar of instant. "Fix your poison. Join me on the porch."

"No, not the porch. In here. It's too quiet outside at the moment. Can't tell who might be listening out there."

"It won't be quiet for long. That looks like Armageddon building up over there behind Fort Myers Beach, and it's looking our way. West. What kinds of storms move west?"

"It's that Dennis thing out in the Gulf. This is the hurricane season down here. It's not a hurricane yet, but it's kicking up its—" He snorted without losing his haunted look. "I was going to say skirts."

Connell sank into the chair near the porch door. Dan retrieved his mug from the porch, then stood to gaze through the glass door and the water-pocked screening beyond. A tall girl in a white bikini bottom and a light-green jacket worked the surfline like an elegant long-legged shore bird intent on treasure shells kicked up by the yard-high breakers.

"Gorgeous broad, isn't she?" said Connell, following Dan's stare. Dan realized he was watching Sandy Adair. An old Groucho Marx quip jumped idiotically into his head. "Why, Minnie, I didn't recognize you standing up!"

"You got a story for me?" He moved from the glass partition to the sofa.

"I've kept this buried for forty years. Now a reporter from a supermarket scandal rag has me in a corner." Connell shook his head morosely.

"You might not believe this, but I came down here to warn you, not to do you in."

"But you want the story."

"I won't lie to you about that."

"Off the record?"

"I won't lie to you about that either."

"Sweet Mother of God," Eddie Connell said. He took a nervous gulp of coffee, then stared down into the mug. The ragged front of the storm reached San Carlos Bay. The distant fringe of white condos was swallowed in a gray deluge. The palms edging the unit rattled in the first stir of early-morning breeze.

Then a burst of new wind shrieked out of the bay, boiled the water into whitecaps, and made the palms clatter in frenzy. Their legs stung by blowing sand, the shellers began to race off the beach, a scramble of flopping cellulite thighs and overstuffed bosoms on the bounce. Except Sandra Adair. A gazelle, she disappeared around the other end of the building just as the onrushing wall of rain blanked out the shoreline. It hit the Gulfpride like a bursting dam. Lightning froze Eddie Connell's slack face, restless hands, and collapsed shoulders dead-white. Then the jarring crack of thunder shook him back to life.

"You a Catholic, Forrest?"

"I don't know what I am. No, not a Catholic."

"I should be telling this to priest." And Eddie Connell began.

THIRTEEN

T HE TWENTY-SEVENTH MISSION. That was when it happened. Certain missions had numerical significance. The first, of course. That was when you lost your virginity, learned that nobody sang "The Wild Blue Yonder" up there. The flak was real and ugly and death-laden. The unseen pilots of the Focke-Wulfs and Messerschmidts were there for just one purpose: to kill you.

When you climbed out of the reeking bomber, cramped and smelling of heavy sweat after that first mission, you swaggered a little. You stood around in your baggy flight gear while the ground crew looked for flak holes. Then you saw your hand shake at debriefing when you hoisted the government-issued shot of bourbon.

The fifth mission was notable because after you lived through five, you got an automatic Air Medal, the blue ribbon with vertical orange stripes, to add to the meager strip over the left pocket of your "Eisenhower jacket." The air corps was looking the other way about that particular style, and for not too many occupation *lire* you could get an Italian tailor to refashion your fusty army blouse into a dashing imitation of Ike's customized garb.

The tenth mission was another milestone; all multiples of fives were. The line of little chalked bomb symbols on the tent wall above your cot lengthened as you somehow were miraculously missed by fighters and flak, and the laboring Liberator hung together. The thirteenth meant a lot, of course. Who wasn't superstitious by then? Who wasn't carrying a lucky coin or wearing lucky socks or sneaking his girl's snapshot out of the personal effects you were required to leave behind with the intelligence people?

The fifteenth mission, the twentieth . . . the twenty-fifth. Sometimes they went past by surprise. The Fifteenth Air Force was beginning to award double mission credits for targets that had proved particularly tough. Vienna, for one, where the retreating Germans had concentrated the flak barges that had fled west from collapsing Czechoslovakian strong points on the muddy Danube and Duna.

Everybody had heard of the Eighth Air Force. London was a nifty place to file stories. What correspondent in his right mind would opt for the wind, dust, mud, and flood of southern Italy? There was a song: *It's still the same old story,/ The Eighth gets all the glory/ While we just fly and die* . . .

There was another song. Feisty little Tony Lavella had brought it from gunnery school at Tyndall. Rumor said it had been infiltrated into that particular school by a German agent, but Brice's crew had taken it up as bravado in crew training at Savannah. Now it was their vocal trademark:

Oh take down that blue star, dear mother,
Replace it with one made of gold.
Your son is an aerial gunner—
He'll die when he's eighteen years old.

All six EMs were over eighteen, but not by much except

for Bernie Latza, the old man at twenty-five, a year older, incredibly, than Rolly Brice, their pilot. But pilots were ageless.

That twenty-seventh mission was supposed to have been a milk run to an Austrian railhead in a tiny town near Rattenburg, thirty miles northeast of the Brenner Pass. They felt relief when the bedraggled cloth curtain was rolled up and the line of thick red marking tape on the big wall map behind the briefing platform stabbed no farther north. Not to the bad-news targets: not to Vienna, Steyr, Linz, or Salzburg. This would be an excursion, a holiday. A reward after the grim targets of the previous week. Three double mission credits to an Austrian ball-bearing works, a reported fighter-plane assembly plant, and an oil refinery at three of those four lethal targets. They hadn't hit Vienna.

So far, a miracle, one that made them nervous: there wasn't a scratch on *Brice's Crisis*. Not a fighter bullet-pock or a flak hole. Not even a bruise on any of the nine men who sweated the lumbering, slab-sided B-24H into the air and kept it there with constant attention. Their bomber was one of the few old olive-drab veterans left, a grizzled survivor among the herds of newer, bright-silver Libs coming out of Willow Run. *Crisis* was creaky and smelled of gasoline, stale oil, and fear–sweat. But it stayed up, and nothing had ever hit it.

That March 1945 morning, in a sky so clear the sun hurt to look at, the luck of Rolly Brice's crew dribbled away. Who would have thought so on takeoff into cold air buoyant as water? You could see almost clear across the Adriatic to Yugoslavia as three hundred heavy bombers thundered out of half a dozen airfields in the Foggia plains and jockeyed into tight combat boxes to concentrate the firepower of their three thousand .50-caliber Brownings.

Two-thirds of the B-24 armada, with one broad-winged B-17 Fortress group among them, rumbled north across the

Adriatic toward Prague in support of the Russian ground juggernaut. More than a few of their crews would have much preferred to lay themselves on the line for Patton.

The rest of the heavies, *Brice's Crisis* among them, roared northwesterly, up the center of the Adriatic, both coasts purple-gray on east and west horizons from twenty-four thousand feet. The war was nearly won, and there was almost a dare implicit in their landfall forty miles west of Trieste. The fighter cover, three groups of twin-boomed P-38 Lightnings, had appeared three thousand feet above as they'd passed well east of Rimini.

Nobody on the ground raised so much as a single flak gun to challenge them until Brice's group, with what looked like just a handful of the shepherding Lightnings, veered from the main force as planned, then wheeled around in a wide one-eighty just southwest of Rattenburg to head south and hit the railhead on the way home. That was an appreciated tactic. You had to stay dead on course, straight and level, through the bomb run, but at least you were already headed home—if you accepted a leaky pyramidal tent in a stunted almond grove as home.

The flak over the minuscule target was thin and ineffective, a scatter of flashes that etched sharp black blots against the sky's brilliant blue. The bursts expanded to dirty gray smudges that drifted past high and off to the left. To defend Vienna, Linz, and other major targets, there were deadly accurate radar-aimed 88s. Here in the Austrian boondocks, they'd probably given the boys and old men of home defense whatever leftover, burned-out guns could be bootlegged out of tightening desperation.

Behind his turret perched smack on the nose of the howling B-24, Eddie Connell knew that Lieutenant Heinie Volz watched the lead B-24 to the left and slightly ahead of them. When Morgan's lead ship dropped, all nine heavies in A Flight would drop. Only Morgan and Kraft, the deputy lead beyond and behind Morgan, carried the Norden bombsight that the correspondents were so fond of touting. "It'll put a bomb in a barrel from thirty thousand." So it would—if the air was dead smooth, if there was no prop wash from preceding aircraft, no flak to distract the bombardier, no worry about fighters, no discomfort from the electric bunny suit beneath your alpaca-lined poplins that burned your arm if you leaned against something and your butt if you sat. Even if all that perfection existed, what would the correspondents say about the drop-on-leader technique? The lead ship might indeed hit the barrel. The rest of the loads went their own way, spread out as far as the nine planes in the flight were spread.

The doors of Morgan's cavernous bomb bay slid up along their fuselage tracks. Down the undulating line of flight, all bays opened. Eddie felt the vibration and knew that from the rear of the flight deck above and behind him, you now could see down through five miles of empty air.

Then Morgan's bombardier dropped his. And everybody else salvoed theirs. *Brice's Crisis* bucked upward, lightened by three tons. Twelve chubby five-hundred-pounders fell away.

The bomb bay doors rumbled closed.

"Hits!" Walt Rose yipped moments later from the vantage of his ball turret beneath the belly. "A good straddle."

Eddie remembered the target recon photos at briefing. The railyard nestled in the center of the village down in a mountain cleft. A nice straddle. Wonder where the rest of them went off? The war was winding down fast, and there was a hollow moment now and then when you thought of things like that.

"Lovely, lovely. That's a take!" That was Tony Lavella in the tail turret with his announcement that everything was clear back there. All they had to do now was get this drafty boxcar back to Cerignola. Tony was a dark little

213

hotshot of a Boston street kid with a hard yearn to break into some kind, any kind, of show biz once this was over.

The rest of them jammed the intercom with the hoots and hoorahs of tension on the drain. Helluva bunch, these guys, Eddie reminded himself—as he did every time they had come out of the bomb run and were home free. Beanpole Bernie and built-like-a-truck Phil on the waist guns, away from their engineer and radio op duties during the bomb run. Skinny Mickey Mouth up there in the top turret over the flight deck, ready to sell you anything from the winged phallus pendants he'd picked up on a quick trip to Pompeii to the silk scarf his brother had mailed him from Hawaii.

Coming off a bomb run like this one, with the only flak a laughable mile away and still not so much as a pinhole in the bomber's aging hide, gave you a lift that beat adrenaline. Like winning the statewide playoff with a touchdown on the last play. A bases-loaded homer in the ninth. The prettiest girl at the dance murmuring, "Let's go out to your car." God, this was wonderful!

Then Eddie stared straight ahead. What in hell was that! First nothing on the lavender horizon. Then a fly speck. Then the speck grew wings. Above the heavies, three P-38s broke off their essing at twenty-seven thousand and slanted down.

He depressed his mike switch. "Twelve o'clock level. Something coming in—Holy Lord!"

The onrushing aircraft raced toward them, more missile than airplane, deflected upward, whistled not two hundred feet above the echelon of B-24s, was gone.

"My God! What was *that*?" Mickey's awestruck voice.

"Damn, never saw—"

"Quiet down! Call the clock." That was Brice. Cool, but there was an undercurrent in his pilot's voice that Eddie hadn't heard before. The American fighters roared past in belated pursuit.

"What was that thing?" Hen Rigby's voice was conversational. Did anything ever shake their copilot? When Brice had threatened Tony and Phil with procedural mayhem after they'd soaked up all that Christmas vino in Bari, it had been Hen Rigby who'd taken the pilot aside. "It was just a friendly little toot, Rolly," Eddie had heard him say. "You don't want to blow the crew apart over a bottle of Dago red." And it had been Hen with his Brooks Brothers good looks who had taken Walt to Foggia when Walt hadn't thought he could force himself down into the cramped and frightening ball turret one more time. After the two of them came back, Walt never again seemed to have the problem.

"Rolly?" Hen prompted.

"ME two-six-two," Brice finally said.

And that sent a cold rush of fear through everybody on board. A jet! The Messerschmidt Bf.109s with their 30mm cannon and the armored Focke-Wulf 190s had been bad enough. But they had faded away as fighter interdiction and strategic bomb strikes demolished the logistics of parts replacement and fuel supply.

But an ME-262! In briefings, the intelligence officers had said, "If you see one, start firing as soon as you do. Don't expect to hit it. You'll just let him know you're awake. Top speed: five hundred forty."

Five forty! That meant the jet and *Brice's Crisis* had just closed at something around eight hundred miles an hour! Fire as soon as you see one? Nobody'd had time even to think of pulling a trigger.

"He's coming back!" Tony screeched. "He's swung around, and he's coming back. Where in hell are those thirty-eights?"

"Fat lot of good they did," Bernie snorted.

"Call the clock, damn it!" That was Brice again, maybe a militaristic pain in the ass, but he knew how to keep them on the job.

"Five o'clock level," Tony said. "Here he c—"

"There he goes!" Eddie broke in as the jet screamed past. He saw belated tracers from somewhere down the echelon. But nobody aboard the *Crisis* had yet gotten off a shot.

"He got Morgan!" Walt yelled from his miserable elbows-between-knees position below the belly. Eddie swung his turret hard left.

The big plane only fifty yards distant drew a trail of white vapor behind number-three engine. Fuel. Then it blew. Exploded in Eddie's face. He thought he felt the fireball's heat right through the plexiglass and his oxygen mask.

Morgan's B-24 disintegrated in a boiling shower of metal and men, shrieking down and away in the long inverted arc illusion you saw from high up.

Nobody said anything for a long moment. Then Brice broke it. "Where is that son of a bitch now?" He hardly ever swore. Nobody had a total view out of the bomber. They had to use each other's eyes.

"Three o'clock level, swinging around behind us again." Tony, at the far end of the long fuselage. "The P-thirty-eights are a mile behind him. Two miles."

"Must be a green pilot," Hen Rigby guessed. "No fancy pursuit curves. Just dead-level firing passes from the rear."

"He's smart enough to know our fighters don't mean doodly," Mickey pointed out.

Eddie was struck by the irony of this. Twenty-six mission credits with nobody hurt, the plane and everyone in it untouched by fighters, flak, or mechanical failures. Now the war was about closed out, the Luftwaffe was a pathetic shell, and this misguided son of the Fuehrer had been given a deadly new toy to play with. And he was trying to be ace-in-a-day for a cause already lost.

On its second firing pass, the dull-green jet concentrated on the B-24 at the far right of the echelon. He was more than a mile past when the clumsy Liberator fell off to the right. It bled a black rope of oil. Number-four engine seized. The bomber rolled ponderously on its back. A dark little object hurtled from a waist window. Another. Chutes blossomed—too soon at this altitude. Maybe they'd be lucky and not die of anoxia or the below-zero air temperature.

"Three out," Walt reported. "Four."

The dying Liberator completed its roll, struggled to stay level. The right wing dropped again. The big plane rolled faster this time.

"Five out. Come on, come on . . ."

Now a thousand feet lower, the B-24 dropped its nose in a fatal spin. Its incongruously long tapered wings whipped over and over. Nobody else would get out. They were glued in there by hundreds of pounds of centrifugal pressure. Only Walt and Tony saw the now toylike bomber slam the base of a mountain just south of the Brenner Pass and wink bright orange. The others were searching for the screaming nightmare that had done that.

"Behind us, behind us!" Mickey shouted.

"Where o'clock?" Brice insisted.

Is his mouth as dry as mine, Eddie wondered? Am I the only guy up here trying so hard not to piss my pants?

"Six o'clock high, diving."

"For God's sake!" Brice yelled, finally turning human. *"Shoot at him!"*

The tail and top turrets cut loose, the four heavy machine guns shivering the fuselage. Eddie heard metal snap and ping behind him.

When the jet broke away a terrifying instant later, he

shoved the heels of his gloved hands against the double-handled turret control. The twin gun muzzles elevated. He jammed his thumbs on the firing buttons. The .50s banged on both sides of his head. Tracers leaped after the dwindling jet, blinked out. The bastard could outrun bullets!

The jet climbed away. Its shark-shaped fuselage and low-slung twin-engine pods merged into a pinpoint high above the decimated bomber echelon and the frustrated P-38s. Then it was gone.

"Call in, call in!" Why was Brice's baritone so strangled now?

"Tail okay."

"Waist to pilot. Okay here, both of us."

"Ball turret still hooked on."

"Took a chunk out of my Plexiglas, but missed me," Mickey said.

"Nose turret, f-fine," Eddie managed. Was that *his* voice so scratchy in his own earphones?

Heinie Volz said, "Navigator still navigating." Poor bastard had no gun where he was. What a sweat he must have been through.

"Hot damn!" Tony chipped way back in the tail. "Fought a jet and hardly a scratch!"

"No," Brice said much too quietly. "He got Hen."

Eddie jerked his turret around, struggled out of his bulky steel flak helmet, and craned over his shoulder. He could see Brice behind the pilot's window, but Hen Rigby's side was vacant. Then he saw Mickey drop out of the top turret onto the flight deck behind the pilots' seats and rush forward.

"How bad?" Brice's intercom voice was muffled.

"Twenty millimeter right through the seat armor into . . . into his back. Didn't explode."

"Didn't have to."

"Solid ball armor piercing, I guess."

"He's . . ."

"Yeah. 'Fraid so, Rolly."

Nobody wanted to hear that conversation between pilot and gunner, but they listened.

"I'm coming forward," Bernie said from the waist.

Together he and Mickey lifted Hen's slack body out of the shattered seat and lay him on the flight-deck floor. There was hardly any blood at first. Then when they dropped below freezing level at ten thousand off Ancona on the way in, there was a lot.

How many times had Eddie seen the drab ambulances race down the taxi strips to other hardstands? He wondered how those crews had felt when they had to unload a dead or dying gunner or navigator or pilot onto a stretcher. Now he knew. Numb. Disbelieving. Not like the movies. No glory here. Just blood, pain, and the fierce effort not to weep.

Bernie, Mickey, and Brice lifted Hen's body carefully, such tenderness from men who had thought themselves really tough bastards. The tenderness didn't matter a damn. Hen's eyes were open, staring straight up at the clear blue sky where he'd died. His mouth sagged.

The medics reached into the gaping bomb bay and manhandled the body onto their stretcher as Hen was lowered from the flight deck. The rest of the crew stood around uselessly on shock-weakened legs. The ambulance rolled away, no siren needed.

The debriefing officer, Captain Lessing his name was, tried not to show his fascination with their having encountered a jet, but it came through. Attack procedure? Firing technique? Number of passes?

They reported what they could. Tonelessly, not really caring. Thinking about Hen. He'd told them his dream was to teach at a girl's prep school after this was over. "It's all set," Eddie remembered him saying as if he'd said it not ten minutes ago. "And I'm going to buy one of those little English sports cars. Low to the ground. The closer to the ground, the better I'll like it."

Hen was—had been the "rich kid" of the crew, the one with the private-school polish, but he'd had a knack of making you feel like he welcomed you right up there with him. Hell of a lot that meant now.

"Get off this base," Brice ordered the six of them after debriefing. "Clean up, put on your ODs, and go somewhere."

Cerignola was only a few miles from here, an hour's walk through the poverty-scarred countryside. They set out through the now soft midafternoon, each struck by its contrast with the harsh killer air they had fought through just hours before. None of them had been able to force down army C-rations in the tin-roofed mess hall. Each had accepted the ritual double-shot of bourbon when they were handed back their personal effects.

On the hardpan dirt road, two miles from the airfield, they encountered the woman, a quirk of timing, an accident of fate. Afterward they would blame what ensued on a lot of factors, but ultimately on themselves.

Six once-cocky, unconquerable young American airmen walked disconsolately north on an obscure Italian dirt lane and met a drably dressed twenty-three-year-old woman standing outside a dilapidated stone farmhouse. A little four- or five-year-old boy in ragged shorts and shirt hung on her skirt.

"*Buon giorno,*" Tony Lavella said. The rest of them were proud of their squatty tail-gunner's Boston-hardened Italian.

She barely glanced at them, a probably pretty girl, but it was hard to tell under the ragged scarf. Quick as her look was, it conveyed a hatred that was like a slap.

The insulting glare wasn't enough. She spit out rapid-fire words.

"What did she say?" Walt asked Tony, his pudgy face screwed into a baffled frown.

"She said we are, well, 'bastard sons of whores.' Come on, forget it. Let's go."

"Wait a minute," Bernie said, his face hardening. Maybe if he'd eaten something on top of the raw G.I. bourbon, he wouldn't have reacted so aggressively, Eddie thought, but Eddie himself felt anger rising.

"What the hell's her problem?" Mickey growled.

Tony shrugged and rattled back at her. She stuck out her jaw, parked her hands on the hips of her tattered gray skirt, and snarled a burst of Italian in reply. The exchange seemed to go on and on. Finally Tony waved his hand in her face. Then he roared in English, *"Shut up!"*

"What's she saying?" Mickey's angular face had clouded.

"She says this was her brother's farm. The *Facisti* forced him into the army. Then the Germans came and used the house for some damned thing or other. Then we came and took his orchard for the airbase. The U.S. Navy sank her husband's submarine and he drowned. And last week we killed her brother in an air raid on Bologna."

"What was he doing up there? The Italians are supposed to be on our side now."

"Forced labor for the Germans."

"Tell her we're sorry. Ask her if she has any wine in the house. *Vino,*" Phil Helmsgaard said.

"Come on, Phil," Tony said. "I thought we were going to Cerignola."

"What's in Cerignola? Vino and some crummy whores. Why walk there if there's something to drink here? Ask her," the glowering radio operator demanded.

More Italian snapped back and forth.

"She says no," Tony translated blandly. But the venom of her response had been obvious to all of them.

"She says she came from Sicily two days ago to see if anything was left after she found out the brother had been killed. She says Americans looted the place."

"Americans?"

"She says she found a soldier's cap in there. An American cap."

The woman spat out something more.

"She said we're no better than the Germans."

"Damned bitch!" Phil cried. He pushed past her and strode toward the house. "Come on, let's see for ourselves."

With that, the woman bent down, snatched a roadside rock, and threw it at Phil. It caught him on the side of the neck.

"Damn!" he roared. He whirled, grabbed her arm, and propelled her into the house. The boy ran shrieking after them. The other five airmen trailed into the small building not quite sure of what was happening.

The place did look as if it might have been looted, as she'd claimed. The few pieces of furniture were battered. There were light rectangles on the dirty plaster walls where pictures had been removed. The bare wooden floor was covered with a gritty layer of footprinted dust.

They heard Phil's growls and her disdainful foreign responses in the rear of the house. Then Phil emerged with a shout of triumph. He held four bottles aloft. "She lied! Dago red!"

She stood in the doorway behind him, her eyes ablaze. That didn't slow them down. In fifteen minutes the heavy wine on top of the government bourbon plus the late-afternoon heat had made them all drunk. It was then that the woman, who had leaned motionless against the doorjamb through all their ribald bottle-tipping, pulled the Lugerlike 9mm Glisenti Italian Army pistol from under her skirt, pointed it straight at Phil Helmsgaard with both hands, and pulled the trigger.

The explosion deafened them all and shook a fall of white dust from the ceiling. They stared. She brought the pistol down level again. This time she aimed it at Tony.

"Damn you!" The inaccurate bullet had nicked Phil's left earlobe. The front of his flight jacket was speckled with blood. "Damn you!" he yelled again. And he launched himself at the woman. He crashed into her just as the pistol detonated a second time. The slug bored into the floor.

Then Phil crushed her against the doorjamb, slapped her face with his right palm, left palm, right palm. The scarf fell away. Her stringy dark hair whipped across her eyes.

He grabbed her blouse, yanked. The worn fabric split up the back. Her breasts flew free.

"No better than Germans! *You bitch, we just lost a guy fighting the Germans so's you could have your frigging farm back!"*

She shouted some Italian obscenity back at him. Then she twisted an arm free and slammed him in the nose with her fist. Phil kicked her feet out from under her. They fell together, his hands pinning her wrists. Her legs flailed, and her left shoe caught him on his wounded ear.

"Hold her legs, damn it!"

"Phil," Tony cried. "For God's sake, Phil!"

Phil shook Tony's hand off his shoulder. "No wop bitch is gonna shoot at me and get away with it!" Phil shouted drunkenly. "Hold her legs, Walt."

She kicked him again. Walt scrambled to grab the flailing ankles. Phil managed to hold both her thin wrists with his left hand. With his right, he seized the waistband of her skirt and wrenched it down. She wore loose tan bloomers. He tore them away, too.

Then with his free hand, he yanked open his trousers and

223

olive-green army shorts. And with Walt still holding her legs, he raped her.

She screeched in pain and outrage at the hard, dry jabs. When he rolled off, there was madness in the dusty air of the isolated farmhouse, a drunken, overpowering ferociousness.

She lay naked, spread-eagled, bleeding slightly. She stared up at them and yelled, *"Nazis!"*

She couldn't have chosen a more infuriating epithet. Driven by anger and a compulsion they were never to understand, the others raped her too, almost assembly-line fashion. All but Tony. She didn't resist now. She endured, eyes slitted and hard as agate. Tony turned his back, walked to the open front door, and stared into the deserted road.

Not until the other five stood above her again, buttoning up, slapping at dust, did they notice the boy. He stood saucer-eyed and barefoot in his droopy shorts and shirt in the narrow doorway across the kitchen.

"Hey, Tony," Phil called. "Tell her brother to get the hell back where he was."

Tony turned, muttered something. She sat up, looked behind her, and answered in a tone so lethal they all felt it.

"She says he's not her brother. He's her son."

After that, nobody said anything until they were nearly back to the base.

"I don't think she can do anything," Mickey finally offered. There was no life in his voice at all.

"Guess again." Tony pointed at their jackets. They all realized at the same time that they wore an identification that could get them God knew how many years in some military stockade. Neatly stenciled across the left pocket of each poplin jacket in half-inch letters were the words

"Brice's Crisis," the product of a rainy-day standdown and time on their hands in January.

But the axe didn't fall. Twenty days later the group had flown its final combat mission, a rough one through dense flak to Linz. Then it was over. They flew a few supply runs to the Udine Valley, tins of biscuits and meat to starving civilians up there at a hazardous grass airfield northwest of Monfalcon. Then Brice's crew was high over the Atlantic in one final three-legged pull from Cerignola to Marrakech to the Azores and then Connecticut.

They never told Brice or Heinie Voltz. They never spoke about it among themselves. They were reassigned in six directions at Bradley Field, and they all were relieved at never having to face each other again.

FOURTEEN

THE TROPICAL DOWNPOUR blew through the porch screening and soaked the glass partition. Dan picked up his mug and scowled. The coffee was cold.

"It was the war," Connell said. "The damned war. They talk about it now like it was a lot of clean-cut kids on a glory road. Nothing like the grubby mess in Vietnam. But it had plenty of grubbiness of its own. The USAAF told us we were the best there was, the elite. That's how they got you up there to get your face shot off or to burn or freeze or die from anoxia."

He stopped and stared at the rug. "My God," he almost whispered. "They told us we were the best, then we gang-raped a girl because she insulted us."

"And because you'd just lost the best-liked man on your crew when you'd thought you were home free. Shock takes a lot of forms."

"You don't have to make excuses for us . . . for me."

"I don't know how to excuse rape."

"I don't need to be judged, either. Not at this late date."

"Somebody's judging all of you, Connell. And the verdict has come up guilty with the death penalty five times."

"Who? Who in hell would know? Only the six of us. I'm sure nobody talked. I'm positive of that. Only the six of us. And the girl."

Thunder exploded out in San Carlos Bay. "She must have told—" Dan began. Then he saw it. Of course! "The boy. You said he was, what, about five? He'd be forty-five now."

"That spindly little kid in baggy shorts?" Connell frowned. "But why now?"

"I guess we may never know that. But two to one it's the boy avenging his mother for the gang-rape he witnessed."

"Do you know what's going on with a thing like that when you're only four or five?"

"I'm sure something sticks with you. Maybe a nightmare she had to put in focus for him later. Now."

"My God." Connell's face sagged. "If you're right . . ."

"I'd say the evidence is pretty strong."

Connell spread his hands. "What the hell can I do? Going home makes no sense. He can find me there easier than he could find me here. I'm better off here."

"I found you here," Dan said. "At least send the girl home. He doesn't want her, but right now she's sleeping with a target."

The wind sounded stronger. Out in the Gulf, the horizon had turned black as oil smoke. The cloud mass was shot through with serpent tongues. Dennis.

Connell stared. "My God, you got any idea what a hurricane can do to a barrier island? This one's only three to five feet above sea level."

Dan automatically looked for a phone, found none. Then he remembered there were no phones.

"Get the girl out of here, Connell. Take her to the airport. Then we'll figure out what to do next."

He flicked on the TV set. Surely there'd be storm bulletins. The set was dead. Advancing blackness dimmed the room. Dan flipped the switch for the overhead light. That was dead too.

"Power's out."

"Take care of the girl," Dan said. "I'm going to the office."

He ran the two hundred feet through the glowering, rain-shot morning in slacks and shirt. He sure had packed poorly for this kind of thing. He yanked the door open, banged it closed behind him, and stood there dripping.

The clerk with the pink burn was adjusting a yellow slicker's parka hood around his face.

"Just getting ready to knock on doors, Mr. Forrest, with late word on the weather."

"Why don't you put phones in this place so we wouldn't have to drown to find out what's going on?"

"Had them in. Too many people stuck us for long-distance calls they never paid for. Took them out. Couldn't call off the island now, anyhow. The phone and power services come across the bay on a pole line, and there's a break in it somewhere out there."

"Have you looked out in the Gulf? What the hell is that?"

"Tropical storm."

"A hurricane?"

"If it was a hurricane, we would have been evacuated hours ago. It was technically a hurricane for a couple hours last night a hundred miles out. Now it's downgraded to a tropical storm. Nasty, but only a one- or two-foot surge expected. We'll have limbs down, more debris on the roads. Best to ride it out in your unit. We've been through plenty of these."

He sounded as if he was thriving on the excitement of it all. "Alligators'll be out of the swamps today for sure."

"Alligators?"

229

"Sure. A lot of this island's a wildlife refuge, and it's illegal to kill alligators anywhere anymore. We got some dandies back in some of these sloughs. Now and then, they'll walk right up out of a canal or mangrove swamp, go on across people's lawns. Police show up and see that nobody gets hurt or hurts the 'gators. They go on back where they came from or sometimes on into the Gulf."

"You're a regular Chamber of Commerce booster."

"Hey, listen, most of the time this place is as close to paradise as you can get without wings."

"Not today. You got an extra slicker I can borrow for the swim back?"

It smelled like old oil, but it beat another soaking. When he rounded the far end of the intervening Court Building a big Mercury veered around him, rain pelting through its headlight beams like streams of molten glass. He glimpsed Connell behind the wheel, the girl beside him. The Merc's taillights shimmered through the entrance portico, then were swallowed in the downpour.

When Connell returned, then what? Dan had glued this whole thing together from a patchwork of guesses, Casey's computer work, and sheer bullheadedness. He'd found the sixth man alive, and now he was sure he knew the reason it all had happened. But it was still a handful of loose ends.

Connell had turned out to be pigheaded, and his bedmate had been an extra complication. And now that he was down here with Connell, Dan himself wasn't sure what they should do when the big insurance man returned. He had the crawling suspicion that Connell was safer bucking through the storm to the airport than he would be when he returned to Sanibel.

Arbalesta had missed a turn where 275 wound through St. Petersburg streets. He lost more than a half hour ramming through a savage squall searching for a way to get back on the interstate. When he did manage to pick it up again near Pirellas Park, a dismal fish-belly dawn had crept out of Tampa Bay. He crossed the long Sunshine Freeway Bridge bone-tired, eyes grainy with the need for sleep. This had been a drive *diabolico* through wind and black rain.

On the south end of the bridge near Palmetto, he found himself on 41, the Tamiami Trail. The highway was easy enough to follow with its big orange 41 signs, but apparently it went through every town of Gulf Coast Florida between Tampa and Naples. Maybe that wouldn't be so bad. The thin but increasing traffic on the drenched streets of Sarasota, Venice, and Port Charlotte would force his wakefulness.

His body ached for sleep. Not yet. Not until he reached Sanibel. Then only for a few hours. He would find Connell this day, deal with him swiftly, then force the final hundred fifty miles to Miami and the sanctuary of Alitalia.

South of the bridge over Charlotte Harbor, the highway was empty and bleak. The sun would not shine today. The overcast to the west had darkened again. He had exhausted himself driving through hundreds of miles of rain. Now more rain would come. Out there was tropical storm Dennis, so said the radio which he now turned on only at the hour and the half-hour to monitor news yet escape the detestable music.

At 9:15 the Tamiami Trail rolled him through the loose commercial and residential development of North Fort Myers. Then he crossed the Caloosahatchee River on a long, level bridge.

He nearly missed the sharp turn of the down ramp to McGregor Boulevard along the west side of Fort Myers. At a small restaurant he stopped for coffee. His back felt as if someone had shoved an iron rod up his spine. He'd added nearly eight hundred miles to the Cutlass's odometer. He made a fuzzy mental computation, trying to convert miles to kilometers. *Dio!* It was the straight-line distance from Rome all the way to the English Channel! But this day would end this exhausting search. The debt of honor would be paid in full.

The travel-weary Cutlass paused at the Sanibel Causeway tollbooth at 9:35. The wind had increased. As he paid the toll, Arbalesta watched the whitecaps on the bay explode into airborne spume. He rolled up the window against a fresh spatter of rain and picked up speed toward Sanibel Island.

Where in hell was Connell? Dan wondered. How long did it take to get to the airport and back? The guy had been gone for more than three hours.

Maybe the road had flooded out. Or maybe Connell wasn't coming back at all. That would be cute. Dan now had enough for a *NewScope* story, but it would be a story without an ending. He could wring a couple thousand words out of what he knew, but that wasn't all that he had come down here for. He needed the loose ends tied. He wanted to help nail the killer. And, pain in the ass that Eddie Connell had been at first, he finally had leveled, had told Dan what he had never told anyone else in forty years. Dan wanted to help the guy.

But he couldn't blame Connell, couldn't really fault him if he and the girl both stayed at the airport waiting to catch the first plane that could get out.

Then above the wind rattle of the palms and the rain hiss, he heard tires on the drenched gravel of the parking lot. He stepped out on the balcony beneath the wide roof overhang. The air smelled wet and wild.

Not Connell. A brown car. Oldsmobile. Some poor sunseeker who'd had a reservation for weeks, no doubt, appalled that he and his wife and kids had picked the same weekend that tropical storm Dennis had picked.

Only one person ducked out of the car into the storm. A tall, slender guy. At least he'd had the foresight to bring a raincoat. A somber black one. He reached into the back seat for his bag, slammed the car's door, and plodded toward the stairs below Dan's vantage point.

That was one tired character down there, his head bent, shoulders hunched against the rain. He walked as if he'd driven a thousand miles. At the midway landing where the stairs reversed, the guy looked up. Their eyes met. The man on the stairs looked like a cadaver, eyes sunken deep beneath the sharp ridge of brow. Face lean as a hatchet. And in those haunted eyes, Dan thought he saw the hard burn of imbalance. Or was it just exhaustion? Anybody'd be worn out having driven a distance through this weather.

Dan broke his gaze and returned to his damp room.

Connell showed up around twelve, about five minutes after Dan had written him off and had begun to think about how Charlie was going to take half a story. The big insurance exec shucked his sopping jacket and shook the rain off it out the door. When he turned around, Dan saw the package stuck in the waistband of Connell's water-stained pink sports slacks.

"What the hell is that? A pistol in a Baggie?"

Connell pulled the thing out, unwound the plastic freezer bag, and laid the weapon on the table between them.

"Army forty-five automatic." His voice had a smug edge. "I remembered a friend of mine in Fort Myers, guy I met at a couple of conferences." He caught Dan's look. "Oh, I went to conferences faithful as a priest before I ran into Sandy. The guy's something of a gun nut. I told him I'd gotten some threats, he lent me this little number."

"Just like that?"

"You got to know Art to understand."

Dan eyed the big automatic. "You ever fire one of these things?"

"Had to. In the service. USAAF required proficiency with the carbine and with this."

"That was forty years ago, Connell."

"Like riding a bike." He picked up the .45, tripped the magazine release. The heavy clip slid out of the grip into his left hand. "Seven big ones. This thing was designed to stop hyped-up Moros in the Philippines, so the story goes. Don't tell me it won't handle a nutty Italian with a ladies' popgun."

He palmed the clip back home, pulled the slide back to lock a round in the chamber, then thumbed the hammer down to half-cock. That seemed appropriate for both gun and man.

"Let the son of a bitch show up now," Connell growled. Interesting what more than two pounds of ugly blue-finish automatic would do for a man's confidence.

"You put in any military time, Forrest?"

"I was in knee-pants in your war, a teenager during the Korean thing, and they missed me in the draft after that. Do me a big favor, Connell. Wrap that thing back up and hide it somewhere. We're going to Sanibel City Hall to turn this whole thing over to the police." He'd been mulling over that idea for the past hour. Connell's gun and dumb new jaw set had just confirmed it.

"You kidding? The biggest case they get here is some drunked-up tourist dancing naked on a condo lawn. There's only a handful of cops on the Sanibel force, and they'll be tied up by this damned storm. You ought to see the shape the roads are in already."

"We'll give them a try."

"I'm taking the forty-five."

"Into police headquarters? Maybe that's not a bad idea.

They'll lock you up for carrying it, and you'll be safe for a while."

"I'll leave it in the car while we go in there."

He was one obstinate insurance man, which probably was why he had been such a success at it. Dan had to admire his guts if not his brains.

"We'll take my car," Dan said. Connell was in a hyper-excited state. Dan didn't relish having him behind the wheel.

The insurance exec put the .45 back in its loose plastic bag, jammed it most unprofessionally dead-center down the front of his atrocious pink slacks, and zipped his baggy jacket over it. Dan doubted that the Sanibel cops would notice it anyway, but he was going to make Connell stick to his word and leave the thing under the seat when they got there.

Dan threw on the klutzy borrowed slicker. Connell preceded him along the balcony, then down the steps. The wind had finally slacked off. Now the rain pelted straight down in a torrent of pea-sized drops. Dan flipped up the hood of the slicker. Connell, hatless, just took it. Water ran through his bristle cut behind his ears, down his neck.

The parking area was awash in two inches of water. They splashed through it to the Toyota. The slicker's big hood obscured Dan's side vision, but he sensed that some other poor sopping sucker had come down the stairs behind them. Terrific day for the beach.

He slid into the little car and reached over to unlock the passenger door for Connell. When he straightened, he heard a tap on his own window.

Dan shoved back the obscuring slicker hood and stared through the rain-streaked glass straight into the muzzle of an automatic. A little round eye. A .22.

The thing wasn't a cannon like Connell's borrowed artillery. But Dan knew it had the power to drill straight through the safety glass, then plow into his brain. His blood jelled to ice.

Arbalesta had fallen into bed in his wet clothes and had collapsed into near-instant sleep. When a thunder crack jarred him awake, his Rolex told him he'd slept only two hours. But even that respite seemed enough to free him of the near-hallucinatory state exhaustion had brought on. When he'd dragged himself up the stairs after registering as "Carmen Bianco"—the name had come out of no-where—and paid in cash for one night's lodging, he'd thought he'd glimpsed Connell on the balcony above him.

Then he realized his overextended brain had superim-posed the memorized photograph of Edward Connell on the head of a casual bystander. Had Arbalesta actually stopped and stared at the man? Had he detected a flash of more than idle curiosity in the tall, muscular man's eyes? Arbalesta had found the encounter unsettling.

Now he was chilled and his clothes were clammy. He should have undressed before sleeping, but he had been too drained of strength and coordination for that, even seem-ingly drained of the need to complete his mission. But just two hours of rest had changed that.

To dispel the late-morning's grayness, he flipped the switch of the bedside lamp. Was the bulb burned out? He rolled off the bed and walked to the bathroom. The switch was ineffectual there as well. A power failure?

He returned to the bedroom and opened the slats of the small venetian blind above the bed. The little window overlooked the parking area. He didn't see a light any-where on this monsoonlike morning. A failure of power for certain.

Then he did see lights, the headlights of a car as it rounded the building between this one and the office. It pulled into one of the numbered bays. The lights flicked out.

Now Arbalesta's chest thudded almost audibly. From the vehicle emerged a big man in a rain-soaked greenish jacket and hideous pink slacks, a man with unusually short-cropped white hair. No hallucination this! From Rollo's clandestinely obtained photograph, Arbalesta recognized the man instantly. Edward Connell.

The girl Arbalesta had panicked in New Orleans had been truthful and accurate. Now that he had managed his brief sleep, Arbalesta knew that his decision to drive here had been the correct one. He patted the breast pocket of the sports coat he had tossed on the other bed. The compact lump of the HK-4, loaded, waiting, and undetected by any airport scanner, told him he had again done everything right.

The girl. What of the girl Ginny Landstreet had mentioned in her terror-induced outpouring? Arbalesta would wait and watch. Opportunity would present itself. All factors were again falling into place. He had opted for this unit in the Gulffront Building because he decided that an old man bent on impressing a young girl surely would take beachfront lodgings, the best he could buy. Arbalesta congratulated himself again. He had been right about that, too.

He stood at the bedroom window, intent on the parking lot with its scatter of cars. Connell had not looked like he had spent much time in the sun. Surely the girl would be seeking a tan, though. That appeared to be an American fetish. He had admired the well-tanned women in Phoenix and Los Angeles. If the weather would break and Connell's woman would take to the beach, leaving the man alone in the unit . . .

Then Arbalesta stiffened. Two people had just started down the rain-slicked balcony stairs. The bareheaded one in the jacket and pink slacks was Connell again. The other wore a floppy yellow slicker with its hood up. Too big and with too agressive a walk for a woman.

When the pair reached the landing halfway down where the stairs reversed, Arbalesta stared. Beneath the slicker's hood, he made out the face of the man who had watched him climb the stairs earlier this morning. The man on the balcony. Now here he was with Connell.

A prickling sensation broke across Arbalesta's shoulders. It was written all over them: in their tight expressions, the sets of their bodies, the way they moved down the stairs. They *knew* . . . something.

Was the other man some sort of law officer? No, not in that stained and unkempt slicker. But anyone could see with certainty that both men were responding to perceived danger.

Were they bent on escape? If they moved out of Arbalesta's reach, then what? Would he be forced to return to New Orleans and wait out Connell's return? The man would have to go home sometime. But a man who so flagrantly deceived his wife might not feel the need to return to her for days. Weeks? Arbalesta intended to complete the vendetta and return to Miami tonight.

A deviation from the plan structure could do it. If the other man had somehow recognized the danger when Arbalesta had clambered up the stairs below him, then he was the only "witness" in this entire thirteen-day sequence who posed a substantial threat. The other man had to be disposed of also. That would wrap it up, as Americans said.

There was not another instant to lose. Arbalesta dived across the bed, jerked the HK-4 out of his jacket, grabbed his raincoat as he rushed out of the unit. He threw on the coat and pocketed the little pistol as he slowed to a fast walk along the balcony to the stairs. Then he trailed the two men, he hoped, with the apparent disinterest of a stranger.

If they continued out of the parking area down the drive to the office, this opportunity would dissolve in the downpour. But if they were headed toward an automobile, that eventuality could be seized upon.

He found himself smiling without mirth. They approached a white Toyota.

His timing was excellent. He pulled out the gun, held it close to his body, strode to the car, then centered the muzzle through the window on the slickered man's forehead just as he straightened from unlocking the car door.

The man appeared properly frightened. That was good. A frightened man was easier to control. Connell had sunk below roof level. The door over there slammed. Arbalesta motioned downward with the .22. The driver complied, rolled the window down.

"You will unlock the rear door. Slowly. One error and you are a dead man."

He opened the rear door, bent in quickly, then pulled the door shut. "Drive."

"Where?" the slickered man asked. His voice was steadier than Arbalesta had expected.

"This gun is a small one," Arbalesta said, "but it will easily penetrate your skull. Drive. I will tell you where to turn." He held the pistol level with the top of the seat back, to the right of the headrest, unnoticeable from outside.

"*Sinistro*—left."

The little car swung left at the motel entrance. At the intersection of East Gulf and Lindgren, he directed them right, toward the main road, Periwinkle. But at the four-way stop there he hesitated. He did not enjoy working blind like this, without a carefully structured and well reconnoitered sequence. But he had no choice now. He was committed. There could be only one outcome.

"What is that way, to the right?"

"I have no idea," the driver said.

"If you lie," Arbalesta warned him, "it can end here."

"Residential area, then the Lighthouse Beach," Connell threw out. His voice did sound properly panicked. Did he realize he was the primary target?

"And the other way? To the left?"

"The main part of the island. Shops, stores."

"The whole island is like that?"

"Up to the wildlife refuge," Connell said. And when he said it, the driver's shoulders tensed. He had recognized Connell's slip and knew Arbalesta was seeking a place of isolation.

"Turn that way."

The driver obliged. They rolled along dead-level Periwinkle Way. Its puddled blacktop was littered with palm fronds and pine branches torn free by Dennis's still impressive power. For a stretch, huge feathery pines arched over the narrow road. They splashed through a green tunnel, then emerged in a commercial section.

The road was flanked by frame shell shops, restaurants, gift boutiques. They passed several well-landscaped shopping centers, their parking lots sparsely occupied in the heavy rain. A church on the right, then a less pretentious L-shaped shopping strip on the left, and the driver stopped at the T-intersection of Periwinkle with Tarpon Bay Road.

Arbalesta glanced down Tarpon Bay toward the storm-whipped Gulf. Houses. No good. "Turn right," he ordered.

Another T-intersection came toward them out of the rain, this one less than a quarter-mile later at the Sanibel-Captiva Road.

"Where does this road lead?"

Silence.

"You!" he snapped at Connell.

"Up the island, to Captiva."

"What is that?"

"The next island. A smaller one, across Blind Pass Bridge." Connell sounded as if he were strangling.

"*Buono.* We go that way."

To Arbalesta's growing satisfaction, they now traveled a deserted road cut through dense tropical growth on both sides. Occasionally they passed little residential clutches carved out of the lush vegetation on the left. To the right, according to a sign they had just passed, were the inviolate wetlands of the huge J. N. Darling National Wildlife Preserve. It looked wild and deserted, but it could be patrolled.

Soon, Arbalesta realized, they would reach Captiva. A smaller island, Connell had said. Possibly less opportunity there than here in this wild area of Sanibel. But he had to get them off this main road. He had glanced down each side road to the Gulf as the Toyota had sped past. But he had spotted houses or low condominium buildings—or the side road had appeared too open.

Then they passed one that was different.

"Stop!" he ordered. "Back up."

He looked down the narrow macadam lane that angled sharply off the Sanibel-Captiva Road. He nudged the driver with the HK-4's muzzle. "That way."

The blacktop of Bowman's Beach Road ended at a wood-post barrier a half-kilometer into the scrub. To Arbalesta's dismay there was a row of two-story condominiums on the left behind a fringe of palms, their stained-wood exteriors wet and somber. His brain began to race until he realized they were empty, their windows boarded against off-season weather.

The driver pulled to the barrier and stopped. Arbalesta peered past him through the windshield. A path led from the road through a grove of tall pines. Then the path met a long wooden footbridge that crossed perhaps fifty meters of swampy slough. Beyond that lay another, much denser pine woods. Then, through a narrow rift in the trees, he saw a sliver of rain-beaten beach and the boiling surf of the Gulf.

The second stretch of woods was the obvious, even ideal, place. Surely no one else would be in this secluded area in such a downpour. There was no other car. He would finish them both with the muzzle of the gun against the skull so quickly the first man would have no idea what had happened to him, and the second man would not have time to react before he, too, went down.

Then Arbalesta would drive the Toyota back to the Gulfpride Inn, park it, wipe it free of prints, lock it. He would leave for Miami immediately in the Cutlass. It was probable that the inn's manager would not be aware of his absence until check-out time at midday tomorrow. He would assume, of course, that Arbalesta, having paid in advance, had simply forgotten to leave the key.

Until these two were found, there would be no suspicion at all. And when they were inevitably discovered by some wandering shell collector or suntan seeker, Carmen Bianco, a man who had never really existed, would have long disappeared.

"You will get out," Arbalesta told the driver. "You also," he directed Connell. "I have the gun at this man's head, so be careful. Walk around to me."

When he stood beside the car with the two men in front of him, he said to the man in the battered slicker, "Give me the keys."

And now they knew.

Dan had never been so terrified and so totally angry in his life. Not when he'd been tossed out of the little Long Island community newspaper on his drunken ear, not when he'd awakened in a Garden City hospital with crawling DTs. Those times, he had indeed been overwhelmed with fear, but nobody had stood a yard away with a gun in his hand and madness frozen into his gaunt face. At his elbow, Dan could smell Eddie Connell's sweat.

"You will walk to the path, across the bridge, then into the woods," the man ordered, his voice cold as steel. An Italian voice, all right. There had even been a scatter of Italian words.

"You," their assailant ordered Connell, "you first. I will be right behind both of you."

Single-file, they trudged along the path. Dan cursed his stupidity. A tall man with a black coat. Walter Rose had given that description to his partner and to his wife. But when Dan had seen the man, he hadn't even recalled Rose's sparse clues.

He had never been so acutely aware of the scent of pine, the feel of wet needles cruching under his shoes, the fresh smell of rain. Was it all to end here, all the wonderful odors of life, the sounds of wind and rain and the distant wash of surf? The vivid colors, the ochers and greens of ground and woods? All to end here beside this coffee-colored slough on a remote barrier island?

In front of him, Connell stumbled up the path's rise to the level of the bridge. His shoes clattered on the bleached rain-sodden boards. Dan followed him onto the foot-bridge, his legs leaden. It was six feet wide with waist-high wooden railings. Below, the slough's sluggish surface was dimpled with rain. Ragged scarves of dark brown scum floated motionless, and there were knots of driftwood—

No, not driftwood, Dan realized. Those were the twin bumps of an alligator's eyes. Watching. One silent witness. No, two. He saw another near the middle of the bridge. These final moments were to be seen only by two dozing Sanibel alligators.

What was Connell doing? The big, white-haired man slapped at his neck. Mosquitoes in this downpour? Then he dropped his hand down in front of him. Above the burble or rain into the slough, Dan made out the metallic zing of a zipper.

My God!

He barely jumped out of the way, flat against the right-hand railing as Connell whirled. The .45! Dan had been stupid not to suspect the man's appearance, but the man with the .22 had been equally careless in assuming Dan and Connell were fright-paralyzed and offered no threat to him.

Connell had the big automatic in his right hand, still wrapped in the plastic. He'd gotten it cocked and had rammed his finger through the loose plastic into the trigger guard.

The thing went off right in Dan's ear, a deafening blast that shivered the bridge.

And missed.

Behind their captor, a geyser of tan water spurted above the opposite railing. The heavy slug had gone wide, between the top and lower rails.

Etched in Dan's brain was a flash-frame of the gunman's face, thin-lipped, drained of blood in the .45's yellow-white muzzle flash.

Then that expression of settled madness fell back in place. The lean jaw clamped shut. The haunted eyes glared. And the little pistol barked.

Dan lunged sideways as the bullet snapped past his ear. With a hoarse grunt, Connell sat hard on the slippery boards.

Dan would never know whether he had leaped in reflex out of the .22's line of fire or from the adrenaline of shock upon shock. Whatever impelled him, he crashed full-weight into the skull-faced man. The smoking HK-4 clattered to the bridge floor. Connell was no help now, out of it ten feet away.

Encumbered by the heavy slicker, Dan used everything he had: knees, elbows, fists. Their abductor was wiry and agile, but he, too, was handicapped by his flapping rain-coat.

His fist slammed Dan's cheek, jammed flesh into teeth. Dan tasted his own blood. The man tried for his gun, staved Dan off with one arm, flailed down with the other.

Dan crunched his shoe hard on the scrabbling hand. The bony head flew back. Dan jabbed up with his knee, caught the point of the other's jaw just beneath the kneecap. The awkward slam numbed his leg, but the man fell back. And seized the gun.

Dan ducked his head, forced his legs to piston against the bridge boards, and rammed the black overcoat full out.

A section of railing cracked at the impact of their combined weight. It fell outward, and they fell with it. Dan snaked out an arm. His fingers clawed at the denuded post. His fingernails dug into the wood. And held.

He swung out over the muddy slough, slammed around the outside of the adjacent section. His shoes scraped for a toehold, found it. He ducked under the top rail, heard a crack behind him, and knew the bullet had barely missed.

The man stood chest-deep in the oozing swamp. He aimed the deadly little .22 with both hands. Dan and Eddie Connell were totally exposed, again helpless on the bridge.

The big army pistol! Connell wrestled with it, hampered by a wounded shoulder and the hopelessly tangled plastic wrapping.

The man in the water centered the .22 dead on Dan's forehead.

Then there was a swirl behind him, a sudden eddy. Arbalesta's mouth gaped open for a shout of horror that never came. He flew backward, propelled by an unseen force. Then he was jerked beneath the roiling surface. An arm broke the opaque water. Then another, as his body began to whirl over and over.

Alligators, Dan remembered reading someplace, do not kill large prey by biting. They hook in their rows of teeth, then use their powerful tails to spin oversized victims until they drown.

When the terrible thrashing stopped, only a tattered black strip of raincoat floated to the surface.

They couldn't say anything for nearly a full minute. Dan hung over the rail and struggled for breath. Connell sat dead-center on the bridge floor and stared into the slough. Then Dan forced himself to stand. Eddie Connell began to explore his shoulder with shaking fingers.

"Now we go where we started to go," Dan said. "To the cops. They'll have to believe that hole in you. First, though . . ."

He bent down, picked up the plastic-wrapped .45, and threw the pistol far into what he judged to be the deepest part of the slough.

"Hey!" Connell yelped.

"We don't need that complication. Buy your friend a nice present." He helped the big man to his feet. "I'll split the cost with you," he said.

Charlie Lovett pawed through Dan's stack of receipts in a most preoccupied way. Then he jumped up and actually trotted around his desk to throw an arm across Dan's shoulders.

"Hell of a story you filed, Dan. *Hell* of a story. Runs as is."

So he either hadn't noticed the gloss-overs, or he was going to let Dan get away with them. Most un-*NewScope*-like. Maybe there *was* a heart under all the curmudgeonry.

"Headline's not bad either, so long as the public doesn't realize you wrote it yourself."

246

NEWSCOPE REPORTER HALTS 5-STATE MURDER RAMPAGE. Eat your hearts out, you other supermarket rags.

The gloss-overs? There were only two, neither of them a big deal.

". . . an alleged assault on his mother forty years ago."

That was the best he could do for them, for Phil Helms-gaard, Bernie Latza, Walt Rose, Mickey Josaitis, Tony La-vella.

And: "Connell, vacationing on Sanibel . . ."

The girl with him had had no direct part in this. Let Connell do his own explaining at home and office.

Dan would make sure Cal Josaitis was sent a copy of the piece to amplify Dan's already phoned two-word tele-gram: GOT HIM.

In the corridor outside Charlie's office, Quince Harriss shook Dan's hand. "Congratulations, Forrest. Very astute."

Astute? "Shucks, Ma. It weren't nothing."

"Yes, it was. You're a lot more perceptive than I am."

"Than you? What in hell are you talking about?"

Quince jerked his head to twitch errant hair out of his eyes. "That sly devil Blauvelt, of course. You bet me a ten-spot he'd bong Melody's gong before Christmas. Here's the damned ten. He bonged before Halloween."

"He told you?"

"She told me."

"She tells *you* things like that?"

"You should have bet on me, too."

Another surprise awaited him at home. "A skirt? Is that actually a skirt you have on? And you have legs!"

In his doorway, Casey giggled. "You know I have legs, and more." She looked like a page out of *Glamour*. Frilled white peasant blouse, tan skirt, sleek panty hose, hair a gleaming copper wave. He was awestruck.

"You like?"

"Do I like! The packaging is excellent, my dear." A passable W. C. Fields he'd had no idea was in him.

"Well, good!" She came in and shut the door behind her. "Now let's get to the contents." She began to unzip the skirt.

"Hey, we haven't had dinner yet."

"To hell with dinner, Daniel. It's been almost a week . . ."